REIGN

KETLEY ALLISON

1

CALLIE

Chase and I sprint down the pathway, keeping to the pedestrian trails so our footsteps can't be tracked. Somehow, Chase managed to snag my coat as he struggled to get me out of the building and throws it over my shoulders as we escape.

A sodden piece of the coat hits my cheek.

Ivy's spilled blood is still warm.

My tears are frozen, turning into salted ice that stiffens my cheeks as we fight through the winter chill, but Chase doesn't leave my side. I feel his hot breath on my neck with each exhale, his steady hand landing between my shoulders and coaxing me forward every time a fresh image of a dying Ivy hits the backs of my eyes, and I buckle between sprints.

"Almost there," he says, his breaths heavy. "Keep going."

My exhale hitches on a sob.

"Don't fall apart yet. I promise, baby, as soon as we get to your room, you can fall apart in my arms. I'm right here. I'm not leaving."

I grip his arm as we run, the hard sinew of muscle bulging against my fingers as he uses every ounce of energy he possesses to get us out of here.

There's a tickle of realization as I hold onto him. Chase doesn't have a jacket. The thin material of his white Briarcliff button-up is all that separates him from the December winter moon.

He must be freezing.

I think this fact, but it doesn't register past the surface of my brain. The only worry I can come up with has to do with Ivy. The only anxiety I'm concerned about has to do with my friend.

My former friend.

My dead friend.

"Oh, God," I moan, and Chase takes my weight for his own.

He half-carries me the last few feet to Thorne House and hauls me against his side as we sneak through the back. Chase props me up just inside the door, then exits briefly to use a fallen tree branch to obscure our footsteps in the snow.

He brings the cold with him when he shuts the door and carries me up three flights. I grip his neck like a lifeline, breathing in his familiar scent laced with snowflakes, and work to calm my broken heart.

"Almost there," he says into my ear.

I bury my face into his neck but hear when the lock turns at my apartment door and register the blanket of warmth as soon as he steps out of the hallway.

"What happened?"

Emma's soft voice floats in my periphery, but I've yet to lift my hanging head.

In fact, I've yet to register Chase depositing me on a kitchen stool as he goes to talk to his sister.

"Thank fuck you're here," Chase says, and my eyes lift from the floorboards enough to see him embrace his sister in a hard, emotional hug. "Are you all right?"

"It was the strangest thing," Emma says once they pull apart. "I got a text from Ivy to meet her at the lobster shack in town, but when I went, it was Falyn and Willow waiting for me."

"Goddammit." Chase scrapes a hand down his face. "We thought she had you. That Sabine had taken you."

"Hell no. Just a couple of bitches thinking they could dangle my re-entry into the Virtues like it'd be something I'd desire. Why? What's going on?"

It's here I see the cracks in Chase's glacial demeanor, the stricken lines around his eyes and mouth as he speaks close to Emma's ear.

Emma gasps and rips from his hold. She's immediately at my side, pushing my hair back and eclipsing my vision.

"Callie? Callie, can you hear me?"

I say nothing. Do nothing. Do I blink?

Emma pulls her lips in. "She's in shock."

Chase's presence, as soon as it's close again, fills my soul, and my arms ache to tangle around his neck. Yet no part of me moves.

His voice carries above my head. "What were you thinking, Callie?" His tone dips and dives with emotion. "I should've taken the blade. Not Ivy. Not *you*. Why did you get in Sabine's path? *Why* did you protect me?"

My only answer is motionless lips, soaked in tears.

"It should've been me," he whispers. "It should've fucking been me on that floor. I should've protected you both."

Emma cuts in, "Chase. Please. Look at her."

Chase stills. Gives me the once-over. Something at my middle catches his eye. I curl my fingers, but they're stiffer than normal, like a new layer of skin has caked over them.

Not skin. Blood. Dried blood. Ivy's.

I'm lifted in a *whoosh* of strength and carried into the bathroom where Chase resolutely shuts the door in his sister's face.

I want to tell him Emma's seen me in this state before. Naked, shivering, scared. But I can't.

Chase sets me on my feet, running his hands up my arms as he straightens, so gentle, so barely there. He searches my eyes for a moment.

His stare hardens, coming to a decision. Delicately, he unbuttons my blouse and strips it off my form. My skirt is next, my bra, my underwear.

When I'm naked in front of him, his expression doesn't waver or flush with need. He doesn't grit his jaw or indent my skin with his hard grip before he can't contain himself anymore, covering me with his body.

He does none of that, and I wish he would. I wish for normalcy, for a regular day, for a rewind.

Chase turns on the shower, then strips off his shirt and pants.

Bared, beautiful, he steps up to me, trailing a finger down my cheek. "We'll get through this."

I'm lifted into the shower the same way he swept me off my feet in the main room, the warm spray covering my shoulders and splashing his chest as he steps in.

In silence, Chase lathers my body, his sweeping strokes as effective as sweet, whispered *shushes* against my ear. He soothes as well as he commands, and I wonder if he knows that.

He washes my hair, rubs the blood from my fingernails, and massages the tender spots of my body with athletic expertise. He doesn't stop until he hears a relieved, long sigh leave my lips.

When he's toweling me off, he asks, "Can I carry you to bed?"

It takes effort, will, my every fiber, but I meet his eyes and give him the barest of nods.

His chin lowers. "Okay."

Chase settles me against his chest, his heart beating into my ear.

It's fast, hard, and relentless in its pulse, but it's soothing compared to my erratic rhythm.

I'm laid on top of my covers, my pajama shirt and shorts slipped on with the same ease as when he'd peeled off my clothes.

"I'm staying with her," Chase says above me.

"I wasn't about to question it," Emma responds. Somewhere during our trip from the bathroom to my room, she reappeared. "Sleep, if you can. We'll talk more in the morning. Is there any chance the police will knock on our door tonight?"

Chase sighs. "Likely. Callie was Ivy's best friend."

"I still can't believe it. Sabine's out of control." Emma pauses. Then she asks, in a much softer tone, "Did you leave her body there?"

"Yes, but I doubt Sabine wants Ivy discovered in temple. She could've used some Virtues to move Ivy into the library when we left. These girls ... Jesus Christ, Ems. These girls do anything for her."

"This is what our father has missed for *years*. Even with his own daughter. Sabine grooms us like a predator. She has complete manipulation and control. But..." Emma pauses. "I've always thought, maybe Father knows and encourages it. He certainly encouraged me, in no uncertain terms, to return to the Virtues' fold when I re-enrolled at Briarcliff."

"I had no idea. No fucking clue you were being used like this. And what you did to yourself? What Piper helped do to you? She beat you with your permission. *Emma.*" Chase's tone breaks off at the end, the first, and only, clue of grief he has allowed to permeate the air. "Why didn't you tell me? I could've done something. Exposed the Virtues to the rest of the Nobles. I can guarantee not every one of us would be so accepting of our sisters used as fucking *sex* slaves."

"Some of those very Nobles you speak of stepped up to the side of my bed."

Chase's breaths heave in response, a bull readying his horns for a disemboweling.

Emma continues, "Would it have stopped Sabine from

using you to seduce Callie for her own means? From Piper falling off a cliff? From the Virtues threatening, blackmailing, then killing Ivy? I don't know, Chase. This is what I think about every day. But you've been following Father's rules for so long. I couldn't be sure you'd be on my side."

"How could you think that? I *pulled* you from that goddamned fire!"

"And there, right there, is your damn hero complex bursting out of the gates without any reins. You always have to save the girl, don't you? You ran into those flames without giving a damn about yourself, when really, you should've given thought to the fact that I didn't want to be pulled out."

Chase sucks in air. "Emma. You don't mean that."

But she's relentless. "You even have the gall to blame yourself for Piper's death. *You* didn't push her off the cliff. *You* didn't get her pregnant. It was Piper's choice to dig into the Virtues. *Her* decision to become the Virtuous princess instead of me. But because you just can't stop yourself, now you go after Callie for daring to try and sacrifice herself for you. Maybe she wanted to. *Maybe* it's not all about you, Chase. We need to make our own decisions. I needed to save other girls from becoming Sabine's puppets. Piper needed to save me. Callie needed to save her friend and *you*. For once in your fucking life, allow us to be the noble ones."

"I'm not going to apologize for wanting to protect the women I care about."

"You guys are fighting about who has the right to die first," I whisper, "when Ivy's already dead."

Both go silent.

Emma's the first to speak. She covers her face with her

hands. "I'm sorry. My brain is everywhere. I'm so sorry about Ivy. And I'm terrified for my brother, for you, and I'm taking it out on anything that moves."

"It's okay," I murmur, but the tears well anyway.

Emma lays a hand on my shoulder. "You'll tell me tomorrow. Try to rest." She then lays a hand on Chase's cheek, staring long and hard into his eyes. "You, too."

"Yeah, sis." Chase squeezes her wrist.

Emma steps out of the room and the bed dips as Chase settles beside me. His body molds to mine, and he says, close to my ear, "Can I stay?"

I turn into him, my damp lashes cool against my tender skin as I close my eyes. "Don't leave."

He brings an arm around me, tugging me close. "I'm so —I should've—"

I nuzzle his neck. "Your sister's right. You take on too much. Let us have our faults. I could've saved Ivy, too."

"I wish you had."

I squeeze my eyes shut, asking, for just this moment, that my crying stops. "Sabine was aiming for you. I know it in my bones. And I couldn't stop myself from protecting you if I tried."

"Callie." My name sounds so pained on his tongue. He kisses the hair at my temple. "I hear the guilt in your voice. There's no way you could've saved us both. One of us was dying tonight. There was no way out."

"There's always a way."

I'm surprised at the grit in my tone, the instant anger. Yet, the more I stew on the words, the more certain I become.

"Tomorrow will be rough." Chase fits me against him when he moves to his back. "Rest. Sabine's not touching a hair on your fucking head."

I lick my lips, truly wondering if Chase can claim such invincibility when tonight has shown us there's no such thing.

My best friend is dead. That caring, smiling, bursting-with-joy person is dead. Because she wanted to save her family. Because of Sabine.

Those thoughts grow vulture's feathers until they form into jagged, black wings, and they silently circle my mind, flying lower and lower, ready to eat into the carrion I've become.

But with Chase's arms around me, I manage to slip away and avoid their gnarled beaks, falling into a fitful sleep.

2

———

CALLIE

I crack my eyes open, and for a moment, think they're still closed. Darkness blooms out of every crevice in my bedroom, so blinding I can't possibly be awake. Then it hits me.

This blackness has exploded out of my soul and blanketed the room. Ivy's dead.

"Are you up?"

Chase's soft whisper tickles the hair around my ears. On my exhale, my body molds into his. "Yes."

He squeezes me closer. "You were having a nightmare."

"It's not a nightmare if it actually happened."

"Baby." Chase lifts to his forearm, stroking hair from my forehead and kissing me gently. "Don't take this poison in. It's for me and my sister. We're the ones who brought you closer to the societies. Maybe..." Chase's dark eyes are the only glimmer in the room as he looks down at me. "I wouldn't blame you if you wanted to leave. If you want to run out of these doors this morning and never look back."

The thought occurred to me, but I don't allow any flicker of it in my expression. "I'm not leaving Ivy. She deserves—"

Justice.

They all do.

Piper. Ivy. My mother.

Chase sighs. "I understand. I want to avenge her, too. Fuck, I want to rip the Nobles to their bones and have them grow new, untarnished skin after this. We have to take responsibility for her. Sabine and all her Virtues."

Chase comes to a sit, staring out at the gray dawn coming from my window. "I'll start today. Call a meeting and tell them about what Sabine's done."

"No." I sit up with him, my joints feeling like a middle-aged woman's instead of a spy nineteen-year-old's. "If I've learned anything about Sabine, it's that she excels at grooming her charges. She's prepared for this moment, Chase. She *wants* you to stand in front of your Nobles and accuse her of murder. I bet you she has a plan to discredit you, to make you the enemy and strip your Noble title." I bring my knees up to my chest, digging my chin into the cartilage. "She wants both societies for her own. And while she started with me, she's ending with you."

Chase shakes his head. "I won't allow it."

I approach my next question delicately. "How did she get you to the temple?"

"Ask it like it is. You mean, how did you find me on my knees in front of her?"

"I didn't mean it like that."

"I wouldn't blame you if you did. A fucking pillowcase was tossed over my head when I was at my desk in my room, and I was dragged to the temple to face her. She knows my weakness, that bitch. Sabine used you and my sister against me, said she had both of you locked up in the crypt's cages, and I lost it. Didn't think..."

"You were taken against your will?" I stare ahead, wondering how many Virtues it would've taken to bring down Chase Stone. "They must've caught you by surprise."

"It wasn't the Virtues. These arms were stronger. Broader."

"They were guys," I conclude with him. "You think Sabine's turned some of the Nobles."

"She's not a damn super villain. I *will* take her ass down."

"Did you know about my lineage?"

The sensitive change in topic shuts him up. He swivels to look at me.

"Don't lie," I say before he can open his mouth to do just that. "If you respect me at all, if Ivy's death truly means something to you, don't keep hiding the truth."

His tongue darts out, sliding across his lower lip. In the hue of dawn, his blond hair has become a glimmering sterling, his skin in an alabaster cast, as if his soul is floating just outside the edges of his body. "I didn't know the whole time. I found out a few weeks ago."

My shoulders curve over my knees. "How could you keep something like that from me?"

"Because I had a deep desire to keep you from getting hurt. Or worse."

I ignore his gruff tone. "I deserved to know."

"Callie, your lineage is a *weapon*. One that's been hidden for almost two hundred years. The Nobles hid the survival of Rose's baby for their advantage—so *they* could choose the new queen of the Virtues and regain control, and they did." Chase casts his gaze to the ceiling, his fingers tangling in his hair. "It's been nothing but push and pull with these societies. Who's the strongest. Who's the smartest. Who has the most influence. Theodore Briar convinced his brother—the first Noble King, Thorne Briar, to choose a Harrington woman to become the new Virtue queen after Rose died and squirreled away his own daughter. Why do you think that is?"

"Theodore didn't want his daughter, his secret baby with Rose, to inherit the Virtues."

"Exactly. The Virtues were already poisoned at that point, even at their origin. Without Rose to guide them, competition with the Nobles flourished. In protecting his daughter, Theodore didn't anticipate that once the Harringtons took control, it turned into a covert war of who could become more powerful and gain more allies as they grew in size and influence."

"Did the Harringtons have Rose killed so they could take her spot?"

"I don't know. Her death was ruled a suicide."

"Yes, the story is that she killed herself because she was desperate for a child and she couldn't have one. But she *did* have one. After what Sabine's—after how she—" I swallow. Collect myself. "I wouldn't put it past the Harringtons, even the two-hundred-year-old ones, to commit murder."

"You could be right. Hell, everything I've studied and memorized in the Nobles' rulebook could be nothing but lies. The Nobles overlooked the Virtues, convinced that women would never come into the kind of power they possessed. They didn't consider the Virtues' drive for success and the motivation that can provide—needing to claw themselves to the top. The Nobles didn't have that type of drive. We were men of privilege, of high-class riches, meaning we never had to consider what it was like to prove ourselves over and over again. I'm coming to understand that in an effort to manage that kind of desperation, the Noble successors never told the Virtue Queen about Rose's surviving lineage. If they did..."

It takes a moment to sort through everything Chase explains. "In hiding Rose's surviving bloodline, the Nobles maintained the power to choose the queens, instead of leaving it up to the Virtues. What I don't get is, why continue to hide it? The Virtues were under a new rule. Since these societies are following the rules of the monarch, a hundred years later, it's not like the power of Rose's bloodline could derail that kind of history."

"Actually, it can. Secret societies are sworn to their rules and oaths. Especially the original law. Think about the US Constitution. It's like that. We strictly follow the will of the founders. *Including* Rose's will, which was to have her heirs be the first in line to rule the Virtues."

I mull this over. "By that reasoning, if baby Delilah Briar ever realized her history, she could replace the queen immediately."

"Worse." Chase searches my eyes. "Think about that baby's blood, Callie. *Really* think about it."

I pinpoint the sparks, the brightness of comprehension he wills in my direction.

It hits me. I gasp. "That baby had *both* Noble and Virtue blood. Theodore and Rose. She came from two of the founders." I rub my fingers against my lips, tearing at the chapped skin. "What does the rulebook say about a member who descends from both a Noble and a Virtue?"

A faint, proud smile pulls at Chase's lips, but he tamps it down. "Congrats. You discovered our problem. If you recall, Thorne never had children with Rose. They were all stillborn or miscarriages. He had kids with his next wives, but that bloodline is diluted. Thorne never thought past his own lineage, so he never wrote anything in our rulebooks about founder blood on both sides—meaning, if the original Noble King and the first Virtue Queen had a child. He had no idea his brother, the next king in line, was having an affair with Rose, or of the baby who came from said affair. So, nothing was ever written about it. When Thorne died, he believed his inheritance died with him. Theodore became king for a time—solidifying this baby's inheritance of the societies."

"Why would he do that? He didn't want his daughter to ever know about the Nobles and Virtues."

Chase cedes my point. "After Rose died, Theodore passed Delilah's real birth certificate on to the second-highest official of the Nobles, a friend and confidant. Theodore knew if Thorne ever found out, the baby would be killed. For her safety, the baby was smuggled out and given to a middle-class family with a forged birth certificate. From then on, the original birth certificate was passed down to only one living Noble at a time—no more. My grandfather was the last one to legitimately receive the information. Then, my father found out. And instead of keeping it safe, he decided to use it to his advantage. He wasn't about to let a Rose Briar descendent languish until someone smarter and more cutthroat got the same idea he did. So, he told Sabine. They traced Delilah's heirs. And they brought you here, Callie, under the guise of recruiting you."

"I can't—I need a minute." I shuffle to the foot of my bed, my feet hitting the floor as I fold my arms around myself. "If what you're saying is ... Chase, was my mother killed so I could come here?"

The sparks in Chase's eyes die out. "Would your mother have allowed you to come here otherwise?"

"*No.*" Even as the denial leaves my lips, the truth wraps around my neck with a stranglehold. "It's not true! My mom wasn't killed over some fake laws concocted by a small-town secret society!"

"Callie," Chase says, his lips barely moving with my name. "Come back. Sit with me."

I stand and whirl to face him instead. "My world—my *everything*—was taken away because of some godforsaken rule Sabine decided to break? Why? Mom escaped. She didn't *want* to be a fucking Virtue Queen!" My palm slams into my chest. "*I* don't want to be queen! She could've left us alone. We would've lived our lives in New York, and I'd've never figured out their existence!"

Or yours, the dark trenches of my mind whisper. *I never would've met you.*

"Sabine and my father couldn't take that chance. Your mom knew of her inheritance somehow. Sabine couldn't let that kind of fatal flaw lingering in the air around her."

"She took everything from me," I hiss through clenched teeth. "And because that wasn't enough, she took Ivy, too."

"Good. Get mad, Callie, because that's the only way we can move forward and leave this fucking bedroom. My father and Sabine wanted to watch you, on their turf, to see if you were malleable enough for them to admit your heritage and rule through you. If they had you on their side, what did it matter that you had the ability to be the ultimate ruler of both the Nobles and Virtues?"

"This is so crazy," I whisper, digging my fingers into my hair. "We're talking of kingdoms and thrones and who has the right to rule, but we're in the twenty-first century! At a college! And *I'm* the one who's told she has a screw loose for thinking my stepdad killed my mom?"

"It sounds ridiculous, but this stuff has been ingrained in us for centuries. I've been groomed as a secret society member since I could crawl. My sister, too. And my father, grandfather, great-grandfather before that." A shadow ripples over his expression. "You've seen what they're capable of. Don't discount their power simply because they covet pretend royal titles."

Ivy's fading gaze forms into the air around me. Her eyes locked on mine, wet with silent pleas as she took her last breaths.

I was so useless in that moment. So benign in my ability

to assume my rightful position and kick Sabine off this so-called throne *before* Ivy had to die.

I think about what that does to a person, when someone they care about dies unexpectedly and violently. It derails the heart, imprinting a permanent mark that trails behind them like an oily shadow...

Even Sabine isn't immune to grief.

My chin jerks up. "Piper died. That wasn't in Sabine's plans when she brought me here, was it?"

Chase takes a moment before he answers. "No."

"It makes perfect sense now. Piper's death really wasn't because of the societies. Sabine and your father didn't know Piper was digging up dirt on Rose. They had no idea she was helping Emma escape their underworld. Addisyn's jealousy was a variable they didn't consider."

"You started looking into the existence of the Nobles and Virtues before they were ready. My father had to pivot hard and fast. That's when they tapped me to do their dirty work." Unreadable lines deepen his frown. "I was already in position."

"They wanted you to gain my trust. Weaken my will." My statement burns my throat, clotting my voice.

"Father admitted why it was so important I keep you close. He told me about your relation to Rose."

"And to Theodore." I massage my neck in thought. "My ancestry gives me control of both societies. Why not kill me, too, and end the bloodline for good?"

"Our pairing meant I naturally maintained more power over you, as a future Noble King. Especially if you never figured out your heritage. But I started caring. And they weren't so sure I was willing to hide the truth of your blood for much longer." Deep crevices form around Chase's full lips. "If they ever figure out just how much I've fallen for you..."

I give him a level stare. "Their plans would change again. They'd want me dead and lose the bloodline forever. Even if the rest of the Virtues and Nobles find out about their duplicity, they won't mind, because I'm already gone."

"Sabine might've killed your mom. She *definitely* killed your best friend. She's not going to stop. I have to protect you."

I peel off my pajamas and start pulling on clothes strewn about the floor.

Chase's back goes rigid. "What are you doing?"

Once I pull the Briarcliff sweater over my head, I turn. "Sabine and your dad are so ego-driven, they never gave thought to the fact that I don't *want* to rule the societies or keep their secrets. I'd rather blast them open and expose them to the world, with Ivy and Piper's ghosts cheering me on. The Nobles and Virtues may not believe you, but perhaps they'll believe me."

The word is strange on my tongue: *believe*. A definition that's been twisted, maligned, and meaningless when it comes to my life.

But this time?

"This time," I say, "I'm not going quietly. I'm showing everybody, the entire *school*, everything I've found out. Piper's diary. Rose's letters. Howard Mason's discoveries. All of Briarcliff will learn about the university's dirty secrets, and then it's up to them to do what they want with the information."

Chase sighs, readying for an argument.

"It's not up to you anymore," I say. "My only friend in the world is dead. I'm not going to sit down or be quiet or *hide* like Sabine wants. She thinks this will shut me up or bring me to her side. But I'm going to do what she least expects. I'm publicly outing her, Chase. And the Nobles. I'm done with this charade." My voice cracks. "*Done* being told what to do. I'm taking it back." I swipe under my nose. "I'm getting Ivy justice. Avenging my mom. Representing Piper. And keeping you. The last person I have left."

Chase's shoulders slope, but he lingers on my face. His lithe body slips from the bed like silk, and he prowls closer.

Cups both sides of my face.

And says, "My sweet, sweet possum. My reluctant princess. My vengeful queen. *My* girl. I am on your side. And I will stay there, whatever you decide to do."

I write long into the night.

The police presence we predicted never comes, but just as quickly as that concern sparks, I squash it and focus on finishing the most important paper of my life.

"Got it," Chase says behind me.

I tilt my head enough to the side without tearing my attention from my laptop. "Dr. Luke got back to you that fast?"

"He's willing to give us his copy of the Briarcliff email list."

I make a sound of approval, then ask offhand, "He's a Noble, isn't he?"

"He was, before the scandal."

When I don't fill the silence, he continues, "We Nobles are fine with affairs, crimes, acts of idiocy, so long as they're done discreetly. Dr. Luke's blowback carried too far for the Nobles to protect him any longer."

It's comforting that Chase doesn't bother to hide the obvious from me anymore. "Send it to me."

If Chase is concerned over the flatness of my tone, he doesn't say anything. My email *dings* with his message, and I toggle to my inbox and copy it. "Thanks."

Chase comes up behind me, laying his hands on my shoulders and bringing his mouth to my ear. After a light kiss, he says, "I'm only going to ask this because I feel it's warranted. Are you sure you want to do this?"

I spin to capture his lips with mine. When I pull away from him, I stare dead-on into his eyes.

And in answer, I click *send*.

Chase blows air out of his mouth. "Fuck. Lady Luck be with us."

"We don't need luck," I say when I stand. "All we need is desire. And I have the crushing need to fuck that woman over in spades."

3

———

CHASE

I leave Callie drifting between her sheets, but not before smoothing the lines of grief on her forehead until she at last fell asleep.

Dawn floated away with her, the glaring blue of the sky taking its place as I sneak out of Thorne House and prowl into mine, taking the side stairs where security thoughtfully (and with enough bribery) turns their back until I reach my door and stalk in.

I prod a sleeping Rio with my boot, right in the ass. "Up."

Rio twists in his bed, mumbling something close to "No, motherfucker," before throwing his arm over his face.

As a Plan B, I rub the gray sludge of former snow from my soles onto his exposed abdomen.

He screeches, bolting upright. "The fuck, man?"

"I said up."

"Fine. I'm up. What do you want?"

"Out."

"Multiple syllables not your forté today, huh?"

"Last warning."

"It's my room!"

"And mine. Which I'm commandeering. As your prince."

Rio stares at me a moment, the brown of his eyes resembling murky, hazy sludge, likely remnants from smoking last night. "Pulling the Noble card on me at the ass-crack of dawn. Thanks a bunch, *Prince*."

I eye him as he slides out of bed, his footsteps as heavy as the headache I'm sure he's nursing. When he scratches the top of his head, his dark hair tangled and unkempt between his fingers, I wonder if he knows.

If he participated.

"You seeing Ivy before exams?" I ask casually.

"Nah." Rio steps into his pants, then goes for his belt. "Meeting her after, though."

I make a sound, though if you ask me, I'm not sure what it's supposed to communicate. All I can see is Ivy's diluted blood circling down the shower drain beneath Callie's bare feet.

After buttoning his shirt and throwing his blazer over his shoulder, Rio says, "Whatever you have planned this morning, she better be worth it. You haven't even shaved. Do you think she has?" He winks.

Hell. He thinks I'm kicking him out to receive some pre-exam fuck from some faceless co-ed, like we used to do before freshmen year reared up and sank its fangs into my neck.

Or ... before Callie showed her face at Briarcliff.

Her eyes, rimmed in gold and filled with shattered jade, cloud my vision until I blink them back, but the beauty of her refuses to be dimmed.

Growling, I follow Rio out of the bedroom, my glare so tangible, it should leave marks on his back.

Rio opens the door, where Tempest is not so surprisingly leaning against the frame. He tips an imaginary top-hat the moment Rio notices him and jumps back in surprise. "Howdy."

"You assholes keep ruining my morning. This is your booty call?" Rio turns to me. "I'm disappointed, man. I was hoping you were back to your old ways. Then, at least, we could all get back to ours."

"Go find Ivy." I spit out the words before my better judgment can properly contain them, but Rio, senseless, ignorant jackass that he is, doesn't blink at the undertone.

"Great idea. *She* follows our rules. I can fuck her and not have Mommy and Daddy be angry at me," Rio says, then dips around Tempest before I can think of a proper retort. Or better yet, before I can grab him by the back of his collar so I can drag him back in here and invert his goddamned nose.

"I see he's his usual maggot self," Tempest muses as he strolls in, shutting the door behind him.

I dart a final look at the door. "He's not our problem."

Tempest grows serious. "Talk to me."

I gesture to our kitchenette, where we start to sit on the two stools, but I pop off, unable to contain the tight wiring of my body for one meager second. "What do you know about last night?"

"Last night?" Tempest cocks a brow. "I studied, drank a tumbler of smuggled whiskey, then curled up in my bed and slept like a milked kitten. But I assume my bedtime routine isn't why you texted me so early."

I get to the meat of it. "Sabine killed Ivy last night."

Other than his body going still, Tempest doesn't react.

"I was there. So was Callie. I'm convinced the bitch was aiming for me, but..." *Callie stood in front of the blade* "...she changed her mind last minute and stabbed her current princess instead."

"Why in the fuck would she do that?"

I shrug, but it doesn't convey nearly enough meaning, so I scrape a hand down my face instead. Fathoming the unexpected death of Ivy rubs me raw, but adding Callie on top of it—a girl who dove in front of me, whose vanilla-scented hair cascaded over my face with the force of her jump, and the heat of her haggard breath dampened my neck as she clutched me—is another thing entirely. I don't feel things for girls. I *never* feel the need to claw them off my body and throw them behind me, teeth bared for battle.

Yet I wanted to do all that and more for her. To end her heartbreak. To rewind those moments until I'm holding the knife and cutting out Sabine's heart instead.

"I'm not so dense as to believe murder doesn't happen in our ranks, but to do it so outrageously? Sabine believes she's invincible, Temp. She doesn't think anything will come of this."

Tempest stares at the dark marbling of the countertop, his gaze hooded and unreadable. "Who else knows?"

"No one other than Callie."

He sets his jaw. Looks up. "Good. We're gonna keep it that way."

"No," I correct, "we're going to kick down Sabine's doors and drag her out in front of all our members and behead her."

"That's a quaint image, but you and I both know if you take her actions to the king, nothing will come of it."

"I'm so sick and *fucking* tired of nothing coming of shit! First, my sister's mutilated and nearly killed. Then Piper dies. Now Ivy. We swore to lay low until the right time, and I was with you on that oath—but this? This makes three. I can't let this go on any longer."

"Here's how I see it." Tempest rises and tucks his hands in his pockets. "Sabine went into last night with the sole motivation of ending your life. Likely she had a plan for when you were a corpse at her feet. I'm thinking, Callie's psychiatric history got the better of her, and she stabbed the shit out of you, and Ivy, poor dear, tried to intervene but was gutted for her efforts, too."

"That's cold, T."

"Forgive me for the brief summary, but even you have to admit that Callie's mental history is like catnip. Using it isn't even diabolical. It's such pluckable, low-hanging fruit."

I do my best to control an unwanted eye twitch.

Tempest sweeps out a hand, continuing his one-man, fucked-up Shakespearean theater. "But alas, circumstances occurred, and variables came into play that Sabine didn't quite plan for, like your girl throwing herself in front of you. Death by literal backstabbing can't work if Callie's supposed to be the villain wielding the knife. So, Sabine used quick-thinking and switched gears, deciding to sacrifice her top girl because sending you a message was more important. Think on that, Stone. The consequence of killing someone close to her was less important than screwing you over. There is no way you and Callie can stay together after this."

"Stand down." I curl my lip at him. "This isn't some Romeo and Juliet moment where I take a vial of poison and sacrifice myself for a love story. Our society is under threat. Our ranks put into question. My *princedom* at stake."

Tempest grips my arms, not to shake sense into me, but to assist in having me sink to his level. "I certainly hope you see it that way," he says, his lips barely riding over the words. "Because from an outsider's point of view, you're doing a helluva lot to fuck up your takeover of the Nobles for a girl."

"You know who she is." I shove out of his hold. "You're the *only* other person who understands the dangers of Callie's legacy and why I kept up the charade of seducing her to keep my father happy, and why I'm still keeping her close. We need her on our side, T. And after last night? She's gone rogue. And that's not a benefit to any of us."

I tell him about Callie's mass email that's likely hit everyone's inbox by now—including his. Tempest's expression grows shadows, but he stays quiet.

"Why'd you let her do it?" Tempest asks after I finish.

"Because I need her to trust me. Her best friend was violently murdered in front of her. How would it have looked if I tried to convince her to do nothing?" I start pacing the room, my veins throbbing, my arteries pumping. "She was silenced when her mother died. Labeled unhinged and kept separate from any information regarding Meredith Ryan's murder. Who was a former Virtue, by the way."

Tempest doesn't flinch at my fact-drop. He wouldn't, since unearthing long-forgotten, scandalous secret society mysteries is part of his deal as my second-in-command. Tempest is the sole recipient of my wants, theories, and terrible truths. He alone understands the desperation behind my goal to steal the Noble reins from my father.

"I had to give Callie some control," I say through his silence. "Some ability to seek revenge. Otherwise, she'd be kicked down, locked up, voiceless, and betrayed. She may not have gotten back up this time."

Tempest studies me. "Are you sure your concerns for her are surface level?"

"I'm protecting her as I've always done." Then, to cover any missteps I may have made, I add, "Causing her to become strangled and unsure again does neither of us any good. We need Callie at the top of her game, ready to do anything we ask. Curled up in a ball and wailing at the walls isn't her ideal state."

"There will be a lot of blowback because of that email."

"How about another girl's murder? You think there'll be issues with that?"

Tempest ignores my sarcasm. "I'd bet my parents' next blockbuster movie that Sabine has prepared for this moment. And that's fine, because you're coming out with your own story."

Tempest stops any retort by lifting his hand, silently asking me to hear him out before I lose it.

"As your only ally, my duty is to keep *you* safe. Not her, not Ivy, not even our boys. You first. Listen to me, and listen well. This is how we'll play it—you're going to resume making Calla Lily Ryan's life hell."

I lift my brows, sucking in breath for a sweeping denial, but my throat constricts before I voice sound.

Tempest senses the opening. "If you want to keep her safe, this is how you'll do it. Callie's figured out her heritage. Great. Sabine saw her as a threat before, but now it's an impending avalanche. And there's also you to contend with. You care too much about the new girl, and she's developed feelings for you, too—which, thank you both, was show-cased in front of our evil queen last night. With that kind of proof, Sabine's on the warpath. She's so keen on ending you, she was willing to sacrifice Ivy to prove her suspicions that you've continued ignoring your father's instructions, despite the public lashing."

The sound of the dagger sinking into Ivy's skin, then Callie's piercing scream, stirs the air around me. For a minute, I think I'm holding Callie's weight again, bracing her against my chest as her tears drip from her chin, cold by the time they hit my collarbone.

I blink, and Tempest comes back into focus.

"We can't take their perception of your treachery at face value," he continues. "In order to get Sabine to back off, you need to shut up about Ivy and distance yourself from Callie.

No—that's not enough. You have to make Callie hate you, Chase. Like *fucking* despise you. If Sabine can kill her princess without a thought, she'll kill you and Callie with just as much ease and take the Nobles and Virtues for herself."

I rub my fingers against my lips, air heaving from my nose, but I can't argue his points. "Sabine has my father. She's taken the Virtues and made them into her playthings. She has powerful men at her disposal by placing key girls in positions to annihilate them. Why isn't that enough for this cunt?"

Tempest's pale eyes pin mine. "After Piper's death, this runs deeper for her now. I don't think she'll rest until she has you by the balls. Your sister was first, but I'm confident Sabine's ultimate goal is your destruction. Do me a favor, don't help her along."

I grit my teeth, my jaw aching with the force. "I won't rest until I avenge my sister and keep Callie from the same fate. That clear?"

"Crystal. And we can do all that. Intelligently and without this whole cocked-and-loaded thing you have going on right now."

"I have to warn her."

Tempest's eyelids lower to half-mast. "Do what you must, but don't draw any more attention to yourselves. You two are done. Do *you* understand?"

"Yeah." I massage the back of my neck, staring at nothing but seeing everything. "I have to ruin her at the same time I'm falling in love with her."

4

CALLIE

By the time the sun crests over the polished stone landscape of Briarcliff University, I'm dressed and on my third cup of coffee.

My hand shakes as I set my mug on the counter for the final time, my stomach growling for more sustenance. I tried to satiate it—with cereal, a string cheese, a banana, even a damn cookie—but I vomited every time.

Ivy's not alive.

She's dead because of what I represent. Some fake queen meant to rule a concealed class of pompous, psychopathic assholes.

And my mom died for it, too.

No wonder I can't keep anything down. How am I supposed to reconcile that kind of mindfuck with a complete breakfast?

Emma's door creaks open, and I break out of my vortex stare into our granite countertop.

"The craziest thing just happened," Emma says in greeting. "I got the most hilarious email this morning."

I give a curt nod, then push away from the counter and toss my backpack over my shoulder.

"Holy shit, Callie. What have you done?"

"Told the truth."

"You've outlined *everything*." Emma holds up her phone. "Rose Briar's letter. Howard Mason's journal. *Piper's* diary. Jesus—Ivy's murder last night."

"It's the only way I know how to fight back and protect us at the same time."

Emma gapes. "How the *fuck* is this meant to be a defense? Who did you send this to? Everyone? The entire school? The national news stations? *Callie.*"

I don't react to her heightening panic. "Did I ever tell you that Ahmar and my mom used to catch up over coffee some nights?"

"I can't wait to see where this is going. Did my brother agree to this?"

I ignore her question. "Most times, I slept through their meetups, since it was largely them decompressing, shooting the shit, that kind of thing. But one time, I couldn't sleep. I went into the kitchen to ask for a glass of warm milk, but right when I reached the threshold, I heard Ahmar say, 'Seriously, Mer, you can take all the photos you want, provide all the evidence, but sometimes, the cops just can't act. Funds are too thin. Man-power too spread out. So, you know what I gotta do sometimes? Take it public. *Nothing* makes a commissioner act faster than throwing scandal at the press.'" I shrug. "So that's what I did."

"There are no facts. Everything you collected was stolen from you. How is anyone supposed to believe this?"

"I don't need truth. I need panic. Interest. Rumors. The Virtues can't touch us while the gossip swirls."

Emma's phone dangles at her hip. She takes one step back. "I don't know whether to admire you or fear you. You don't ... sound right."

I respond colorlessly. "I don't know how I'm supposed to act. Sabine wants to take everything from me until I can't rely on anyone but her or the Virtues. I'd rather face public ridicule than become her next princess. And with these kinds of accusations sent to parents, faculty, and the Briarcliff University staff and Board of Directors? I'm dragging her out of her protective cave and feeding her to their stockholders. She can figure out how to explain Ivy's blood on her hands. Because, after this semester, I'm out." I breathe in deep, then level my shoulders. "I'm going home."

"I don't blame you," Emma says quietly. "Though I don't think it'll remove you from danger."

"My mother knew she didn't belong here. If she were alive today, she'd never have let me step on this soil to even glimpse the university."

"What about my brother? Does he know you're leaving?"

Chase. *My* Chase. He left soon after I fell asleep, deciding that if the police came, he probably shouldn't be here. Haskins never knocked on my door last night, but that doesn't mean he won't find me this morning.

But Chase is different. I can't let him find me, because if I do, I'll break. I'll fall into his arms. I'll stay.

"He'll understand," is all I can say.

"He might say he does, but he's lying. You're the one person he doesn't have to play games with or be one step ahead of. You're real—you're showing him what an *actual* person is like outside these walls and away from Briarcliff's chains. If you leave, I might lose the remaining piece of him that's been able to withstand our father's tampering."

My lips twitch in hesitation, but I don't think Emma notices. "Chase will be fine. He's strong."

I turn for the door.

"Hey, Callie?"

"Yeah?"

Emma sucks on her cheek in thought. "This may come out strange, even though we *are* here for a diploma. But I feel like I should remind you: exams are today. Assuming your mass email doesn't screw over the curve to epic proportions, that is."

With any other person, I'd be concerned over Emma's mention of exams the day after I watched Ivy die. But Emma isn't any person. She has her own tragedies inside her and her own ways of dealing. Sarcasm and compartmentalizing are the top tools in her box.

But the calculus final? Neither of us has the mental bandwidth to handle that this morning.

I say to Emma on a sigh, "Fuck."

Ahmar calls me on my walk to the university's main building.

"How's it going, kiddo?"

I choose my words carefully, while clomping along in the snow. "Have you found out more about the Nobles and Virtues?"

Ahmar reacts to my cheerlessness with a short, "Calla."

"It's bad here, Ahmar. Really bad. Ivy"—It *hurts* to say her name—"Ivy was killed last night."

Silence.

My story comes out in a rush. The knife. How it cut Ivy's throat. How she bled to death in my arms. And just ... how.

"Ahmar?" I ask, once the sickness surrounding my words subsides. "Are you still there?"

"Kiddo, I'm working on processing all you've said."

"It's a lot, but it's true. I was *there*, and so was Chase, and Ivy ... Ivy..." I end on a sob.

"Baby girl." Ahmar's sigh is filled with love. "I think I gotta come over there."

Nodding vigorously, I blurt into my phone, "That's a great idea. I don't know if Haskins is in the societies' pockets, but a lot of the Briarcliff PD sure are, and I'm positive they're working on covering up Ivy's death. She was *murdered*, Ahmar. Just like my mom." I halt in the middle of the walkway, the overnight snow clumped and packed to the sides. "Oh my God, Ahmar, I haven't told you who did it —*Sabine* had Mom killed—"

"Callie. Honey. Take a breath."

"I can't, Ahmar! Don't you see? It all comes back to the Virtues. I have the blood they've been looking for! They don't want me to—"

"Jesus Christ, honey." Ahmar's voice grows thick before it cracks. "Please stop."

"No! They can't kill any more people I love, okay? I won't let them. I can't let them take Chase!"

"*ENOUGH!*"

Ahmar's yell has me careening, but I right myself before tripping over a mound of plowed snow.

"Sweetheart, think about what you're saying. *Think* about how crazy this sounds!"

"But it's the truth!" My voice shreds into the air.

"You can't go down this road again. I won't let you. I'm coming over there, and I'm taking you home."

"What?" I blink, staring into the blinding white until tree-tops blur into the horizon.

"You're scaring me," Ahmar whispers. I've never heard him whisper before. "All this crazy-talk ... I thought I was helping you by listening to your theories and letting you work them out until you came to the solid conclusion. The *right* answer. But you're not. You've spiraled, and I'm taking the blame for that."

"*Spiraled?*" My shock echoes through the landscape. "Ahmar, please. This isn't like last time. This *is* *real*. I watched my friend die last night. I-I felt her die. I'm not making this up or chasing wild theories or seeing things—don't come." My lower lip, dampened and chilled with sudden tears, wobbles. "Don't come to try and put me away again."

"Anything I do, *anything*, is because I love you. I even looked into these societies you keep mentioning, and yes, they do exist."

"See! I told you!"

"They're as legitimate as skulls and bones or locks and keys or whatever those Ivy Leagues call their secret clubs. Calla, what I'm saying is, they are the Ivy League equivalent of massive donations from their alumni and ego-stroking meetings and dumb rituals well after graduation. These exclusive clubs are nothing but a way to reward over-inflated, privileged egos for being rich and contributing to the success of capitalism."

My heart sinks. "Ahmar, don't say this. The Virtues are so much worse than that. There are sex rings involved, and pay-offs, and blackmail."

"That may be, but it's impossible to prove."

"*I've* just proved it! I saw everything!"

I hear Ahmar's slow inhale and exhale. "Sweetheart, I love you with all my heart, but you are not a credible witness."

"Then find somebody who is! Dr. Luke. He was a Noble but was kicked out for getting involved with Piper. If you talk to him, I bet he's pissed enough to—"

"Baby girl, I'm gonna stop you right there."

My face crumbles, the collapse made all the easier by the crippling cold. "You've always been in my corner. Believed me when no one else did. So, *believe* me when I say my mother was killed by the Virtues for her automatic inheritance of the society. Ivy was killed to teach me a lesson. And Sabine only wants me alive to become her puppet. I'm in danger, Ahmar, and you're the only adult who will help me."

"God. *Damn it.*" I can picture Ahmar's internal arguments with himself and the way he'd be running his hand down his face. Balling a fist in his hair. Punching a nearby wall. He did all those things directly after we found my mother. "I wish you would hear me, kiddo, loud and clear. I want to help you. I do, and that's why I'm offering to come get you before I call your Dad and let him know you're falling apart."

"Do it!" I dare him. "He and Lynda will *both* admit the danger of the Virtues."

But ... will they?

Blair's in the picture now. A baby girl they have to protect better than they did me.

"Calla, I've been threatened with losing my job if I pursue this any further."

That has me whirling. "What?"

"I'm not supposed to be messing with other jurisdictions. You and I both know this. But now my lieutenant is involved, and he's telling me if I keep looking into Briarcliff crimes, I'm out on my ass. We're overloaded as it is. He can't afford to have me split my efforts."

"But ... you're doing it during your down time. He can't relegate the hours you're not working."

"It's come from the top. The commissioner has told me, point blank, to end my research on Briarcliff."

"I don't..."

"Baby. You do. You do understand. This is out of my hands. You have to let Briarcliff PD do their jobs, and you have to come home."

It's amazing. Not ten minutes ago, I'd told Emma I was going home. Leaving. Escaping. Into another cage, all the same. "I can't. I won't. Ivy's body is barely cold, and my mother's has been cold too long."

"Ah, sweetie." Ahmar sniffs, and I swear to God, I think I'm making him cry. "You're breaking my heart. You scare me so much. More than I've ever felt fear in my life. I need you to come back. You can't be there anymore."

"If you can't see what's in front of your eyes..." I take a deep breath. "There's no reason a commissioner and lieutenant would be so concerned with your off-hours, especially if it's not affecting your work, and I know you. It's not. They're probably former Nobles. And you know what? One is likely been back to the Virtue temple and used that bedroom with underaged girls—"

"Do *not* keep going with that line of thought, Calla Lily."

Ahmar's use of my full name brings me up short. He's never, in all my years of knowing him, released my birth name like fire escaping his mouth.

"Mom *went* here, Ahmar!"

"That doesn't mean she was killed because of it. Your momma photographed a lot of crime scenes, mainly gang-related. We've looked into Briarcliff, and to put it simply, the evidence just isn't as strong as possible gang retaliation."

"What about my roommate being pushed off a cliff? Are you going to disregard that, too?"

"I'm not dismissing you, honey. I'm laying out the facts—"

"People are dying all around me!"

My yell causes the few Briarcliff students heading to exams this early to falter and look back at me.

"Everywhere I turn," I continue, aiming for calm, "somebody I care about dies. You can't pretend not to see that."

"You are not the reason, honey."

Instead of a comfort, the sweetness in his tone only angers me further. "Stop saying that like it's true. I *am* the cause. It's my bloodline that's done this."

"We are not in the stone ages. You can't expect me to buy this descendent business like it's a bona fide recipe for murder. Your momma was in a high-risk career. Your roommate was involved in multiple affairs and was knocked up by her sister's boyfriend, thus becoming a victim to her sister's rage and jealousy."

"And Ivy?" My question is nothing but a tremble of sound. "What about her?"

"That, I don't know. I haven't heard anything. Baby, I'm sorry."

He doesn't believe me.

My voice comes out softer. Flatter. The Briarcliff forest dulls in my vision. "I understand. I'm on my own. If you won't believe me now, then I have to gather more evidence. I'll do just that."

"Calla, don't you dare hang up on m—"

The phone drops to my side.

I trudge the rest of the way to school with the same misery I carried when I found my mother, massacred on the floor.

5

CALLIE

I should be on a first-name basis with the Briarcliff prefects at this point, but to be honest, when I'm summoned by yet another one as soon as I enter the university, her face doesn't even look familiar.

Her expression, however, does.

Callie the troublemaker, drawing the attention of the Chancellor. Again.

Shoulders hunched, I make a left into the faculty wing, not bothering to toss my things into my locker.

With each step, a viscous film grows around my heart, becoming thicker and slimier the more time that passes between Ivy's last breaths and bringing her murderer to justice.

Like today, for example. Why is everyone still in school? Shouldn't we be holding a memorial or an assembly for another tragic victim at Briarcliff?

I hate to think on the reason for the silence, but it's

obvious in the roots of this university. Unexplainable events, secrets, lies, mysterious deaths ... all of it grows in Briarcliff soil, yet everyone just steps over the weeds.

Marron's door is open, leaving me exposed in his door-frame before I'm ready.

"Ah. Miss Ryan. Come on in."

I jolt at my name. A quick scan of his office leads to further confusion.

Haskins isn't here. And now that I think about it, I didn't pass one patrol car on my trek to the university.

"You're looking rather pale," Marron says as he rustles papers on his desk, flicking a glance in my direction. "Do sit down."

With stiff legs, I do as he asks, dropping my bag at my feet before taking a visitor's chair.

"Now." Marron stacks the same pile of papers. "I assume you're curious as to why I've called you in this morning right before your first exam."

"Actually, I know exactly why I'm here."

At last, Marron's gaze steadies on mine. He arches a brow. "Am I correct in assuming you will take responsibility for the dissemination of complete misinformation *and* the unauthorized use of parent and faculty email addresses last night?"

"I'd think you'd be more upset that your secret societies are outed," I observe, neither confirming nor denying. "But in this place, I guess it takes a lot more than attributing a second girl's murder to the Virtues to deepen your frown."

"Excuse me?"

"Ivara Alling." My voice shakes, and I fight for control. "Ivy. She was killed last night by Sabine Harrington."

Marron leans back in his seat. His stare doesn't leave my face.

I continue, "You know who Sabine Harrington really is. The queen of the Virtues, a secret society created by Rose Briar, and after her death, continued on by women anxious to claim power in a man-driven world. Namely, the Harringtons, which Sabine married into."

"Good gracious, you have quite the imagination. I'm not surprised that it's largely in line with the anonymous email sent out."

I squint at him. "The Virtues weren't the first. Thorne Briar created the Nobles, an elite secret society meant to groom and prepare boys for the ultimate status within college, then the workforce, and ultimately, key positions of political power."

Marron sighs. "Miss Ryan, as much as I enjoy a good story-telling—"

"You're one of them."

A muscle under Marron's eye twitches.

"A Noble Viscount. I saw you in your red robe, telling what I can only assume are high-class escorts to strip for the freshmen initiation this year. I also heard your talk of soul-mates—a lame attempt at controlling the Virtues, if I've ever heard one, but I'm guessing you Nobles haven't mentally surpassed the whole 'let's marry the woman and that'll keep her out of trouble' trope."

I wait for my theoretical mike to drop—I'm so angry, so

helplessly enraged, that all I want to do is affect someone, hurt someone, *wake them the fuck up.*

"Why, yes." Marron lays his forearms on his desk. "I read all this in the elaborate, paranoid rambling you sent to all faculty and parents last night."

"There's nothing delusional about an anonymous email I happen to agree with," I hedge.

"You are treading such dangerous waters." Marron clucks his tongue. "And I sincerely don't think you care." He lifts a sheaf of stapled papers, turning them so I can read the first page. "Indeed, your psychiatric transcripts assure me of your inability to discern fact from fiction when you're in such a dissociated state." He holds up a hand to prevent argument. "Allow me to elaborate."

Marron licks his finger, turns the page, and reads, "'The patient suffers from paranoid personality disorder. On a recent occasion, extreme paranoia occurred in the form of the patient's insistence that her stepfather killed her mother. PPD can also include an unrelenting mistrust and suspicion of others, even when there is no reason for those suspicions to be cast, of which the patient also displays.'" Marron looks up at me over the top of the paper. "Does any of that ring a bell?"

"You bastard," I hiss under my breath. Marron doesn't react. "Ivy was stabbed in the neck by Sabine because that woman is so starved for power that she'd rather traffic, maim, and kill the girls she enlists, while you just sit there and preside over your over-priced, over-privileged, garbage dump of a school, uncaring of the senseless deaths of your own students."

"Although you have yet to admit it, you've caused quite a stir with our parents. I assure you, I have easily quelled the hurricane you've attempted to create with one, simple attachment to your diatribe." He lifts my hospital transcripts again. "This."

"Throw my past at me all you want," I seethe. "That doesn't change what I saw last night. I had Ivy's blood under my fingernails—"

"Ah." Marron sits back, giving me the once-over. "You're looking rather clean from my perspective. Did you shower?" His expression grows coy. "Did Mr. Stone help with the cleanse? Indeed, did he convince you to write this email that can so easily be discredited with your fragile mental state?"

My heartbeat kicks up, pounds, slams in my throat, but I keep my voice level. Pray for it. "My friend's *body* is in your library. I saw the police lights last night. Soon, you'll have to answer for another death on your watch."

"Hmm." Marron puts his index fingers to his lips and turns his attention to his desk. "I don't normally break confidentiality, but I believe I have something you should listen to."

I balk. "Why isn't anybody *hearing* me? There's no time for more stupid games! Your Virtue Queen is out of her—"

Ivy's voice fills the room.

"Hi Chancellor, um, I'm sorry to call so late, especially before finals, but my mom's sick. Like, really not doing well. She's been diagnosed with ... with ... ovarian cancer, and I'd really like to be with her. I hope you can understand. I'll defer this semester in hopes you will allow me to repeat my freshmen year. You under-

stand, family comes first. I need to be with my mom. Please send anything my parents need to sign through email. Thank you."

Once the grief at hearing her one last time runs through my veins, once shock filters through my head—"No. *No!* Can't you hear the fear in her voice? Ivy's terrified! Sabine must've made her say this before she put Ivy on her knees. Sabine plunged a knife into her while Ivy had her back turned! And she *trusted* her! All Ivy wanted to do was save her family!" I stand so abruptly, my chair falls backward, knocking into a side table and scattering picture frames across the floor. "How could you defend such a woman? How can you encourage such hate against children?"

Marron watches my tirade in such a bland and non-reactive state, I'm actually terrified.

"Chancellor..." It comes out as a whimper. "Please."

Marron purses his lips. "I'm sure you won't be surprised when I say, as soon as I can prove you were the one who sent that baseless stream of consciousness to Briarcliff's parents, you will be expelled from these grounds."

"Don't fall in line. Just once, do the right thing. Sabine can't get away with this."

"I'm afraid, Miss Ryan, that your disorder has clouded your better judgment. You're an adult now, so there's no possibility of forcing you to get the help you need, but I implore you, seek that rehabilitation. Not only am I genuinely concerned for the students around you, I'm also concerned for your well-being."

"*Fuck you,*" I spit.

Marron *tsks*, then sighs. "Do I need security to escort you out?"

I turn my back to him in answer.

"Good girl," he murmurs, but his voice no longer registers. "And I wish you the very best of luck with your exams today."

I have to step over the scattered pictures, quelling the urge to kick and stomp on them until they're as destroyed as my insides feel, but one overturned frame distracts me enough to pause. There's a strip of masking tape on the back, and the name MR. MARRON, AKA HOWARD MASON, circa 2001, scrawled over it with black marker.

I'm bending and picking it up before my mind accompanies the movement. When I turn it to see the picture, my mouth drops open in awe.

"Who is this?" I whisper. Most of me doesn't care if Marron heard me or not.

Yet, he stops his mindless shuffling of papers as soon as he registers what I'm holding.

"My old faculty photo," he snipes. "I was a teacher here before I became Chancellor. Do put it down before you ruin it further."

"You ... you're Howard Mason?"

Marron licks his upper teeth. "I haven't been called that since my attendance here."

I ask through the massive lump in my throat, "Why did you change your name?"

Marron's expression hardens. "Miss Ryan, you've vastly overstayed your welcome. Leave my office before I'm forced to initiate a school lockdown and have you dragged out by police."

His overdramatic warning doesn't affect me. "You were

against them. When you went to school here, you made it your mission to expose the Nobles, but now you're one of them. Why? How?"

"Miss Taskin!" Marron hollers. "Allow security to escort Miss Ryan to her first exam, of which I have no doubt she will excel."

But I'm not finished. "2001 ... that's when my mother went here. Did you know her? Were you her teacher?" My face goes numb. "Were you involved in her—?"

"Miss Ryan, you're to come with me."

I look over my shoulder to where a beefy school security guy in a dark suit stands nearby. And he looks ready to drag me out by my hair.

"You're not getting away with this." I whirl on Marron, even as security moves to stand between the Chancellor and me. "You're just as culpable as Sabine. You covered up a murder last night, and the fact that you can just sit there and pretend an innocent girl isn't dead *sickens* me. You're pathetic. Disgusting. And when justice finally comes for you and you cry out your last words, I hope they're the same ones you wrote in your journal—"

Marron's eyes flicker.

"—*Help me.* This time, no one will. Nobody will come to your rescue. I'll make sure of it."

Security's broad body wrestles me out simply by shadowing my smaller form, but I make sure my eyes are bright, that they're made of starlit fire, for every second Marron holds my stare, until security pulls the door shut.

6

CALLIE

I join the swell of students heading to class, having no choice but to merge into the mass and become as inconspicuous as possible.

Anonymity turns out to be insanely difficult when all I hear is talk of the email last night and the big reveal of secret societies on campus.

This psycho says Ivy's dead, someone whispers.

If dead is going home and avoiding finals, then I guess she's gone to fucking heaven, another says and laughs.

Do you think it's true?

Nobles and Virtues? What the hell? Why wasn't I chosen?

Piper and Addy's mom? Are you serious? The asshole who wrote this ruined my MILF moment. I don't want to have my cock slit while I bang her.

Fake news. Total bullshit.

No proof.

Gossip Girl wannabe.

Russian hacker for sure.

As we progress down the hallway and my exposé turns to fodder, my heart sinks to the deepest chamber in my chest. I was so convinced that all Briarcliff University needed was a rumor. It's fueled so much before—Piper's death, Addisyn's arrest, Rose Briar's mysterious disappearance...

Why *shouldn't* more uncertainty taint student thoughts and cause faculty to second-guess their career choice?

They should be rewinding their memories, where sudden inconsistencies become obvious, now that I've given them context. Like the university's hidden rooms and hallways and the random disappearances of their roommate at night. The sudden propulsion of their average-grade friend being awarded all A's in every single exam. The pairing of two people who are complete opposites, yet now call themselves soulmates.

Something.

... yet, nothing comes out of these mouths except ridicule.

Don't they know what they're treading over every day at this school? Can't they feel the ghosts they pass or notice the dried blood under their feet when they go to the library to study?

I clamp down on the banshee that wants to wail its way out of my throat and into these ignorant, stupidly neglectful ears.

If clear words and accusations will never convince these people ... I need the blood on my hands.

My tongue feels like a swollen lump in my mouth, a

useless muscle mass that's done nothing to help. I'm at a loss on what to do, other than retrace last night's steps, so I can personally witness what they've done to clean up the library and temple.

My best friend. My *lost* friend.

Tears well, but I sniff hard and order my eyes to stop getting so hot. As soon as I'm able, I'll find Chase. As soon as I can talk to someone who saw what I did, things will be better.

I step into calculus in an anonymous wave of movement, silently taking my seat, yet staring hard at the vacant chair across from mine. My eyes don't leave Ivy's permanently empty spot until that special part of me that seems to conjure him when I need him the most flickers to life.

On a hitch of breath, I look up.

Chase meets my eyes and holds on, giving a single, imperceptible nod before he takes his seat.

Professor Dawson passes out the exams and calls for us to begin, but all I can focus on are Ivy's last words. All I hear are her wet gasps for breath as blood fills her lungs.

And the only picture on the backs of my eyelids is of my mother, interposed over Ivy in the same helpless, dying state.

"Time!" Dawson announces. "Pencils down."

The hour went by with nothing but one breath filling my lungs. Blinking, I study the stapled exam, apparently sifted through by my fingers since the pages are dog-eared and fanned through. My hand aches from my prolonged grip on my pencil, and for the first time, I notice the lead is worn down to the nub.

Curious, I go back to my exam, staring at the answers for each equation.

For every single question, I wrote the same answer: **2.**

For a pair of unanswered deaths. Ivy and my mother.

Over and over, scrawled on each page and on the backs, in cursive, then block numbers, until there's nothing left but faded scribbles as my pencil wore down.

As Dawson comes by to pick up my exam, he frowns, yet says nothing as he tucks it in with the others.

I stare at his back as he continues to gather exams.

Has Chancellor Marron already warned the professors of my disintegrating mental state and imminent departure? Is that why Dawson's so unaffected?

He's a Noble, too.

Once finals are collected, the classroom bursts with noise. Voices pile on top of one another, discussion of the strange midnight email quickly overtaking any comparisons over the toughest equations.

Chase finds me through the crowd. "With me."

We don't create the stir we normally do when Chase hooks my arm and escorts me out. Too much attention remains on the anonymous email.

"Where should we go?" I ask him under my breath as we filter through the students in the hallway.

"Our Vault."

I almost trip over my feet. "You mean, back to the—?"

"Yeah. I do."

We veer around a corner and stop in front of a custodian's closet. After a brief scan of the area, Chase uses his keycard, and the lock beeps green.

"What about the rest of your finals?" I ask, genuinely concerned. My grades, I've all but given up on and passed over to Marron for the final F, but Chase? He has roots here. Priorities. Loyalties. *Rules.*

All I get from him is a steady, "It's fine," before he shuts us into the black.

I don't bother to ask more questions, relying on my sense of touch instead. I keep my hold on Chase's arm as he navigates seamlessly around shelves of cleaning items until we reach a wall.

Another small light flashes green, followed by a low whine of hinges.

"Of all the places," I whisper as he pulls me deeper. "I wouldn't have thought to search the janitor's storage space for hidden access to a Noble room."

"This didn't used to be a supply closet. It was Thorne Briar's office before the faculty wing was created, moving the Chancellor's office."

The mention of the word *Chancellor* has goosebumps skittering under my skin. "Chase, Chancellor Marron's not who—"

"Shh. We're in the walls right now. If we talk loud enough, people can hear us in the hallways."

Good to know. I hunch forward and keep my hands on his shoulders as we traipse through the darkness.

"Steps ahead."

I feel around with the tip of my shoe before descending the first step, Chase's tight, reassuring grip on my hand leading me the rest of the way down.

After what feels like fifty steps, Chase finally begins

lighting sconces with his pocket lighter, the dampened stonework of the walls gleaming into focus.

It doesn't escape me that the Nobles have largely stuck to old traditions and their original rooms, unlike the Virtues. Granted, the Virtues' original temple was destroyed in a fire, but Sabine allowed it to happen. She shut Emma in and never called 911. She was probably glad to sacrifice the rotting, mildewy nineteenth-century architecture in favor of more modern amenities.

And be gifted a circular room where she could be the center of attention by her future husband.

The thought gives me pause. I wonder if the name of the new library ever gives Sabine hives.

I certainly hope so.

"We're here," Chase says as we step into a low-ceilinged, stone-lined room with rows of wooden pews laid out in front of a large, skull-framed hearth.

"Holy shit," I murmur, breaking away from Chase to wander closer to a fireplace taller than me. Above it is a life-size, iron insignia of the societies' raven. "I've been here before. Snuck through there to get to you when you were—" I glance at him.

"In the cage. I remember." Chase throws his lighter into the fireplace, the dried, corroded wood igniting with a *whoosh* of heat.

I watch the fire dance. "This was also in Howard Mason's journal. A fireplace rimmed with the skulls of English nobility."

"The nobility part is suspect," Chase says behind me,

"since a lot of these skulls were found through local grave robbing."

I shy away from the fireplace and sit in the first pew. "And Howard Mason?"

Chase glances in my direction. "What about him?"

"First the renovations, then the trivia of your skeleton hellmouth over there. You're chock full of information. You must know what happened to him." I search his face for clues of knowledge and if he knows who our Chancellor really is.

"I'm more concerned with your well-being right now."

"If you're truly worried about me, you'll tell me about Howard Mason."

"Callie, what are you getting at?"

Shoulders tensed, I decide to just get it out. "Chancellor Marron. That's not the last name he was born with. He's Howard Mason."

It's imperceptible, microscopic, but Chase's entire body stiffens in front of the fireplace. "How did you find that out?"

"By accident. He called me into his office this morning." I explain what Marron said and how my reaction tipped over a few pictures.

Chase curses, a blasphemous echo seeping into the hollowed-out eyes of the skulls.

"You knew, didn't you?" My accusation doesn't reach nearly as far. "This whole time—when you threw that journal at me in your father's study, disguising it as something else, something *important*."

Chase's response is quiet. Monotone. "I told you, when

you first came here, I was under strict instruction to lead you astray."

"And you were so good at it, too." Now, oh now, my voice reaches echoing levels. "Dumping garbage on me, harassing me in the dining hall, encouraging the bullies—Piper—to do their worst. And then stripping me naked and sleeping with me." I swipe at the sudden dampness under my eyes. "I could've handled a quick fuck. It wouldn't have split my heart open. You could've turned me into an entertaining story for your buddies the next morning, and it would've sucked for me, but I understand some guys are just rotten. And I would've gotten over you."

The barest wind flutters through Chase's lashes, and I tell myself it's coming from the fireplace. It can't be from a flinch of hurt.

"Instead, you used me in all the ways you could. Mentally. Physically. Emotionally. *Verbally*, the way you tossed around 'soulmate' like it meant something. When now, here we are, and you've kept another piece of the society to yourself. Marron was a teacher when my mom went here. Another key to my past you refused to give. Why? Because you want to control me? Just like Sabine?"

Chase jerks like he's been slapped. "Don't you fucking come at me like that."

"Why not?" I stand, my voice reaching a terrible, gut-wrenching level when I do. "Why do I have to peel you like a goddamn onion in order to get the answers I need? What kind of hold do the Nobles have on you that you want to betray them one minute, then protect them the next? Choose a fucking side, Chase!"

"*I choose you!*" he roars, and I shrink at the decibel. "I chose you. I made a promise that I wouldn't keep anything else from you, and I—Chancellor Marron *is* Howard Mason, but I—there's not—I didn't want you to—*ARGH!*" Chase digs his hands into his hair and spins away. His shoulders hunch over, and his voice shreds when he screams, "FUCK. THIS!"

Adrenaline leaks into my bones, the joints of my fingers trembling, my teeth chattering with invigorated fear, but I force myself to be strong. "I've learned a lot since coming to this godforsaken place. About this school, the people here. But I'm noticing a common thread, and it starts with my mother."

Chase says nothing, so I continue, "I learned the hard way that mistakes don't define a person. Their choices do. She left Briarcliff behind when she became pregnant with me. Meredith Ryan ran from the place that tried to hold her prisoner because she couldn't stand still and let the Harringtons kill me or recruit me. My mom *chose* me. And Piper? Piper helped Emma, even though it was to her detriment—even if she put her family's legacy at stake by discovering Rose Briar's hidden bloodline, buried by her ancestors. That was *her* choice. Then there's Ivy, who defied Sabine despite the great risk that *her* family would be forever indebted to the cruelty of the Nobles and Virtues."

When Chase *still* doesn't react, I spit, "Hell, while I'm at it, my stepfather found out about my mom's affair and confronted her, slapped her, and she ended up dead that night before they were ever able to forgive each other. And you? You bowed to your father's mysterious instruction to distract the new girl while they figured out whether I was worth saving. Do you see where I'm going here?"

Chase, breathing heavy, lifts his head enough to peer at me through his fallen strands of blond hair. At last, his lips move. "Yes. We've all been defined by our choices."

"I thought so, too, at first. This whole time, I thought my mother's death was mutually exclusive from this university —from *me*. Until Sabine forced me to figure out perspective. A person's actions ... they can be seen as choices *or* mistakes. So, I'm asking you here, now, *please*, how I am supposed to interpret yours..."

Chase eats up the space between us, his hands clamping on my upper arms and yanking me against him. His hot breath sweeps over my cheeks, his sweet, minty smell nearly buckling me to the ground. I don't—*can't*—let the impact of his proximity show on my face.

"Listening to my father without question was a mistake," he whispers harshly, his eyes burning against mine. "It's ingrained in me, to emulate him. I nearly lost my sister because of it, and it was with her in mind that I targeted you. But you changed me, in the moment, at the end, fuck, with your first steps into this school. You were traumatized innocence, and I couldn't make sense of you or of the reasons why my father wanted such a delicate, bruised, wide-eyed thing under his watch. But I listened—to you, to him, and I learned. And when you and I slept together, that wasn't part of his plan—that was my *choice*. Opening myself up to the true origins of the Nobles and Virtues was my choice. Deciding to protect you instead of manipulate you was my choice." He slides his hands to my shoulders.

"Standing with you, in this room, in direct opposition to the shitstorm going on upstairs, is my choice. You, Callie, are what defines me these days, and that is why I decided to keep Chancellor Marron's true identity from you."

His face is blurred into a faded, bleak watercolor, and he uses his thumbs to wipe the teardrops from under my eyes. I start to say—

"I'm not finished," he says, tilting his head as he searches my face. "I get to say my piece, too. Your accusations against your stepdad were a mistake. And you not being at the apartment to meet your mother for dinner when you were supposed to was a mistake. Your friend's overdose came from the choice *she* made to shoot up and wasn't the result of your decision to go to that party. Piper is not your fault. Ivy is not your fault. Your mom—no, Callie, look at me."

I dove down in defense, my chin digging into my chest, my shirt dampening with my tears. Chase lifts my head by curling a finger under my jaw, urging my gaze to his.

"Your mom," he continues through my soft sobs, "isn't dead because of anything you did. So, now I'm going to pose the same kind of question to you: Are you going to let other people's choices and mistakes define you?"

"Stop," I say, pushing against his chest. It's too hot in his space. Too real. "You're not—that's not—"

"The point you were trying to make?" Chase offers a small smile. "Next time, don't spar with me thinking you have an automatic win."

"I'm damaged," I croak. "These deaths, the destruction that comes in my wake, it's because of my DNA, the blood in my veins—I'm mentally unstable, unreliable, a loser at making the right decisions. I can't even write a detailed letter and email it to every possible person in Briarcliff existence without it being discredited or erased."

"You are so much more than that."

"Oh yeah? Then why am I hiding out in the basement with a guy who thinks keeping me blind and isolated is the best way to protect me?"

Chase's expression goes stiff, his fists clenching as they rest on my shoulders, his internal war made starkly apparent with the forced calm he's etched into his face. He stares at me, looks away, then stares at me again.

"Chase, what—?"

He crushes his lips to mine.

7

CALLIE

Chase uses a distraction tactic as old as time—sex, feelings, touch—and I'm a slave to it, craving the euphoria of pleasure, the ease of forgetting, every time his tongue slides over mine.

"I need you." Chase's breathes into my lips, searing them with vicious, demanding fire no hearth could ever match. "I need you so bad right now."

"Chase, we're not … this isn't the…"

His lips skim to my neck, while his fingers travel to the hem of my skirt.

I grab his waist in automatic reaction, but I'm not pushing him off.

And so, I give in.

My fingers claw. My nails dig into his skin. They work together to rip his shirt out from his pants. With his hot exhales coating my exposed cleavage, and his trailing touch on my inner thighs, it's hard to imagine a time I'd ever say no to him, unfathomable that I'd ever tell him to stop.

I try to pull away, to separate our mouths, but each time I do, my arms yank him closer, my body molded to his.

I wrench at his collar and his shirt rips open, buttons scattering to the floor. As soon as his gorgeous, firelit chest is exposed, I lick between his pecs.

Chase groans, his fingers tangling at the back of my head, ushering me down until my lips are at his belt, and I make quick work of removing that, too.

He kicks his pants off, and in those freeze-frame seconds, I realize my shirt and blazer have somehow been pulled off as well. A black lace bra, plaid skirt, and tights are all that remain between us, but I find I'm not cold.

I'm not chilled at all.

I grip his dick in my hands, familiar, hot silk sliding against my palm, and when his tip beads with pearlescent shine, my tongue darts out and catches it like a dewdrop.

"Fu..." Chase can't even get the full curse out.

His eyes turn into burnished flames as he looks on, urging me with his hips to take him all in. When I do, his upper lip curls in satisfaction before his head falls back, and he groans to the ceiling.

I'm desperate for more warmth, more soft fire. My other hand massages his balls, pulling gently, and I dip down for an experimental lick.

"Callie ... I can't..." Chase's voice is nothing but a twinkle at the back of my mind, so focused am I on the now, the him, the physical instead of the pain.

"I want you," I say between sucks. "Only you. Just this. I

don't want to think about anything else or remember even five minutes ago—"

Chase clasps the back of my neck, tilting my head back as he comes to his knees. His body follows his push until I'm prone on the ground, and his naked, hard body covers mine. "Don't even put the thought of it into existence. We're here, and you're mine. Let me take you."

I nod, my tongue poking between my lips to taste what remains of him on my lips.

His eyes flare. He reaches under my skirt and yanks at my tights until they're around my ankles.

"Chase!" I yelp when he pushes then holds my legs straight to the ceiling. I have a thong on, but I've never felt so exposed, lying on the hard ground in the middle of a forbidden, forgotten room.

"There's no time to be precious with you. I need your pussy *now*." He palms his dick, his eyes never leaving my center.

In one sweeping motion, he's gripping both my ankles in one hand while scooting my panties to the side with the other.

My hands smack into the ground on either side of me when he plunges his fingers deep into my folds.

"So wet. So fucking wet," he rasps, pumping his four fingers, in and out. "I could see it through your G-string, and I'm feeling it now. *Fuck*, I want to taste you, but if I eat you out..." He bares his teeth and slides his tongue over the top row, his stare anchored to mine. "I'll come all over this goddamn room."

My eyes roll to the ceiling, pure bliss settling at my core, then spreading. "Then fuck me," I grit out, "before I come all over your fingers."

He repositions, growls, then slams all the way in.

I cry out, cupping and squeezing my breasts in an automatic will to spread the pleasure, my ankles still held up high by the bulging muscles of his arm and the athletic stability of his hand.

I've never been fucked with my thighs clenched together, and now I'm wondering why I ever left that kind of sex as a question and not a fact.

I can feel every inch of him, sliding in and out, thrusting, every curve of his dick branded on my skin, in my folds, hitting my G-spot with target expertise.

Chase experiences the same ecstasy, a barely contained loss of control lining his face as he plunges, harder and faster, then moves to hold my thighs, keeping my legs clenched together and my knees falling to my chest as soon as he changes the angle and...

HOLY.

"*Chase,*" I wheeze through scattered breaths, my fingers curling against the gritty stone floor.

"You're so tight." He groans. Pauses. The sound of my shoes leaving my feet then hitting the wall registers in my ears, then Chase tears off my tights. "Wrap your legs around me. Now."

Legs quaking, I do as instructed, and somehow, though it seems impossible, pull him deeper.

"Come on my cock," he says, rocking his hips, but his restraint is loosening, the imminent unleashing bright in his eyes.

One more thrust and the smallest tilt of my hips is all it takes for my thoughts to explode and my vision to coat with an inner swirl of color.

Chase yells, then collapses on top of me, his breath exploding in short bursts on my breasts, then my neck, until he holds on and kisses my lips.

"I needed this," he says as he lifts his head, drinking me in with a starry haze. "I needed you."

I thread my fingers around his nape. Touching his lips with gentle, velvet kisses, I whisper, "That was a choice?"

I feel his lips curve as an exhausted chuckle leaves his lips. "That will *never* be a mistake."

8

CHASE

I could lay on a dirt-cold stone ground with Callie for decades, taking the aches and pains as a natural consequence to her warmth, but our circumstances could never allow for such an escape.

Even hidden behind walls and down secret staircases, we can't avoid danger.

"Is this why you brought me down here?" she murmurs as she plays with pieces of my hair.

I kiss the top of her head, her vanilla scent a welcome substitute to the dirt and grime of Noble deeds. "No, but it came as a welcome surprise."

She's molded to my side with the artistry of a Renaissance painting, her milk-white thigh curving over my tanned skin, and her hair luscious and streaming across age-old floors.

If anyone deserves an imperial title, it's her. *And she has it.*

"Will anyone walk in on us?" she asks. "I hear this is a place James likes to frequent."

My lip quirks. Yet another detail she's uncovered on her own. "James hasn't convinced a girl to descend to his level in quite some time." I roll until I'm on top of her, nuzzling her nose. "And you're never to use yourself in the same sentence as that fucktard again."

"He's your friend."

"Allegedly."

Sadly, the sparkling amnesia of sex fades. There's nothing quite like the mention of James to give me a flaccid cock.

I push up, then flop into a sit beside her, my forearms resting on my knees.

It's almost non-existent, but I catch the stiffening of her joints as she senses the growing distance between us.

"Chase, have I done something?"

"Nah." I rub my hand across my mouth, staring at the back wall. "It's me that's the bad guy."

"How do you mean?"

Callie doesn't ask the question with surprise, likely because I've proven many times over that I'm not the hero of her story.

But I've yet to explain just how much of a villain I have to become.

She rises to her elbows, her tits covered with black, sexy lace. I'm itching to squeeze them, pinching her nipples through the scant fabric and soaking the peaks with my tongue. It's a much better vision than the future I'm about to give her.

"I brought you down here so we could find the privacy we lack above ground."

"Okay." She sits cautiously.

I stare at my hands, dangling as uselessly as the fucker I feel like I am. "You know we can't do this anymore."

"I'm aware." She tucks a strand of hair behind her ear, a surprisingly enticing movement that I follow. "I'm having issues resisting you, though."

She tries to curve her lips, but her smile hasn't reached her eyes in a long time.

I put my hand to good use and touch her too-soft skin, scraping my thumb down her cheek. "Baby, I couldn't resist you the second I saw you. It's why what I'm going to say next is so hard."

"Tell me." She holds my wrist, pausing my movements. "Just get it over with."

I hate being responsible for capturing the light in her eyes between my fingers and snuffing it out. "I'm no good for you. Look at me, I've taken advantage of you when your friend just died. In front of us. Murdered."

Callie closes her eyes. "You gave me a burst of happiness in an otherwise awful existence. I can't regret something like that, especially when the force of her loss came back the minute we finished." She presses her free hand to her heart. "I feel emptiness, right here, all the time." She lowers her eyes, then whispers, "Except when you fill me."

I stare hard at the top of her head. "Say that again."

She blinks, those wide eyes of hers traveling back up. "I said ... I don't know if I'll ever feel full."

This is the point where I'm supposed to argue with her

—grab her by the shoulders and shake the truth out of her. That currently, she can't live without me. A strange, foreign flutter of yearning at the center of my ribs tells me I should.

I don't.

"Do you recall the moment you came up to me and asked me to be cruel to you?"

Callie drags her thighs against her chest, wrapping her arms around her legs. "I guess. Yes. I asked you because Sabine was growing suspicious of us meeting up with each other when she ordered me not to."

"And did we?"

"Fool her?" Callie raises a brow at the same time she rests her chin on her knees. "What do our current events tell you?"

"Mm. Which is why I'm coming to you now and asking you the same thing."

"For me to be cruel to you?" Her voice doesn't carry any intrigue or acceptance. More like the monotone of a girl who knows the opposite is true.

Twisting, I find my shirt nearby and pull it on, but I don't stand. I don't shuffle away from her. The subtle breeze of her sweet cream smell every time she exhales is all that keeps me intact as I share the news that I intend to destroy her.

"I'm warning you this time," I say, knowing full well Callie understands where this conversation is going, "that I will not stop at one event. Or two. Or nine. Sabine intends to implode my life if I don't do what she wants, and that is to separate myself from you."

Callie's fixated on something over my shoulder, but it's with the attention of a woman who's looking so inward, nothing on the outside matters. "So, it's true, then. Everything I've done up until this point is worth nothing. My uncovering of the societies. My attempts to solve Piper's murder. My hope to shield Emma and Eden from more pain and humiliation." Her eyelids lower to half-mast. "To avenge Ivy. You're no longer on my side, are you?"

"Don't put words in my mouth."

"My reputation is gone, too. Any opponent could point to my breakdown after my mom died. Without you backing me up, that transcript has all the merit it needs to erase my side of the story."

"I'm not too worried about your reputation when I'm focused on saving your *life*." It comes out sharper than intended, and I bite my tongue, sending the heat of temper into my eyes instead of through my lips.

Callie lifts her chin from her knees, the gold of her irises growing heated with a glassmaker's perfection. "My reputation is what's holding my life *together*. Without it, I'm unstable. Obsessive. Crazy. And *Sabine* is the sane one."

"I'm not questioning your sanity, but I can't risk Sabine doing to you what she did to Ivy."

"So, you'll make me miserable instead?"

"With or without your permission." I force myself to stand. It should feel exceptional, staring down at her as she's splayed at my feet, but all I cling to is the numbing belief that this is for her own good. "It's not only you I have to protect. It's my sister, my brothers, my society. Sabine is crushing all three—four, including you—between her fists, and I can't sit back and watch my father gift her a kingdom of ruin. We used to stand for something. The Nobles were remarkable, apex humans who could flip the world over with one flick of their finger. This room?" I sweep my arm out. "It has harbored riches you wouldn't believe. Minds that would blow you away. We encouraged capitalism, free-thinking, revolution, and innovation. Astronauts stood where I am. Presidents and bio-scientists. And our sisters, the Virtues, were encouraged to do the same. We operated as one, Callie, and if I don't find a way to bring them together again, I represent nothing. Was raised by nothing. I am *not* nothing."

I say it through clenched teeth, but low thunder accompanies my words. One with erratic lightning.

Callie flinches, but she unfolds and pushes to her feet. Her plaid skirt covers her sweet spot as she rises, and her hair conceals her nipples when she straightens.

Creating a shield of her own sort.

And when her eyes flick to mine, they display a burning, inner core.

"You are so far from zero," she says. "I wish you'd see that. Instead, you're pushing me away. Intending me to suffer."

A sharp rebuttal forms against my lips, but I temper it into a sneer. "I'm sorry you see it that way, because all I'm aiming for is the sacrifice of one chick in order to gift my secret society the limitless power they lost."

She gnaws on her lower lip, a faraway look cresting over her face. "Will you stop Sabine from trafficking girls?"

My gut clenches at her sharp swing into acceptance. I eye her suspiciously because of it. "I said 'reform,' didn't I?"

Callie doesn't wince at the callousness. "With your plans in play, no one will believe I'm the descendent of Rose Briar. My ravings will be solidified by your aggression toward me. I'll become the nothing Sabine wants."

I'd rather you become nothing than lose you.

The words tickle the back of my mind, but don't dare come forward. Instead, I hold her stare, this half-dressed, tousled, prep school reject in a way I can't hold her with my hands. "It's the only way to bring Sabine to my side without destroying the societies."

Callie steps back, and with slow, stilted movements, she gets dressed. I watch her in silence until her last shred of clothing is slipped on, then follow suit.

"I want them destroyed. You want them reformed," she says as I'm fixing my jacket at the collar. "Maybe you're right. We can't be together with such opposite goals in mind."

"We can't be together for a lot of reasons. I'll admit I'm hot for you and have trouble keeping my dick in my pants every time I see your tits, but it stops there. I can control myself for the greater good."

I brace for Callie's reaction, knowing I've hurt her. As expected, her inner flame flickers out, yet I wonder, while her heart turns to cinders, if any embers of protest remain, like how I lost myself in her heat, or the way her strokes create tremors across my skin, and she makes me see stars.

Perhaps it would mean something to her if she knew no one else has ever been so successful in my undoing.

I sling my bag onto my shoulder. "I assume you know the way out. See you around, possum."

Then I turn my back on her.

Unfortunately for both of us, I'll never be the one to confess.

9

CALLIE

Chase's abrupt departure allows me to make it to my English Lit exam with one minute to spare.

I huff into my seat, still smelling like him, the tips of my hair carrying his cologne and my body lingering with the sweat of our sex as I fish through my bag for a pencil.

As the professor hands out exams, floating through aisles with the flutter of paper and the expected, monotone speech about the consequences of cheating, my heart sits like a spade at the bottom of my stomach, its sharp edge spearing me with every fidget, every thought, every frown, involving Chase.

He wants to make my life hell from here on out. Little does he know, I've been living in that fiery pit since my mother was killed.

What will a few more rumors do? Or heightened forms

of harassment? Christmas break is coming up. I'll escape, regroup, and find the calm I need to *slit Sabine's fucking throat.*

I tell myself this as the exam is slipped onto my desk. Simple essay questions meant to revolve around our reading assignments for this semester, but all I see is, *You might be able to handle more Briarcliff trash thrown at your face, but what about Chase's cold, soulless stare? How will you handle the facets of his smile as it transforms into a sneer, or the blackening of his heart the longer he tortures you? Explain these points as thoroughly and with as much detail as you can in the section below.*

For bonus points, elaborate about your dead best friend and how it feels having her dried blood on your soul.

The pencil snaps in my hand.

"Here."

The soft, wispy voice comes from my left, accompanied by a manicured hand dangling a spare pencil.

I follow the thin fingers to the delicate, pale wrist, all the way up to bottle-clear, gray eyes fringed with black lashes.

My lips part on a scoff. "I don't want your lead poisoning."

Falyn flicks the pencil with a perfect arc of her fingers and falls back into her chair. "Suit yourself, possum. I was only trying to be nice to my new sister."

Hate fills my body so fast, it leaks venom through my teeth. "You talk about sisters like it means something, when the blood of one of them is still wet on your marble floor—"

"Ladies!" the professor barks from her desk, the lenses

of her glasses flashing white with her sharp look. "One warning. That's it."

Falyn's lower lip juts out, feigning proper chastisement, and she goes back to her exam.

I no longer have anything to write with, and we're not allowed to go through our bag once the exam starts. There's no sense of panic in my chest, since leaving an exam blank is the least of my problems. I bury my head in my hands instead.

When the bell goes off, I pry my eyes open, away from the soothing black, and return to the overly bright, obnoxiously loud classroom, the remaining students popping out of their seats or feverishly scribbling the last of their desperate attempts onto their papers.

"Pencils and pens down!" the professor calls, while students jostle each other and scuttle from their seats.

My limp hands lay on my exam, palms open and empty.

"Nice try, possum," Falyn says as she passes, her perfume singeing my nostrils. "Can't blame you, though. It must be hard to focus after the trauma you experienced."

Red coats my vision, turning my papers scarlet and my nails into ruby talons. I rip my gaze up and into Falyn. "You're a cold-hearted bitch. Do you even mourn her? Did she mean anything to you?"

"Who?" Falyn arches a brow. "Ivy? Of course, I feel bad for her. She's in Philly nursing her mom back to health. Or waiting it out until her mom croaks. Whichever. Either way, her vacant spot has to be filled." Falyn shrugs. "She left it up to me to bring our sisters together, which I'm trying to do with you, if you weren't so bitchy about it."

My entire body goes cold. "Falyn." I rise from my seat. "It's all a lie. Ivy's dead, and you can't take her place."

For a brief moment, Falyn's stare turns unsure, but a fast coating of disdain erases the fracture. "There's no guarantee Ivy will make it back next semester. Somebody has to become captain of crew, and I'm next in line."

I grab Falyn's wrist. Cling to it. "You don't want it. Tell Sabine no."

"*Ow.*" Falyn tries to yank her wrist from my grip. "Let *go*, psycho vermin."

"I will if you promise not to be the next princess—I mean, captain." I glance around at the lingering students, some whose attention we caught. "I can't explain right now, but being a captain is so much worse than you think—"

"Get your claws off her, possum," a deep voice comes from the doorway.

My body responds automatically. I release Falyn, but a sickening dread prevents me from looking toward the door.

"Falyn," Chase says. "With me."

Falyn purses her lips, throwing a pert, "It is *so* obvious why you don't want me to be the next captain, Callie. And pathetic," before she sidles over to Chase ... and Tempest, and Rio, the three of them waiting for her in the doorway.

I swallow, collecting my things as if I don't feel Chase's assessing, dead-eyed stare on the body he ravished not two hours ago. "Touch her again, possum, and I'll have to make you pay."

Glancing at him through my lashes, I pull my bag tighter to my chest. "Tell me, is this Prince Charming coming to protect his new princess, or am I staring at the evil sorcerer about to lay the same curse on Falyn that fell on Ivy?"

Chase's jaw tics, but otherwise, he's stone. His family name. His future. "You and your fairytales. Wake the fuck up. Your life would be so much simpler."

"I'm wide awake," I retort, my eyes growing hot. "And you are not taking me down. Do whatever you want, protect the assholes, defend the bullies." I point at Falyn. "They break so much easier than the underdogs. If Ivy couldn't fight it, there's no way Falyn can take the weight of the title. Don't put her in that position."

"Briarcliff has enough saints lording over us," Chase says with his infallible stare. "Do I need to cut you into the glass windows, too? Stay out of it. I've warned you once."

I search for the boy laying in my arms on a stone floor, draped in Briarcliff colors but heated by my kisses alone. I really do. Not one flicker of inner pain mars his perfect face. I'm met with calculated hate. He's nocked his poisoned arrow, and he's aiming for my jugular.

"You have no one, Callie," Chase continues quietly. Falyn floats to his side.

He throws his arm around her shoulders. Falyn's cheeks flush with surprised delight, and she loops an arm around the front of his torso, tipping her chin up at him, then leveling me with a triumphant look.

I pretend like my heart isn't already dust. I respond, through numbed lips, "I certainly don't have you."

Chase tips his head in acknowledgement, then swivels around, dragging a lopsided Falyn with him as she tries to keep up with his strides.

Tempest salutes me, his eyes betraying nothing as he follows Chase into the halls.

Rio, damn him, grins at me with his teeth and says as his parting shot, "When I talk to Ivy tonight, I'll give her your best, you fucking freak."

10

———

CALLIE

Biology is just as big a mess as English Lit, and calculus before that.

I risk being kicked out before my last semester even begins, but I can't find the inner turmoil necessary to kick my ass into high gear.

Maybe leaving is for the best.

By staying on, I'm putting myself in danger.

If I leave, my Briar legacy won't matter, Sabine will live on as a vindictive queen, Falyn will become a porcelain plaything like she's always wanted, and Chase will...

Chase will...

Ivy won't...

My mom will never...

I shove into my dorm, my winter coat puddling to my feet as I storm into the kitchenette, throwing open cupboards and searching for the bottle of vodka I know Emma stashes here somewhere.

Emma's quiet voice sounds at my back. "I'd ask you what was wrong, but that'd be a stupid question."

The top cupboards don't provide me with anything, so I bend down and pillage the bottom shelves. "Where's your —" *Goddammit. Why must everything be so hidden all the time?* "I need—" *There.* My hand scrapes across a frosted, cylindrical surface. It's in the corner cupboard, behind the lazy Susan. I twist off the cap, fall onto my haunches, and chug on my knees.

"Are you sure getting drunk is the best way to handle this?"

The burn of room temperature vodka at my throat is my answer.

"Oh, Callie." Emma shuffles closer. She crouches to my level and puts her hands on my shoulders.

I meet her eyes through a blurred haze. Vodka dribbles from the corners of my mouth. My cheeks are hot, warm and sticky like the vodka dripping from my chin, but my head's not tipped back that far. There shouldn't be vodka on my cheeks.

It's because I'm crying.

My cheeks are wet because I'm crying.

A wet hiccup leaves my mouth, and I pull the bottle from my lips and gag. Then I sob, the half empty bottle leaving my lifeless fingers, clanging to the floor beside me, spilling clear fluid across our floors, spreading like blood.

Emma's forehead crumples, and she pulls me into her chest. "Let it out."

My lips rip apart, my teeth going dry from the sudden suck of air, and I wail.

I howl in her arms, my nails digging into her flesh, and I weep for my mom. For Ivy. For Chase.

For me.

11

CALLIE

I'm meant to be thankful on Fridays.

TGIF, right?

It's the last day of school before Christmas break, and my final exam before I can exit these halls and find relief in New York City for two weeks. All I have to do is make it through three more hours, then by lunch time, I'm on a train back to meet my new baby sister.

I hold onto that flash of goodness as I roll onto my back but hit something soft on the way.

"Oomf," Emma moans, frowning as she pushes me off her.

"Oh. Sorry." I sit up, pushing my hair out of my face and taking stock of my surroundings.

Emma's shelves stare back at me, barren of pictures but full of knick-knacks like vintage My Little Ponies and various POP figurines of Disney villains.

It hits me at the same time I tuck my hair behind my

ears and cock my head at a miniature Darth Vader. I've never been in Emma's room before.

And yet here I sit, in her bed where she comforted me for hours last night as I drained the last of her smuggled alcohol and tore out my heart for the third time.

The headache hits me next.

"Ugh," I moan, leaning my forehead into my hand as I struggle to stand.

"Good. Alcohol poisoning didn't take you like I thought it might." Emma sits up, her blonde hair a scraggly mess on top of her head.

"I'll deal," I groan, then stumble out of her bed, cutting through our central area and into my room.

We don't talk much as we get ready, Emma showering first while I funnel Tylenol and find a piece of bread to line my stomach. Neither of us mention last night or the way Emma patted my back and stroked my hair, offering comfort where her brother couldn't—or wouldn't.

It's not in Emma's nature to rehash her sincerity, and I don't expect it from her as we finish putting on our uniforms and head out the door.

She was there for me, like she always is, in my worst moments.

Emma's glued to her phone as we wander down the hallway, glowering so hard at it, I'm surprised the screen isn't forming cracks under her glare.

"Do you have plans for the holidays?" I ask her as we wait for the elevators. The look on her face instantly makes me feel dumb for asking it, but what am I supposed to do? Ask her how she'll handle Ivy's murder and Sabine's revenge over the break in a public hallway?

A few girls cluster behind us, instantly putting hands to mouths as they whisper to each other and slide glances at me, but I ignore them.

"I'm going to my mom's in LA," she answers, but twists her lips. "It's been a while since I've seen her."

"Is Chase going, too?" I ask, then frown as the girls' giggles get louder.

The elevator dings open, and we step in. The three girls follow.

"He usually hangs back with our father. They're Scrooges on Christmas day, but they go to the Harringtons on Christmas Eve. Father and Sabine might go on a couples' vacation. My brother might just be the Grinch this year, alone in our lake house, instead of Scrooge."

"How nice." My voice comes out hoarse. "I'm sure it'll be extra special for everyone this year."

"She wishes he was the baby daddy, just like Piper did."

I turn sharply to the voice. One girl catches her breath in surprise, then grins. "Can I help you?"

"What did you just say?" I ask.

Emma pockets her phone and grabs my arm. "Leave it. Let's get through the morning."

The girl responds anyway. "I didn't say anything, you furry whore."

My brows jump. "Excuse me?"

"Do you even wax down there?"

Another, braver girl asks, "Or is that what Dr. Luke liked so much about you?"

"He's hot, sure, but he's so fucking old. He probably enjoys a full bush," the last one adds.

I gape at them. "What the hell?"

The elevator slides open, and Emma latches onto me so hard, I trip over my feet as we exit. Emma wears a look of such determination as she pushes through the front doors, I'm forced to ask, "What are they talking about?"

"Another dumb rumor," is all she says before I stumble out of the building and into the blinding white of day.

Emma leaves me in the West Wing, wishing me an aloof "good luck" before she heads off to her Global Studies exam.

It's with the listless trail of a ghost that I make it to biology and take my seat, aiming to be just as invisible.

I'm amazed I've made it this far, considering the trauma that keeps replaying behind my eyes, the dulled, vodka-induced headache acting like a macabre music track replaying over Ivy's dying body and Chase's coldblooded dismissal.

Is this all that's left of me? I wonder as I stare at the black laminate of my desk. *Am I nothing but a vessel of death and loneliness?*

"Baby killer."

I jolt at the hiss at my back, then turn.

The guy meets my confused look with a morbid grin, adding, "Teacher fucker."

Pointing to my chest, I ask, "Are you referring to me?"

"Ain't no other chick I know that gets herself an abortion on a teacher's salary." He licks his top row of teeth.

"Huh?" My vision grows smaller with all the brow-furrowing I'm doing.

A *slam* makes me jump in my seat. Falyn's dropped her books on her lab desk and slithers onto her stool across from me. "Secret's out, possum. Might as well own up to your hideousness."

I shake my head, but only a confused fugue follows. My email about Ivy's murder goes unnoticed, yet what Emma dubbed "another stupid rumor" gets the spotlight?

"What now, Falyn?" I ask, but I'm conscious of the growing stares, and the curious, car-accident attention that's directed my way as more students filter into the classroom and take their seats.

"At least Piper still had the kid in her belly when she died," someone in the back mutters, but it's loud enough for the entire room to hear.

"Yeah, this one decided to have her womb scraped out instead of 'fess up to fucking Dr. Luke, too," his friend responds.

My palms slam against my desk as I stand. "The hell?"

Falyn pipes up. "Admit it, you got an abortion in a desperate move to hide your sluttiness before you went after Chase."

"I did no such thing!"

"Oh, no?" The tip of Falyn's tongue pokes out between her smirk. "Prove it ... 'cause the whole school's talking about you fucking Dr. Luke the second Piper was out of the way. Does the man just not use a condom?" She cackles. "Or do his gray-haired pubes just taste that good?"

This has Chase written all over it is the first thought to sink into my brain as my knees turn to gel, and I fall into my seat. *He swore it'd be worse this time.*

"All right, class!" The professor wanders in, clapping his hands for attention. "Are we ready for our final exam before our highly anticipated break?" He scans the classroom, his hands clasped in front of him. "Who's excited for Santa?"

The class groans in response.

"No? Your teenaged years have jaded you all, sadly. Well, here's your first sack of coal. Grab an exam from the top of the pile and pass it back."

Falyn cuts one last gleeful look my way before turning to the front.

I work hard to focus on the questions, do the experiments, and write down the answers, but whispers and fake coughs keep getting in the way.

Possum probably used tweezers...

So pathetic...

Like Chase would ever want her saggy pussy now...

Loser.

Fugly Piper wannabe.

But it's the last one. Oh, the last one. That gets me.

Murderer.

I fly out of my seat, my stool toppling onto its side. It skids across the floor with a metallic shriek.

Heads pop up from papers, most mouths agape. Falyn props her chin in her hand, watching me with a hungry menace.

I ignore them all and storm to the front of the room, tossing my unfinished exam on the professor's desk.

"Miss Ryan, what on Earth...?"

"I don't feel well," I mumble, then career out of the classroom before the redness creeps from my cheeks into the whites of my eyes.

The hallway's deserted, the usual proctors either completing their own exams or hooking up in custodial closets and empty classrooms.

Briarcliff University's lack of supervision was always obvious, but now I'm disgusted by it. My steps echo through the hallway, and a cold draft follows my every move. None of it dissipates the heating of my bones or boiling of my blood.

Ivy's dead. Piper's dead. Both murdered, and all they can talk about is a malicious rumor about a fake baby I had while fake-fucking a fired professor.

My coat's in my locker, so I brace myself for the long walk ahead of me to get to the opposite wing before the clocktower tolls, signaling the rush of students out of classrooms and the start of winter holidays. I don't want to be caught up in the tide. My shoes squeak against the flawlessly polished floors as I hurry my steps, but the vicious energy sparking against my joints doesn't subside.

"Dipping out early, huh, possum?"

My rubber soles shriek on my abrupt halt in the middle of the hallway.

"Probably a good idea, considering what's leaked to the student body," the deep voice—the *familiar* baritone —continues.

I don't turn around. Counting the tiles at the tips of my shoes, I whisper, "Leave me alone."

"I won't."

With a slow, aching arc, I swivel to the voice.

Chase's smooth, undeterred features stare back at me.

My expression is probably war-torn and famished compared to his, lost in a battlefield where neither side won. He sees it, he must, but there's no reaction in that untarnished expression of his.

"Did none of what we had mean anything to you?" My voice, though low, curls around the thick stone columns and wisps its way into Chase's ear. "Or did it mean so much, you have to eviscerate me in order to separate yourself from any sort of warmth whatsoever?"

I search for a flinch of understanding, a tic of emotion, but he gives me nothing. "I'm doing what I have to."

"No." My heart thumps, filling in the spaces between our breaths.

"You don't see the value in it?" Chase angles his head, resembling a beautiful demon he'd kept so well hidden until now.

"How can I see value in filthy rumors and disgusting gossip?"

"The worse I torture you, the better it is for both of us."

"Says the guy who comes out a king for it."

"Callie." He steps forward.

I skitter back. "Don't you dare come near me."

"I told you what would come next. We talked about this. If your dignity is more important than your life, then I'm sorry to say—"

"It's *erasing* Ivy!" My shout bounces off the walls, the portraits of alumni in their gold-framed paintings seeming to hurl my words right back into the heart of me.

And there it is. The flinch I was waiting for. Yet, instead of being satiated by it, I'm starving for more. More hurt. More humiliation. More pain.

I rake him from head to foot, this golden boy with eyes drenched in liquid bronze, who blinded me and freed me all at the same time.

I'm desperate to stride right up to him and throw him against the wall. Toss him across the floor. My mind begs to break his heart the way he's shattered mine.

One foot steps forward. Then the next.

Chase doesn't react, preferring to observe my performance with cold disdain.

My eyes skate to the side where a large trash bin is nestled beneath an old painting of some benefactor or another. Chase follows the movement and arches a brow of careful disinterest.

That's all it takes for me to storm to the bin, throw off the lid, pick it up, and hurl the contents at Chase.

Crumbled paper scatters across the floor.

Half-empty coffee cups splatter against his shirt and pants.

An open ketchup packet hits him in the chin, leaving a trail of red under his lip.

The empty bin makes a hollow, clanging sound as it hits the floor at my feet, followed by my heaving breaths.

Chase doesn't move. Doesn't twitch.

As the trash floats, then settles around him, the clock-tower bell clangs some distance away.

We remain in a brutal lock of eyes, his smoldering, mine alight with rage.

Doors crash open as students sprint out of classrooms, their first taste of freedom since the semester began, but shoes skid to a stop almost instantly. Cries and hollers die out in favor of ogling the Briarcliff prince covered in trash. Some search for hidden phones in their bags and blazers.

A few dare to come closer.

I expect Chase to unleash. To unhinge his jaw and punish me for daring to malign his perfectly pressed appearance. Or at the very least, to drag his hand through his hair and shake off the used tissues and cold noodles dangling there.

He does none of those things.

Just looks at me coldly. Brutal and haunted.

Haunted?

No way. I have to be hallucinating the fragments of misery in his eyes. Misery he caused. Happiness he refuses to consider.

We can beat this together ... I tried to will his way in the Nobles' crypt, but Chase refused, considering me a weakness, an unnecessary accessory to his plans to overthrow his father.

I've never wanted to punch someone yet wrap my arms around them at the same time. The ache is real, and it sits right at the base of my ribs.

Chase parts his lips, his tongue coming dangerously close to the stains I put on his face when it darts out to suck on one of his canines. "You will come to regret this day, possum."

"Do your worst," I retort. "I guarantee it'll never be as bad as watching the guy you loved bow to a woman who brutalizes and kills."

This time, I step all the way up to him, raising my chin one notch. Then two. "All because he's scared."

Chase's mouth twists into a snarl, but I don't wait around for the mushroom cloud of consequence. I turn my back on him and stride down the hall, my quaking limbs for once shrouded and protected by a Briarcliff uniform.

12

CALLIE

I told him I loved him.

What the *fuck* is wrong with me?

Sitting back in my seat on the train, I watch the afternoon swirl into greens and blues as we chug toward the city, my duffel squished between me and the window as I pretend not to smell the pastrami sandwich a businessman eats beside me.

My stomach rumbles in protest. I mentally remind it that these vicious swings between nausea and starvation can't be good for it, so could it kindly shut up?

The snack cart comes by, and my stomach shows no signs of quieting down. I cave and buy a bag of mini pretzels. As soon as the salt hits my tastebuds, my stomach revolts.

See? Told you.

And now I'm arguing with an organ.

"*Argh*," I moan in frustration, smacking against my

headrest. The guy beside me doesn't flinch at my strange behavior, instead licking remnants of mustard off his fingers before settling in with his tablet.

I'd lost it on Chase, very publicly and with a lot of witnesses. My heart was all-in, but not in the way I'd fantasized. Dreaming of Chase's public declaration of protection, his claiming of *me*, crept into all corners of my mind most nights. Never did I envision a scenario where I'd make *him* the possum with garbage clinging to his body the way his tailored uniform usually did.

He must hate me now. Possibly he always did. Maybe, there was never any love to be lost between us. Just sex and pleasure. Either way, it's all gone now, dust and ash I've left behind at Briarcliff, a two-week reprieve where I don't have to breathe the fumes.

I should be relieved, but I'm worried instead.

Anxious over Sabine. There hasn't been a whisper or a flash of movement since ... since...

I shut my eyes tight as images of Ivy splayed across the temple floor flash forward.

My body's thrown in the darkness, and my eyes pop wide at the train's sudden stop. Pulse beating like a drum in my ears, I cling to the window, allowing its cold to seep into the heat of the moment and dissipate the horror.

"You okay, sweetheart?" the businessman asks with a thick Queens accent.

After a single gulp, I nod, unable to yet turn my head. A brownish stain colors the back of the headrest in front me, serving as a stark reminder of my final words to Chase.

All because you're scared.

It's becoming awfully clear who that statement was really meant for.

"This your stop?" the man tries again. He's moved—standing above me and grabbing his overhead luggage. "'cause I think you have about five seconds before this sucker moves again."

Nodding, I shuffle out of my corner, hugging my duffel to my chest as the man steps aside and allows me through first.

I land on the platform in a dusty fugue, blinking fast and searching for my bearings before anyone I know sees me and asks me the dreaded question I wish to avoid the entire holiday: *What's wrong?*

It's impossible to put into words what haunts me, or even words that make sense. I tried with Ahmar and failed. The entire university backs Sabine's story of Ivy's sudden departure ... not death. Chase makes clear his willingness to sacrifice himself to save the Nobles, and all *I* want to do is nuke the Virtues and take the Nobles down with them as collateral damage.

At the same time my thoughts circle, I'm scanning the crowd for a familiar face, taking tentative steps forward as I enter my old world.

I spot Ahmar after the second sweep, my footsteps picking up, my duffel swinging on its strap against my shoulder as I release it and start to run.

He glances up from his phone at the sudden blur of movement, then stretches his arms wide.

I fly into them with an *oomph*, clutching Ahmar close

and smelling his familiar woodsy cologne as I bury my face in his chest.

"That's the kind of welcome I was waiting for!" he says, his chin digging into the top of my head.

I resist the urge to bawl, knotting my fingers in the fabric of his jacket instead. Ahmar's warm. Safe. He's home.

"Ah, Calla." His arms wrap tighter once he realizes I'm not letting go. "I gotcha, kiddo."

Sniffling, I untangle my hands from his coat, stepping back and swiping under my eyes. I take a few deep breaths, too, clinging to normalcy instead of another breakdown.

"Come on." Ahmar throws his arm around my shoulders and directs us to the exit. I'm thankful he doesn't press for more information or ask how I've been doing since our last, frantic phone call. "Pete and Lynda are waiting for you. I'll drop you off there."

"Sure."

In another time, I would've asked him to stop at our usual diner—*our* being his, Mom's and mine—for coffee and pancakes, but as my stomach insists, I can't keep up an act for very long. I'd rather have the distraction of my new sister, the flurry of newborn attention, than searching eyes across the table, cataloguing my every twitch and wondering if it's time for a longer stretch at a facility.

Ahmar takes us to his double-parked car on 42nd Street, opening the passenger door on his unmarked police vehicle so I can slide in.

It hasn't yet snowed in NYC, but the brisk, icy weather turns into condensation on my cheeks as soon as I get into the heated car. Ahmar hops into the driver's side, and in seconds, we're merged into congested city traffic and honking with the rest of them.

I allow Ahmar's curses at pedestrians and derby-bound taxis to settle around me like a comforting blanket, happy to make the ride in the city's version of a quiet evening.

When he pulls up to Meyer House, I straighten out of my relaxed flop against the passenger door.

"Here you are, kiddo."

"Aren't you coming in?"

"Nah. Not today. This is a moment you should enjoy with Pete and Lynda."

I ask, while reaching through the middle console for my duffel, "Have you met Blair yet?"

"Sure have. She's a cutie." Ahmar winks. "But you'll always be my baby girl."

The endearment pulls at the leaden chain in my chest. "Thanks, Ahmar. For the pickup, for the ride, for the..."

"Lack of interrogation?" Another wink. "You deserve a breather. Enjoy your time with your new baby sister. We'll meet up for coffee in a few days."

I'm not so mixed up that I can't sense the promise in the question. *We'll be having a serious talk* is all but scrolling in blinking red lights under his brows.

I nod, leaning over to kiss his cheek. "Got it."

Ahmar hasn't shaved in a few days, his scruff grating against my lips more than usual. I pull back, inspecting him and noticing the purple crescents under his eyes. "Are you sleeping okay?"

"Child, leave." He shoves me affectionately on the shoulder. "We'll have our mutual *come to Jesus* moments when I pick you up for pancakes. I'll text you."

"Okay," I say, but I leave him behind with great reluctance. It's not often I witness Ahmar appearing less than put-together. He uses his tailored appearance as somewhat of a shield to the murder and mayhem he witnesses constantly, taking his time grooming and making weekly barber appointments to counteract the ugliness of other humans.

I've seen him scruffy and unkempt in only one other situation, and I prefer not to dwell on it as I step up to Meyer House's stoop and watch his headlights disappear into the evening haze.

I take the rest of the stairs on a sigh, then stop, hovering near the door. Three months of residency doesn't give me the confidence to saunter in, nor am I considered just a visitor.

My fingers curl over the iron knocker, and I swing it against the door a few times before turning the knob and pushing in—falling somewhere in between.

"Hello?" I call, sliding my bag off my shoulders.

No answer.

Leaving my bag in the foyer, I take the curving staircase, my palm brushing against the cold, solid brass of the railing. "Anyone home?"

The lights are dimmed but not shut off. They have to be around here somewhere.

When the second floor gives me nothing, I make my way to the third, and that's where I find them.

"Hi—"

"*Shh!*" Dad shushes me, though it's seemingly not enough because he also elbow-wrestles me out of the nursery. "We just got her to sleep."

"Oh, sorry," I say in a much softer voice, but peer over his shoulder.

"You want to see her?" he whispers, then nudges me forward. "Go on. But *carefully*. And with *no footsteps*."

Cautiously, I creep into the room, the white trim of the curtains and bassinet framing the shadows with lace.

Blair's face comes into view as I stop beside Lynda, a slip of white cheek peering out of the blanket wrapped tightly around the tiny form.

Impossibly small fingers appear under Blair's neck, sneaking out of her wrapping as she spreads them wide, then clenches them closed again. She coos, her eyes crescents of slumber, and does a little wiggle in her pink cocoon.

"She's like a dancing burrito," I murmur, but the smile crossing my face is warm, real, and wide.

Lynda adjusts one of her nightgown's straps as she straightens and notices me. "Callie! You're here!"

My eyes widen at her excited shout at the same time Dad's face pales.

"Relax, Pete," Lynda says as she envelopes me in a fragrant hug filled with baby powder and ... something sewer-like I can't identify. Baby poop? "Blair rivals an alcohol-induced fraternity hazing once she's down. It's so good to see you, honey."

"You, too," I say, squished against her suddenly voluminous breasts. Our relationship, while cloudy, seems to have cleared into a light fog since Blair was born, and I accept her embrace.

Her Briarcliff roots don't escape my thoughts, nor her high school connection to my mother, but mustering the strength to confront her while she's in day-old pajamas with her normally sleek blonde hair in a sagging top-knot doesn't seem like the best time to create stormy skies again.

Plus, I'm fucking exhausted. Like traumatically, face-down-in-the-dirt, knocked out.

Lynda must sense the direction of my thoughts. "You look so piqued, honey. Long day? You can meet Blair when she's awake in the morning. Or in two hours. How was your last exam this morning? Oh—there's dinner waiting for you downstairs. A crown roast of some sort. Lamb? Help me out here, Pete."

"We've now reached the time of night where my wife is inexplicably ripe—with energy." Pete smiles tightly, his eyes a little wild as he rests his attention on her. "I mean *blooming* with energy. She's filled with chatter. Might I leave you two to it?"

"Sure, Dad." I give him the exit he so desperately needs. "I'll hang with Lynda for a while."

"But not too long," he admonishes. "Lynda's right—you look as tired as we do."

"Exams were ... a lot."

"I bet. Briarcliff doesn't pride itself on poor test-taking. Glad you survived. I'll see you in a few."

His word-choice beats against my skull. *Survived.*

Barely, Dad.

As my dad escapes to the fourth floor of the brownstone

to face-plant somewhere, Lynda latches onto my hand and drags me down to the first, where the dining room and a re-heated crown roast await.

"Are you hungry? I'm *starving*." Lynda hops a few steps in front of me. "I'll eat the whole lamb if they let me. They don't teach you in breastfeeding school how dang starved you become."

"Breastfeeding school?"

"Oh yeah. I made Pete attend three of them with me. And swaddling, baby massage, pregnancy yoga..."

As she prattles on, my lips pull into what I hope is a smile as I follow her into the expansive, nineteenth-century dining area, with gold-trimmed panel walls and priceless murals dating back to Lynda's ancestors.

I take a seat next to her at the head of the table, Sophia bursting in just as we sit down.

"Calla Lily! You've arrived!"

Another full-bosomed hug encases me, but as Sophia's heartbeat thrums in my ears, I think this is the closest I've ever come to *home* since Mom.

"Let me get the roast and all the veggies. Good Lord." Sophie pinches my arm as she draws back, clucking. "What are you, an emo hipster? You need meat on these bones."

Sophia heads through the doors to collect our plates. To give myself something to do, I grab the intricately folded napkin from the place setting and smooth it across my lap.

"A little lost?"

I glance up at Lynda's quiet question, surprised to see her red-rimmed but bright blue gaze on me. "I mean no offense—I always feel out of place in crazy-rich rooms."

"Does that discomfort include Briarcliff's classrooms?" she asks.

My hands still on my napkin.

"I realize I'm in a newborn bubble, but I haven't forgotten our phone conversation." Lynda reaches toward me, then lays her hand on the table, palm up.

I stare at her open hand. Watch as her fingers slowly close over her empty palm, a space I was supposed to fill.

"Callie, I don't think I've ever told you how sorry I am about your mother."

"Probably because I didn't give you the chance." I have to stare at the ceiling for this, blinking back the swell of emotion.

"We had a rough start, didn't we? And I don't think I made it any better by keeping my connection to Meredith from you."

My chin falls, and I worry the corner of my napkin. "You told the police. And you hadn't even reunited with my dad yet. That's all that matters."

"No, honey, it doesn't. I should've told you, too, the instant Pete and I grew serious. Now I might be too late. An apology seems so banal, especially considering your worries over your mom's connection to Briarcliff and her…"

"Murder. You can say it." For me at least, it's rolling off my tongue with disturbing ease.

"Yes. Murder. I didn't know her very well, but no one deserves to be treated like that in the end."

I worry the inside of my cheek, glancing at the swinging door Sophia left through. "You said you didn't know Sabine Harrington that well, either."

Lynda murmurs her agreement, then settles against her chair. "She was part of the popular clique. I wasn't." Now it's Lynda's turn to glance at the door. "It was only through the Virtues she really spoke to me, and that was mostly to offer up instructions or chastise my propriety and all the smallest errors I needed to correct if I wanted to keep my membership in the society." Lynda adds quietly, "Even now, she does it."

I lean forward, my better half warning me away from this line of discussion. Lynda's anxious over Blair's safety. She has a new family to think about and a husband who truly doesn't grasp the consequences of Briarcliff secret societies. I should back off, allow her to live a cushioned life where Virtuous membership simply means more perks, better parties, and called-in favors like instructing Lynda to send her newest stepchild to Briarcliff University. But I can't stop. "Were you ever introduced to older men when you were at Briarcliff?"

A tiny line forms between Lynda's brows. "Such as alumni? Maybe. Possibly. At our underground balls and such."

I risk adding more detail with the next question. "Did you ever notice a Virtue quieter than the others? Standing off to the side at these balls or not contributing much to the meetings, but seemingly protected by Sabine or the current queen?"

"There were always girls like those. The sweet and kind ones who were beautiful inside and out."

The opening is there, but my throat prematurely burns

with the consequences. I ask, through thickened tissue, "Was my mother one of them?"

"Meredith?" Lynda cocks a smile. "Not a chance, honey."

My lungs deflate in relief.

"Meredith was outspoken and didn't hesitate to criticize how Sabine was taking on the role of queen before it was earned. I doubt those two ever got along, but in the Society, it was especially tense. In fact, your mom often sought out the girls you're speaking of and made them feel welcome. Experience has taught me that the quiet ones are either the most nervous, or the most diabolical. I think Meredith knew that, too." She gives a closed-mouth chuckle, shaking her head. "Meredith had a knack for befriending the prickly ones, too, but she could never get through to Sabine. Strange, considering the two were matched in every aspect. Academics, sports..."

Not Briar blood, I interject silently. *The trait Sabine covets the most.*

"...boyfriends. Lord, they were cats when it came to boys."

The Meredith she talks about still doesn't connect in my mind. I can't picture Mom as a high-schooler, jealous over boys. I *can* picture Mom seeking out the outcasts and loners and making them her friends. But how much did she know? Was Sabine's future grandmother-in-law in the midst of grooming them for her new, iniquitous project?

I open my mouth to ask Lynda to elaborate, but Sophia chooses that time to come in with dinner, plated on a silver platter.

"Apologies," she says as she sets the professionally

garnished platter in the middle. "It's been so long since we've hosted, and I wanted to make this special on Callie's first day home."

"I love it," I say, and pull Sophia into a side-hug as she stands between us. "It smells freaking divine."

Lies, my stomach grumbles, swaying dramatically. I swallow a ball of saliva, determined to eat a few bites and acknowledge Sophia's hard work.

Sophia squeezes my shoulder with her usual affectionate death grip, then goes about carving the roast and plating. I sit back, allowing the fuss, but desperate to get back to the conversation. Dad could come in at any second, effectively ruining any opening I had with Lynda.

Let Lynda be, he'd say. *She's had a game-changing few weeks and is only now finding her feet.*

Studying the fresh treads of crow's feet around Lynda's eyes and the exhausted sag of her usually expertly filled-in lips, I can agree with him.

But my mother's death matters more.

Sophia finishes, and as soon as the door swings shut behind her, I ask, "Which guy did Mom and Sabine fight over?"

Lynda pauses with her fork in mid-air, the silver sparkling under the chandelier. She hasn't taken her first bite yet. "Honey, it was a long time ago. I can't remember."

"She was eighteen when she got pregnant with me."

Lynda's knife scrapes across porcelain. Her wide-set eyes flick up to mine. "Oh. Oh, sweetie. Here I am being so cavalier when the whole time, you're thinking I know ... oh, gosh, that I might know who your father is?"

Her shock resembles my own. I didn't expect her to say something like that. I only wanted to dig up more dirt about Sabine and Mom's history. With Ivy's brutal killing, my mom's murder, and my alliance with Chase morphing into a rivalry, I don't have the capacity to handle my missing baby daddy baggage.

So why is my stupid mind bringing it up?

"How are two of my favorite girls doing?" Dad breezes in, ruffling the top of my head and kissing Lynda's before taking a seat across from me. "I'm surprised half this lamb isn't gone by now."

Lynda's attention doesn't stray. I freeze in my seat, internally begging her not to bring it up while Dad's here.

She blinks, then breaks our stare and turns to Dad. "Give me time, babe. This meat is *mine*."

Releasing a *whoosh* of breath, I paste on a smile, cutting into my dinner, then chewing and swallowing just like they are.

None of us bring up my haggard phone call for the rest of the meal. The few seconds of weighted study Dad gives me every time he looks up from his dinner is couched with a smile and a wink.

We pretend we're fine.

That Briarcliff isn't strung between us on a butcher's hook.

We're not.

13

CALLIE

Christmas Eve in New York City is snowless, blinding with the sunlit shine of skyscrapers, and colorful with determined workaholics, fascinated tourists, and expertly hung Christmas lights.

The day is mild for winter, and I offered to take Blair on a stroll down Madison Avenue to see the decorated storefront windows. Dad hedged around the offer, blinking rapidly and wringing his hands. It felt awful, watching his trust crumbling away from me like the side of an abandoned building when we'd vowed to try and make it better. I bit back the urge to reason with him that I'd never, for one second, consider harming a *baby* for crying out loud, but my history isn't a shining one, and our relationship is so, so tenuous.

Lynda ended up saving us both. Considering her view of the Virtues, and my valid suspicions over being lied to by my mother's membership, she urged me to take Blair out for fresh air. That, and the purple overtaking the red in her eyes clearly begged for quiet solitude away from the baby, which I was only too happy to give.

Lynda's driver, Clifton, drove us to Midtown, parking in a nearby side-street and unfolding the stroller before hanging back a few blocks and watching my every step.

I don't mind Dad's not-so-subtle instructions to their driver to keep an eye on me. Sabine's odd silence causes a queasiness that has me glancing in every alleyway, hesitating under any scaffolding, and biting down on the back of my tongue every time Blair's stroller hits a pothole in the sidewalk. Sabine must be biding her time—or enjoying her vacation—after so successfully killing my best friend and getting away with it. It's her mind games at work: Sabine's well-aware of her power over me and how small I am compared to her. She doesn't need to end my life to show how easy it is to implode it.

Breathing in cold air, I set my shoulders and push the stroller faster, determined to enjoy this small slice of time with my new sister, even as a dark cloud hovers over my head.

It's not likely a two-week-old will have any interest in the beauty of retail celebration, but my spirits are lifted as I park the stroller in front of each window and admire the view. Blair's bundled tight and slumbers through most of it. I'm thankful for it, since I have no idea what to do with a screaming baby, other than to shove a bottle in her mouth. Every so often I get a text from Lynda making sure Blair's okay, but otherwise, I'm deep in the Christmas drift of

Midtown, pushing the stroller slow and steady through the dense foot traffic of admirers and commuters alike.

A flash of blond strikes my vision just as I pull up to an intersection and wait by the lights. My heart kicks up, beating into my throat, but it couldn't be.

Chase is in Rhode Island.

Another gust of wind ruffles familiar, thick blond hair, and I watch, mystified, as the guy crosses Madison, his gray peacoat flapping behind him.

I shake my head, dislodging the image as the tall blond merges with other, well-tailored, suited men in various shades of black.

"Lady? You gonna walk or you gonna keep fairy-footin' around?" someone barks behind me.

I turn around and glare at the man before Blair and I travel into the intersection.

A screech of brakes jolts me alive, and I fly back with the stroller right before a car blows through us.

"Jesus Christ!" I screech, then point to the pedestrian walk sign at the same time the driver flips me off. "Are you *blind*?"

He rolls down his window, his elbow spearing through as he replies, "Fuckin' use your eyeballs, bitch!"

"I have a *baby,* you turd!"

Something bumps my shoulder—the rude guy waiting behind me. "You fuckin' spunk tissue, that's a *motha* you nearly ran over! A *motha*! What's wrong with you? You got a problem with a lady trying to walk her child across the road? You wanna go? *You wanna go with me*?"

And just like that, an asshole becomes my savior.

Typical New York. I scamper away with an oblivious Blair, appreciative of the Brooklyn man for coming to my rescue, but schooled in the art of disappearing in the midst of a driver-pedestrian throwdown in the city.

The smell of freshly roasted coffee attracts my sense of smell as the men's voices fade into the background. A hot chocolate sounds like the perfect ending to my stroll with Blair, even if it comes at a mere $12 a pop. She bounces along with my picked-up speed, happily dreaming with pursed, rosebud lips, and I wrestle the door open into the warm interior, the sudden burst of lighting and belting of Christmas music doing nothing to disturb her sleep.

I think I like newborns.

The line isn't that long, and I take my place, putting one hand to my hip as the other rests on the stroller, and stare out the storefront window.

There.

Another burst of hair the color of dry sand popping up among sharp grays, serious blacks, and hopeful whites of NYC fashion.

It's not possible. I can't be wishing for Chase's presence on Christmas Eve. Not after what he's done and what I allowed myself to do *with* him. Too much has come between us. Avenging Ivy. Finding justice for my mother. Nuking Sabine. This holiday reprieve with the Meyer-Spencers is nice, but every time I glance down at my sister, I'm reminded of innocence and how easily it can be smothered by evil.

So much more important than *love*.

There it is again: that stupid feeling that creeps into my

mind at the most unwanted times. I don't love Chase Stone. I don't care about him. I *don't*.

Disgusted with myself, I swivel to the front.

"Callie?"

I blink at the girl in front of me, dressed in a boyfriend blazer and pleather leggings, her shins hugged by gray, sheepskin boots with a criss-cross of endless laces. Her features solidify, familiarize, and I swallow a small gasp. "Sylvie?"

"My God, I thought it was you, but the stroller threw me." Sylvie tucks a long, mermaid-length strand of silvery blonde hair behind her ear as she stares down at Blair, her stack of gold bracelets jangling. "She's gorgeous."

"Yeah," I say, latching on to the wonderful distraction of Blair rather than ponder the impact of seeing Sylvie for the first time since her overdose. "She is."

Sylvia giggles when she reaches down to tickle one of Blair's exposed palms and Blair clamps around her finger. "She has your lips for sure."

"Oh—Jesus, no." I laugh too loudly. "She's not mine. She's, uh ... she's my sister."

Sylvie's eyes, anime-large on a normal day, stretch wide when she meets mine again. "Wow. A sister?"

"Yeah. Dad remarried." Shit, this is awkward. I wish for the line to go faster, but this is an artisan coffee shop on Madison Ave. On Christmas Eve. Even their drip coffee is a crazy pour-over method requiring at least ten minutes.

Why did I choose to come here again? Oh, right. Nearly being hit by a car and seeing the Ghost of Chase Present everywhere.

Next thing you know, I'll be seeing Sabine's malicious reflection in mirrors.

The thought of her face haunting me on Christmas Eve, with Blair mere inches away, causes a deep-seated shudder to crawl from the base of my spine. My grip clenches on the stroller.

"You okay?"

"Totally great." I rub my temple, smearing Sabine's image and looking for a pressure-point that could ease my headache. "You? What are you doing on Madison? This doesn't seem like your—I mean, I'm not trying to presume. Maybe you love coming here now, shopping at Saks and sampling rare hot chocolate beans..."

I'm rambling. And I'm *also* here. With a baby snoozing lavishly in the latest $1000 stroller.

Sylvie tucks her hair behind her ear again, a nervous habit she must have picked up after we stopped talking to each other. "Matt and I were looking at the window decorations, and like the little girl he is, he had to pee after we walked five blocks. So, you're still hanging out with Pete as your dad, huh?"

Since I don't know Sylvie well enough anymore to understand if that's a jibe, I respond, "Yep. We've reached a sort of understanding. He's tried to be there for me." It feels like a well-versed script on my tongue, but I keep my expression controlled. Solid.

Sylvie raises her brows. "It's really cool, you know. I love how you still call him 'Dad,' even after..." Sylvie trails off, chewing her lower lip but keeping her focus pinned on me.

"I totally thought after losing your mom, you'd want nothing to do with him anymore."

"It surprised me, too," I say honestly. "But he's all I had left."

Sylvie's brown eyes shutter. Her hand drops from her hair.

"That's not what I—it's been a rough few months, and it's shocking, but Dad's been a steady source throughout it all." I take a breath. Sort my thoughts. Sylvie has no idea about Mom's hidden history, secret societies, and Briarcliff. She's a reflection of last year's life, when I mourned and partied and lost myself in swirls of meaningless, bottomless, blinding glitter.

And she nearly lost her life because of it.

Before I can add anything to this train wreck of a conversation, she says, "But here you are with a baby! It's great that you call her your sister even though you're not related. I'm sure Pete's beside himself with pride that he was finally able to have a daughter of his own. And you don't feel left out? That's loyalty right there."

I literally feel my throat bob as I try to keep my head high. "The opposite, actually. My family feels full."

Shockingly, I mean it. There will always be a Mom-sized hole in my heart, and maybe it takes confronting my past in the form of a former best friend to realize it, but it's Christmas Eve, and I'm actually looking forward to dinner with Dad, Lynda, and Blair.

"Forget it." She sighs, pulling on a hank of hair—a habit I recognize, and I'm wondering where I went wrong in the conversation. "Matt should be out of the bathroom soon.

I'm planning to have our coffees before closing." She glances at the register, where one person stands between her and that promise. "If this lady moves her ass."

The woman hears, and peers over her shoulder to glare at Sylvie and ask where her Christmas spirit is. Sylvie quips, "It's at the bottom of the fucking cup of coffee I'd like to order."

I shuffle uncomfortably beside the stroller.

Sylvie ignores the lady as she huffs and turns back to me. "We were such shits back then, weren't we? Getting into all sorts of trouble. I'm glad to see you looking so great."

I cover my surprise at her perspective of me. "You too, Syl. You look..." *Fantastic. Bright. Flushed, full, and happy.* Yet the words don't come. Instead, I croak out, "I'm sorry. I'm sorry for everything."

Space opens up in front of the register, but Sylvie doesn't move. Just stares at me. Finally, she says, "You never called."

"I was forbidden. And I ... I didn't know if you even wanted to talk to me."

"If you'd tried, you would've figured out I was desperate to talk to you."

"God, Sylvie, I—your parents were threatening to sue. Lawyers told me to stay away. Cops warned me not to go near you." I stop, studying my old friend, a girl so waifish and sallow the last time I saw her, now brimming with health and unfeigned joy as soon as she mentioned Matt.

Ivy. In her I see Ivy, and I falter, my death-grip on the stroller's handle the only thing keeping me upright. The cruel irony isn't lost on me, how a friend I nearly killed picked herself up and righted her life, and the friend who *was* killed had her goodness snuffed out.

I am a magnet of misfortune, that much is clear. I look to Blair and choke back a sob. "I never wanted it to be like this."

"Me neither." Sylvie's soft voice drifts closer as she puts a hand on my shoulder and squeezes.

The register opens, but we remain in a stasis of distant comfort. Sylvie's hand on my shoulder. My eyes to the ground while my arm hangs limply between her squeeze and Blair's stroller handle.

Grumbling sounds at my back. Sylvie looks over my shoulder, blows the impatient patron a kiss, then drops her hand from my shoulder and steps up to the cashier.

She places her order for two coffees. "You?" she asks me.

"Oh—peppermint white mocha."

Sylvie smiles, saying to the barista, "If she hasn't changed since last Christmas, she'd also like whipped cream and candy cane sprinkles."

I smile wanly. "...'tis the season."

Sylvia waves away my offer to pay, and there's too many people behind me to argue the point, so I allow it, shuffling with her to the other side of the counter to wait for our drinks and finagle the stroller to fit between us.

"I forgive you," Sylvie says.

I glance up from Blair—still snoozing, always oblivious.

"Most of all," Sylvie continues, "I forgive myself. It took a long time for me to do that."

Shaking my head, I say, "It was my fault. I pressured you to experiment with me. I hated reality so much, yet I didn't want to enter a forced dreamland on my own—and I pushed you into a nightmare. I'm sorry, Sylvie. Every time I say it, *think* it, it doesn't seem enough, but I can't find other words. The thought of you on that floor..."

Sylvie shushes me by covering her hand on my own. "I take it you haven't forgiven yourself yet."

"How could I?"

"Because we were young and stupid. Still are. My brain is my own, though. I've owned up to my decision to stick junk in my veins. Matt helped me through it, sure—I dunno if I could've gotten through it without him. And yeah, I was mad at you. Ravenously furious, actually. But therapy, and Matt, and rehab, told me a different story where you weren't the villain. You were merely the rabbit hole I chose to fall into. You had your own demons, too. With your mom and being orphaned. Having a stepdad who you were totally sure killed her ... Callie, you were wrung out, too. And we got strung out, together. But we're out of it now. Right? We've moved on." She squeezes my hand. "I want to move on."

I squeeze back. "I want that, too. God, I ache for that."

"Then let yourself."

"I don't know if I ... there's so much I haven't told you."

Another blond flash changes the filter of my viewpoint, and my head snaps up, following the weave of gold through the crowded shop.

And closer to us.

As he approaches, the twinkling aura of my filter disappears. His angles change, a sharper chin emerging from a heart-shaped face. Sandy hair flopping against a forehead rather than a textural sweep across.

"Babe!" Sylvie wraps an arm around Matt's—Matt, *not* Chase—waist, tilting her head and accepting his kiss. "Look who I found! And she has a baby!"

Matt's mental flash-carding of memories can literally be seen scrolling across his face, his eyes popping wide when he puts a name to who I am and hears the word *baby.*

"Not mine," I say, the lighthearted chuckle that follows coming naturally. It ends on a choke the minute I realize how soothing and familiar it was coming out of my throat. "My sister."

"Shit. Callie. Congrats. Uh..." He looks to Sylvie, probably in an attempt to gauge how our conversation is going.

"We were catching up," Sylvie says. "Mainly it was me explaining to Callie that I don't blame her for almost dying anymore."

"Oh." Matt's brows jump, despite being well-versed in Sylvie's bluntness. "Well. Good."

I study him for signs—tics or flashes of anger, any clue of unshed blame directed at me for putting his girlfriend in a situation where she could've been killed.

My knees nearly buckle when I find none. Nothing except open curiosity as he gets a good look at me after almost a year of silence.

Could Sylvie be right? Am I deserving of forgiveness from these two? From *anyone*?

Our coffees come, and I swipe mine up with new fervor, itching to remove myself from the happy couple ... except, the urge to flee doesn't feel natural. Sylvie's question of forgiveness gnaws at the back of my head, shockingly drawing me closer instead of leaping for an escape.

"Sit with us," Sylvie says to me. She gives me the once-over, reading my body language. "Don't leave yet."

"Syl, maybe she—"

Sylvie cuts Matt off. "I won't interrogate you ... I swear. I'd like to catch up for real. See what you've been up to."

Ivy's loss clouds my vision. Chase's unexpected cruelty squeezes my throat. My mom's hidden bloodline stiffens my back, and I'm positive my anguish from the last few months is reflected in my eyes.

Sylvie zeroes in on my expression. "Don't tell me it's gotten worse for you since we last saw each other. How much bad luck can one person have?"

Blair gurgles from her luxurious recline, and grabbing at the opening, I search the attached diaper bag for a bottle. "I should feed her."

"Excellent. You'll do it while hanging out with us." Sylvie pulls me in the direction of a recently vacated table. "Because you've been through a ton of shit, including a dead mom."

Matt, sending me a sympathetic glance, helps Sylvie by nudging Blair's stroller forward.

Sylvie continues, "You deserve to dedicate some time to inane conversation where I regale you with our pointless semester at school and the lame friends I've tried to replace you with. Especially on Christmas Eve, of all nights. This is your second year without her, right? Your mom?"

My heart wrenches open. "I..."

"Sit your ass down, Ryan." Sylvie shoves me into a seat.

Sylvie may have forced me into a chair, but I stay where she put me, delicately nudging Blair's lips open with the bottle until she's sucking contentedly.

And I listen. Hang out. And catch up with old friends as if my mom is waiting for me at home, ordering in our favorite Italian and attempting to make hot chocolate on the stove—this time without burning it and covering up the faux pas with a mountain of marshmallows.

While it feels like I'm tugging on an old sweater a little too small for me, I appreciate the softness, the warmth. Moreover, I accept Sylvie's smile and Matt's deep laugh as they tell me about my old college. And I study Sylvie's complexion, rosy and vibrant, as her hands whip around with emphasis. She resembles the girl I met in elementary school, brimming with mischief and unafraid of the future.

And I wonder if this is what it looks like when someone embraces all the bad they've done. And forgives themselves.

14

CALLIE

The glow of my phone is the only light in the kitchen where I'm plopped on a stool, gaping at the letters scrolling across the screen.

As if I've already formed the habit, my free hand moves to brush against the pendant at my neck while I squint at my phone. It's a piece of jewelry I'd found when I trekked into the attic where Dad said he'd stored Mom's more precious items. It was difficult, almost impossible, to open the first box, then the second, and go through what's left of her. Mom's favorite purple dress was at the top of the pile, and after delicately setting it aside, I found her most loved (but never used) cookbooks, and the one pair of Jimmy Choo's she'd purchased for herself. Her old, ratty t-shirts were next, ones she often wore around the house. They still smelled like her.

Thank you, Dad, for not throwing these away, I think as I run my hand along the softened seams of one. It used to be blue but had faded to the color of an afternoon sky, and I lifted it to my nose. Flashbacks whirled at the scent, Mom enveloping me in a hug, the way she danced in the kitchen, and that time I broke curfew and she'd screamed at me in this shirt and sweats, her hair in a sideways bun and her eyes sparking flames.

The memories broke me and soaked her shirt.

Sniffling, I pulled it away from my face and started rolling it up. Something clanged to the floor, falling out of the single front pocket, and I scooped up the gold, shiny item on a delicate chain, inspecting it closer.

Oh my God.

The raven's crest flashed up at me, so blinding and invasive.

I couldn't put it down.

Without thinking, I clasped it around my neck and tucked it into my shirt, then scooped up Mom's box and tore out of the attic, my heart pounding.

A few hours later, I've calmed down enough that the gold doesn't burn against my skin anymore. I've pulled it out now, rubbing the pendant between my thumb and index finger, immersed the email on my phone and wondering whether I've been hacked.

The under-cabinet lights flicker on. I jump, then scream and fall off my stool at the sudden movement in the doorway.

The shadow screams back.

"Christ on a cracker, Callie!" Lynda cries, clutching the collar of her nightgown as she bends over to catch her breath.

"I—Jesus on a biscuit, Lynda!" I retort, tucking the necklace back inside my shirt.

"You scared the life out of me." She puts her hands on her hips, then arches her back until she's exhaling toward the ceiling. "Usually I'm alone when I'm wandering the halls late at night."

"Sorry." I resume my position on the stool. "Couldn't sleep."

"Don't tell me you're waiting up for Santa?"

I huff out a laugh, but hunch over my phone again. "I wish."

"Blair has me up at such odd hours, my stomach's starting to adapt to midnight snacks. Want to join me for some hot chocolate?"

"Sure. That'd be nice."

Lynda opens the upper cabinet, pulling out two mugs. "Tell me what's going on, honey."

"Nothing. I..."

"Those are your final grades for the semester, aren't they?"

I peer up from my phone, straightening in my seat. "How'd you know?"

"Oh, please, I'm hardly psychic." Lynda chuckles at my expression. "Your Dad was emailed them a few hours ago."

Grades must've come in while I was out with Blair. After the incident at the traffic light, I was reluctant to add another distraction and look at my phone until I got home. Then, Christmas Eve dinner happened, and it was only an hour ago that I'd thought to check my email. That stopped any slim chances of catching any sleep.

"You don't look happy," Lynda observes as she sets a pot on the stove. "If I were you, I'd be ecstatic at those grades. Your dad and I are so proud of you."

I stare back down at my phone, the letters growing blurry the longer I forget to blink. "They're not mine."

"Don't be silly. Of course they are. Briarcliff doesn't make those kinds of mistakes."

Her words hit me in the exact opposite way she intended. My hand clenches around my phone as I glance between the screen and her.

"Lynda."

I use her name forcefully, so she'll stop puttering around the stove and turn to look in my direction.

She does, her long, satin nightgown flowing with her movements. "Cal? What is it?"

"Did Briarcliff falsify my grades because I'm a Virtue initiate?"

Lynda's brows disappear into her blonde highlights. "Goodness, you don't mince words, now do you?"

"That's what they did." I flip the phone so she can see the screen. "There's no *way* I managed a 4.0 GPA. I daydreamed through half my exams and scribbled nonsense on the rest."

"Honey." Lynda's soft voice floats closer. "I'm sure that's not what happened. You're an intelligent girl who's finally been given a chance at a top tier school, and you've excelled."

"I don't deserve these grades, because they're not *mine*."

"But they are." Lynda points to the top of the screen. "Isn't that your student number?"

"It is, but I ran into my friend Sylvie today. Remember what I said at dinner? She looked amazing. Happy and healthy. And it got me thinking, why can't I turn over a new leaf? She's forgiven herself, and I want to try to do the same. I want to forgive myself for what happened between us, and what I did to Dad. I really think going back to school here in the city would—"

"Then those are your grades." Lynda spins back to the stove as if I just answered her question and hadn't poured out my insecurities. "Don't question their origins past tonight."

"But—I'm really happy with you, and Dad, and Blair."

"Callie." Lynda lifts a wooden spoon, keeping her back to me. "Do what they want. Accept the perks and keep attending Briarcliff."

Lynda's shoulder blades spear out of her back as she deliberately sets out to stir the milk and chocolate with awful, jerky movements.

"Lynda," I whisper, "The Virtues' perks come with awful consequences. I don't want to be a part of it anymore."

It's the closest I've come to confessing about Ivy, and my throat swells with the effort.

"Refusing them comes at an even greater cost," Lynda replies, her voice invoking an eerie calm.

My hackles rise. "I'm beginning to think they just do whatever the fuck they want, regardless of whether or not you bend to their will."

"I know you're confused." *Stir, stir, stir.* "Angry, even. But coming at them the way you have isn't going to work out the way you think it will."

"Oh, really? Is someone I know going to get hurt? News-flash, that's already—"

The wooden spoon slams against the countertop. Hot milk splashes with Lynda's arc, but she doesn't react to the boiling liquid hitting her skin.

"Please." Her voice breaks. Placing her palms on the edge of the counter, she sags forward over the stove, exhausted. "No more. Don't put this family through more struggles."

I slide off my stool, clutching my phone to my chest, and step up behind Lynda. Afraid to touch her. "I'm not trying to put you or Blair in more danger..."

"But you are." Lynda straightens, but she still doesn't turn around. "I'm aware of their abuse of power. How well they manipulate and extort. I learned early that it's better to just do as they ask than fight against the inevitable." Abruptly, Lynda spins, then clutches my face between her hands. Her pressure stings. "Honey, there isn't any fairness in it, but it keeps us safe. You're about to become a Virtue, whether you like it or not. Accept the good. The privilege that comes with it. You're primed to attend any Ivy League you want. *Any*. So few students get that kind of chance. And if you do that, if you listen to the Virtues and do as they say, they'll leave you alone. Let you live a life of comfort and wealth in peace. It's really the only way to survive them."

The pot gurgles and hisses behind her, but Lynda doesn't move.

My eyes dart to the bubbling steam spilling over the edges, then back to Lynda. "I don't—I can't do that."

Her eyes well. Lynda's so close, I feel the heat of her breath. Smell the sweetness of milk on her skin. Her fingers dig into the fat in my cheeks, my teeth aching with her applied pressure.

"You know what your mother endured," she whispers.

I swallow, quelling the need to jerk out of her hold and scream.

"It's because she didn't like their rules and went against them. She was forced to run, then live a life as an office cleaner and single mother. She had everything, *everything*, at her fingertips, and they stripped it all from her. Do *not* be your mother."

They killed her just like they killed Ivy.

The accusation is silent on my lips. Lynda looks upon me with such need, I can't voice the truth because I'm certain she won't listen.

"I'm not a Virtue," I say instead.

Lynda blinks. Her arms drop from my face, then she breaks into a smile. "Well, have you had your robing ceremony?"

I shake my head, eyeing her warily as she goes back to the overboiling pot and turns down the dial.

"Then you're right. You're not one of them, yet. However, if they've..." She gestures to my phone dangling in my hand. "It's clearly still in their plans to accept you."

I'm desperate to get through to her and end up deploying the last weapon in my arsenal. "Ahmar's looking into them. If he finds any proof of their history of trafficking, bribery, lies, and murder—"

"Oh, honey, Ahmar will be blocked at every turn. And if

you keep pushing him, he will be the only one that loses. You can't tell me part of you doesn't know that."

Lynda lifts the pot from the stove—there's no way that milk isn't burned—and pours the brown liquid into the two mugs. Once finished, she carries them over to me at the opposite counter.

"It's in his best interest for you to stop feeding him information," she says as she hands me a steaming mug.

I stare at her in horror. "Whose side are you on?"

"The one that's gotten me through decades of living untouched by them," Lynda says sharply. "Now, go on. Drink."

I do, wincing as the scalded liquid hits my tongue.

A faint squeal carries down the hallway. Lynda jerks her chin to the sound, tilting her head. "Damn. Blair's up again. You should get some sleep, Cal. We have a big day tomorrow, now that we also get to celebrate your first semester at Briarcliff." She beams, then sets down the mug. "I'm not lying when I say we're so proud of you. You're so strong, and you're doing great."

Lynda kisses my cheek, her lips cold despite her recent sip of hot chocolate. She sweeps out of the room, dimming the lights as she goes, until I'm left in a room of shadows.

I sag into a stool, staring into nothing.

It was such a stupid idea, thinking I could be happy with Dad and Lynda, that I belonged and had their love. The Virtues will never let me. They've seeped into Lynda's soul, altering her and poisoning her to levels where she can't see clearly enough to know she's tearing me apart with her wish for me to just fall in line.

But, perhaps it's the only way. As a Virtue, I'll gain power. I can claim the status of the Missing Heir.

It could give me the leverage I need to cut Sabine down with the very knife used on Ivy. A blade that could've been used on my mother, too.

The only people who have ever loved me are dead. Anyone alive pretends to care about me to serve themselves.

Glimpsing Sylvie's new life was nice while it lasted.

I know my place now.

The sharp wings of the pendant pierces my thumb through my shirt's fabric.

The only way to end the Virtues...

Is to finish becoming one.

15

CHASE

No music plays.

The clink of silverware and Tempest's loud sips of wine are the sole distractions in this expansive, *stifling* dining room.

Nobody has even decorated it for Christmas, never mind Christmas Eve dinner.

Emma and I were largely forced to my father and Sabine's penthouse in Manhattan through fear of impending doom. The happy couple was supposed to be bound for the tropics, but instead changed their plans last minute to attend all the Christmas parties the Manhattan elite offered, leaving me extremely suspicious of their motives. With Callie too close to Sabine for comfort, I cajoled Emma to come with me to the empty luxury of the five-bedroom apartment, instead of to our mother's in California. I guilted my sister, manipulated her, and told her that if something happened to Callie in the city, she'd never forgive herself.

I didn't give much thought that this would be the first time Emma sat at dinner with the woman who had auctioned her off, then tried to burn her alive when she'd rebelled. The most I offered was to bring Tempest along for the ride, since he never has family around the holidays.

I can be a rat bastard, especially after having trash thrown at my face, but now that we're here, my plan borders on fucking dumb.

My knife screeches against the priceless, gold-embossed plate as I cut into my steak.

"Problem, dearest?"

My attention hovers over my plate, my eyes scraping in much the same way my knife did as I look across the table and meet Sabine's question with a direct stare. "None whatsoever."

Sabine responds with a closed-mouthed smile, returning to her dinner with dainty, calculated bites.

She doesn't take her eyes off me.

A sharp jab to my thigh severs the animosity holding me taut. To further enunciate his point, Tempest clears his throat and shifts his ass in his seat, as if I can't catch his thoroughly subtle way of telling me to stop trying to eviscerate Sabine with my stare.

"I assume exams went well?" my father asks, seated beside Sabine and looking to anyone else who bothers to duck into the dining room that he's enjoying dinner with his family.

"Fine," I bite out.

Even if they didn't, the Noble King would never let his son fail on paper. My exams are likely being doctored as we speak.

"They went okay," Emma murmurs beside me.

I stiffen at her voice. She hasn't spoken since we were forced into the penthouse and asked to sit down for a fake-ass family dinner. And unlike me, her exams won't be forged. She's left with whatever she worked hard enough to achieve—a notion I doubt will ever resonate with dear Dad.

Yet here she is, seated in front of the woman who tried to end her life and pretending like school matters. What Emma went through —what she *hid* from me—boils my blood to demon spawn levels, but rather than directing my barely contained ire at my sister, I'd rather fuse it into my father. He's marrying a murderess. Binding himself to a woman who spites his own children, yet he doesn't bat an eye.

I eviscerate whatever food's left in my mouth, then shove my plate away. "Are we finished with this charade?"

"Son," Father intones. "Try to keep your temper at a minimum. We have guests."

"You mean your fiancée?" The title sits gluttonous, slippery with fat, on my tongue. "Or the dude who's spent every Christmas with us since he was in diapers?"

"Are you calling me a mooch, fucktard?" Tempest asks, cocking his head with a smarmy grin. I know what he's doing, but I refuse to let him defuse the situation before I fuck it up royally.

"I'm not doing this," I grind out. "Pretending all is well when—"

"Chase." Emma's hand clamps down on my wrist, keeping me from rising.

Her nails bite into my skin, but I welcome the pain and her sincere reminder that I shouldn't storm from the table, earning a pissy lecture from my father later, and more importantly, signaling to Sabine that I'm anything but defeated.

Protect Callie won't leave my head. I can't very well do that if I don't have my eye on Sabine at all times during the university's school break. Even during an innocuous holiday dinner, Sabine could be laying a foundation with my father or concocting future plans involving Callie's demise. The bitch never rests, and neither should I.

"Perhaps we should change the subject," Sabine says. "How was everyone's day?"

My lips twist at the same time Tempest says, "Tolerable. Christmas cheer usually makes me sociopathic." Tempest pauses. Grins subtly. Sabine doesn't react, keeping her expression remote while she angles her head with pretend interest. Tempest continues, "But I controlled myself this year and joined Emma to see the tree at Rockefeller."

"Interesting. You all must've seen it millions of times before." Sabine picks up her fork, but before she bites down, she pins me with a look and asks, "Did you all go?"

She's searching for a tell. Any indication that I nearly broke my frozen balls off ducking and diving into blind spots and traffic every time Callie looked over her shoulder, rather than join the masses of tourists in snapping pictures of a giant tree with a bunch of lightbulbs on it.

"We did," Emma says, her voice barely above a whisper.

A worm of guilt inches its way into one of the many holes in my heart. Here is my sister whose every minute is strangled the longer she's forced to dine with Sabine, and I was about to smash my plate to pieces and leave her here.

"Aren't you aware, Sabine?" I ask. "It's a different tree every year. Thus, I'd argue a new experience every time we go."

"Indeed," Sabine says. She draws in another bite, chewing thoughtfully.

I take that as a sign this inane conversation is finished, thank fuck, but she draws my attention as she sucks on the tines of the fork. "I wonder if Callie took the time to see the tourist spectacle today as well?"

My father stiffens beside her. "Darling," he chastises. "Not today."

Emma audibly swallows beside me. I wonder if her twin sense is attuned to the lightning bolt shooting down my spine as I ask, "Why not, Father? You two have won, haven't you? She's no longer a threat to the societies."

My father's hooded gaze meets mine in warning. "And no longer of interest to you, either, so I suggest we move on from Calla Lily Ryan."

"Oh, I'm far from interested." My fork lands on my plate with a clink, and I lean back in my seat. "I've shunned, humiliated, lied, and cheated her. Have I missed anything, Em?"

Emma shakes her head without looking at me. I notice the trembling of her hand as it hovers over her dinner, her silverware held uselessly in her grip. She hasn't eaten a bite, but I refuse to take the blame.

"I believe you accomplished all those on her the last day of exams," Tempest pipes in, then mutters, "and she, you."

I nail him with a glare, which he ignores.

"Should we invite her to our New Year's party, then?" Sabine asks.

My gaze flies to hers. She smiles coldly. "Perhaps she's willing to accept her position now that she's been ... thoroughly convinced."

I take a breath. A cleansing one. A damned centering one. "I doubt she'd have any desire."

"Mm," Sabine murmurs as she brings her wine to her lips. "Too bad. She'd make such a breathtaking Virtuous princess, if only she'd accept our rules."

The tablecloth wrinkles in my death grip. I can't bite down on the instinct enough to quip, "Like Emma was?"

"*Son*," Father spits, the same time Emma's head whips toward me.

She begs, "Chase, don't—"

The temptation to lay out all Sabine's done and how far she's gone—killing Ivy—while dart-boarding a butter knife to her forehead is so strong it's almost irresistible, but I hold myself back.

"Emma made her choice." A vein pulses in my father's forehead. "She decided to forsake her duty as a Virtue princess and betray us by collecting secrets to sell to the highest bidder. Though I doubt we need to rehash this, do we, Emma?"

Emma's jaw locks. She literally can't speak, and my own teeth gnash at the thought of what I've done to her, making her sit here and endure this when she's already become a ghost of her former self.

"Are you really so dense, Father?" I ask.

I stare at him a long time in the tense, frozen silence.

No, my father is a lot of things, but he's not clueless. If he was aware of Sabine's auctioning of Emma, of the reasons she was trapped in a fire of her own making, then he damn well knows what Sabine did to Ivy. The question is whether he understands that Ivy was a spontaneous Plan B, and that his son and only heir was the A-game.

I break our stare, instead grabbing the tongs for a second portion of steak. Tempest mutters his approval of my backing down, and Emma's shoulders sag in relief. Satisfied with my cease and desist, Father asks Sabine how she's enjoying her dinner. She answers that it's delicious.

Idly spinning my fork, I ask, "How far do you think your future wife's willing to go to keep her reign over the Virtues? Besides just marrying you, I mean."

I expect dishes to scatter. Wineglasses topple over as Father hurls himself from his seat, his rage smashing against the table.

Icy derision meets me over the crystal centerpiece. "Are you quite finished, son?"

I smile. "Not in the least."

Tempest throws his napkin on his unfinished dinner with an aggravated, "Shit."

"Do you know what this woman has been through these past few months? This is her first Christmas without her daughters." My father speaks in a silky monotone. If he had a bone to pick his teeth with, he would. "One of which, had she not died tragically, was your soulmate. A wonderful girl, murdered not three months ago, and here you are, shaming her name and humiliating yourself, simply out of jealousy."

"*Jealousy*?" I sputter, but collect myself before my jaw unhinges.

Father folds his hand over his fiancée's. "Sabine is to be my future wife, and she is to have the same respect you gave to Marilee, if not more. This woman has gone through hell, and I refuse to sit here and allow you to disparage her further."

"A hell of her own making," I quip.

"Daniel, it's all right," Sabine says as Father peels his lips back mid-snarl. "He's not wrong. Addisyn murdered Piper. It's awful, and I don't think I'll ever recover from the thought that my girls could've come to that point unless I did something to push them in that direction. A mother's guilt knows no bounds." Sabine raises her demure eyes to me. "I will live with that for the rest of my life. But I plan to change and help the girls I still can, my Virtues, attain the values and positive futures that I can only look back on as an unrealized dream for my daughters."

"Is your simpering supposed to affect me?" I ask her, honestly curious, then turn to my father. "Her daughter was killed by her *other* daughter, Father." I snort. "And if that's not proof enough of her fucked-up mothering, the way she treats her Virtues is by far the worst. Look what she's done to Emma—"

Emma gasps.

"*Get out.*"

If ice could've taken over the walls and cracked into

jagged fractures, it would've had the same effect as Father's voice.

"Sadly, I am so far from done." I push my palms into the edge of the table, tipping my chair on its two back legs. If my father can don an arctic veneer, I'll counter it with the blasé attitude of an asshole son. "We've yet to cover Meredith Ryan. Tell me, Sabbie, did you orchestrate that, too?"

Tempest raises his eyes skyward at the same time Emma swivels in her seat, her eyes stretched to their whites.

"How *dare* you?" my father's whisper snaps across the table. "It's amazing to me that the heir to a fortune and to the governing of a powerful, world-wielding secret society can act with such idiocy. Everything we do, boy, is for *you*. Meredith's inheritance—excuse me, Calla Lily's inheritance—could take that all away from you. Do you understand? *I* am protecting you. Sabine is protecting you. Your sister sits here with us because she knows the truth of our influence. She's paid for her rebellion in the worst possible way, and for that I am devastated—"

"That you can no longer sell off your prized stock?"

"*Chase.*" Emma's whisper is more of a tremulous gasp. She palms the table, much like I do, but squeezes until her knuckles pop through her skin. "Stop this."

My father goes mute. His lips thin to a needlepoint thread. It is through a very small pocket of air that he says, "I do believe you've overstayed your welcome."

"Oh, have I?" I retort, pushing to my feet. Tossing my napkin on the table, I say, "As always, it's been a pleasure, Father," before whirling for the exit.

He says to my back, "Regardless of your prostrating, I trust you haven't said one word to our girl about the little secret we keep, now have you?"

My shoulders level. My feet stop. But I don't turn around.

"Ah." I hear Father's smile. "I'm delighted to know your loyalty remains bound to the Nobles. If Calla Lily were ever to find out you've known who her real father is this entire time ... well..."

Sabine hums in agreement. "Just when we thought such betrayals were finished with. The poor girl would be devastated."

My hands clench at my sides, the skin growing purple with endless, swirling blood.

Another hand comes to my lower back. Words murmur, "Let's blow this place."

After a curt nod, I allow Tempest to push me out of the dining room. We don't stop until we reach my bedroom on the other side of the penthouse, *far* away from the bruises I'm aching to inflict on someone else. Anyone else.

A speck of clarity remains within the red of my vision, and Tempest steps inside it. "Calm down."

"*Fuck* this." I yank out of his hold. "My sister's back there. We have to get her."

Tempest clamps down on my shoulder and shoves me away from the door. "No, we don't."

I bare my teeth. "Who the fuck are you to tell me what to do? You did nothing back there. Didn't have my back because my best friend is suddenly a mute-ass motherfucker—"

"Emma didn't want to leave."

I choke on my own insults. "What?"

He shrugs. "I asked her. She said she'd like to finish her steak."

"That—doesn't make sense." I rake a hand through my hair.

"You tell me. She's your sister."

"Her tormentor's sitting with her. *Both* of them. And we're not there anymore."

"Need I remind you … she was also a mute-ass motherfucker during your shitstorm. Considering the numbers are against you, I'm thinking that was the better way to handle it."

"Oh, come on."

"What were you trying to accomplish?"

I wave him off, choosing to scowl out the window.

"Can't say I enjoy Christmas any more than I did before that remarkable dinner," Tempest muses.

He searches through my desk drawer, humming in excitement when he finds what he's looking for and holds up the blunt.

I grunt my assent. He pulls a lighter from his pocket and fires it up. We sit at my two gaming chairs, spinning them until we're looking out over the Manhattan skyline. A few moments pass, and then ten, before a needed weightlessness overtakes my body.

My smoke ring floats up, widening and embracing my second smoke ring before both dissipate near the ceiling.

"Better, friend?" Tempest asks beside me, reclined in much the same way I am.

I pass him the blunt. "Far from it."

A small nudge at the base of my skull keeps reminding me that Sabine might not have concocted Ivy's—or my—death on her own. I lost my cool tonight because Father might know of my goals to usurp him and might not have objected to Sabine's attempts to get rid of me, or Callie, for good. How could I sit across the table from that man, saying nothing? Ivy was an effective warning but a poor substitute for the real thing. I keep waiting for the final thunderclap. Maybe I was even asking for it tonight.

Giving me an excuse to crush both of them before they get to Callie.

Callie, who I hurt and belittled with a dismissive smile. A girl who deserves better, yet thinks that *better* is me.

I glance at Tempest, idly blowing smoke through his nose—a dragon contemplating the art of burning the village below. "This is the part where I'm going to admit being glad I didn't go to Dubai to spend Christmas with my parents and their crew. You're more entertaining than a multi-mil superhero movie."

I gift him with a bold smile that doesn't reach the essential organ I'm told smiles come from. "I'm glad you were beside me tonight, even though you didn't do shit."

"It's not my job to stir up your childhood traumas with your father. It's my duty to keep you in check. We're not winning over the Nobles by having a temper tantrum at the kids' table."

I drop the ash from the blunt into the tray between us. "Sabine's the one who brought up Callie."

"Dude, I can't keep track of all your trigger words."

The bedroom door bursts open, both of us swiveling to the sound. The only light in the room comes from the surrounding buildings, so it takes a moment for my eyes to adjust to the hallway light rimming the form stomping into my territory.

It's not my father or Sabine, that's for sure. I narrow my eyes at the surprise intruder, who, once out of the shadows, turns out to be my sister.

She snarls. "You're an *asshole*, you know that?"

"Yes."

"Don't be glib with me." She halts in the middle of the room and plants her hands on her hips. "Did you think you were funny in there? Brave? A hero?"

I suppose I have to stand up for this. Pushing on the armrests, I rise, unwittingly towering over her. "Did you really expect me to sit through dinner without mentioning a word after what we've been through?"

"*You've* been through? *You've* been through?" Emma's outrage riddles her cheeks and creates hollows under her eyes. "What about the past two years I've endured under our father's hand?"

"I understand your pain, but—"

"You *don't*. Ivy's dead, and I'm sick over that—over what you and Callie had to witness, how horrible it must be to carry that around when no one's brought to justice for it, but you know what? Same here. I have your rage. I possess your hunger for justice. I've been harboring this shit for years, and the cravings only get worse. But unlike you, I've had time to cultivate. To deliberate. And therefore, to put together a patient, cutting plan that puts your flashbang revenge scheme to shame." Emma takes a deep breath. "I was able to get Callie on my side before you. I had *Piper* helping me before you even knew what the fuck was going on. Though clearly, my efforts mean shit-all to you. You should've given me respect in there or acknowledged my pain and allowed me to speak up when I wanted. And in that dining room, you took away my choice."

I stare at her hard. My jaw clamps shut.

Emma snatches at my silence. "You think you bear all the responsibility, that leadership and reformation fall on you. They don't. *I* am a legacy. *I* am a fallen Virtue. If anybody gets a say in how Sabine's taken down, it's me." She slams her palm against her heaving chest.

"You're right," I say in a low voice, my blood simmering. "I should've handled it better in there."

Emma snorts. "I suppose that's an apology coming from you."

"I mean it."

She looks to Tempest. "Anything to add?"

He raises his hands, palms facing her. "Your argument is sound."

Emma's brows relax. "When we get back to Briarcliff, we're working together. And you're going to let me decide if whatever you're concocting in your vengeful head is the right move. Everything that happens to us starts and ends at Briarcliff. We're not going to decide Callie's fate over Christmas dinner, in a Manhattan high-rise, with anger and spite as our muse. Is that clear?"

Tempest purses his lips. "Crystal, Your Most Respectful Legacy."

Emma cuts him a look.

"Yes," I say, but I'm thinking about Callie on the New York City streets. Vulnerable and exposed, with secrets, lies, and betrayals shadowing her every step.

Emma's wrong on one point—what happens to us doesn't stay at Briarcliff. It can't.

"Now that we've cleared that up," Tempest says, at last rising from his lupine position on the chair. "Anybody going to 'fess up on who Callie's dad is?"

"No," Emma and I bark at the same time. I jolt, then send her a confused brow raise.

"It'll only serve to distract her," Emma says, meeting my stare with a flat one of her own. "I know more than you think, dear brother. Like I said: I've earned your respect."

"Duly noted," I murmur, then watch her as she pivots and exits the room, shutting the door with a punctuated smack.

"Well, that's no fun," Tempest pouts, but reaches for the blunt and takes in a satisfied inhale. "I only enjoy secrets when I'm in on them."

"I'll keep you busy," I say, still staring at the door. "Emma may think she's been biding her time without notice, but she won't protect Callie the way she protects herself. Callie's in incredible danger, and if Callie returns to school"—which, sadly, I know she will—"we have to hunt down Sabine's traps before she falls into one. At the same time, we fuck with her, isolate her, and make her regret ever setting foot in Briarcliff University."

Tempest angles his head thoughtfully. "Okay. I'll bite. That sounds fun."

"This isn't for your amusement. Girls are dying on my watch, and I don't want any more blood on my hands."

Callie's, especially. Just thinking of her slack form in my arms, her chin tipped to the sky, her eyes milky with death, causes an unfamiliar, aching shudder starting at the base of my spine and ending with my stomach plummeting through the Earth.

My lips pull down. I don't like this feeling *at all*.

"Relax, Prince. Callie isn't in immediate danger. Sabine won't kill her on sight." Tempest flicks the end of the blunt into the ashtray. "The whole point of having prey is so you can toy with them first."

16

CALLIE

Every step closer to Briarcliff University makes me shudder.

I force myself to the top, then through the doors, refusing to tip my chin up to the Wolf's Den, in case Chase is up there, lording over the underclassmen as we all return from winter break.

Someone jostles my shoulder. "Did you keep it or scrape it out with a coat hanger?" flies against my ears.

Grimacing, I push forward, ignoring the sneers and judgmental stares.

Chase. Chase did this.

Amid the societal backstabbing, the scandal, and the *murders*, he decided it was a good time to continue the cruelty, giving a forbidden pregnancy a go, since it worked so well with Piper.

The gall of him. The absolute deplorable nature he

would've had to reach for to make this happen and keep it going well after the holidays ... my upper lip curls.

I have to remember what it was like to see Sylvie, and what forgiving yourself for all your mistakes can mean. It doesn't all have to be bad. Good things and happy endings can still happen when we're at our worst.

I don't have to keep being this way.

Turning into my locker area, I'm jostled again. "So, what's it like?"

Without glancing up from my padlock, I snap, "Being pregnant with a disgraced teacher's baby? I dunno ... what's it like embracing yet another unoriginal rumor because your big, bad prince told you to—" I stop as soon as I whip around. "Oh. Hey, Eden."

Her brows jump. "Hey yourself. I just wanted to know what it was like meeting your new sister, but hey, if you've got baggage to unload, I'm your luggage carrier."

Sighing, I lean my shoulder against the locker beside mine. "You haven't heard?"

"That you're preggo? Nope." She cocks her head. "Are you? Because that'd be a twist."

"No," I snap, then draw back my whip. "It's another of the Nobles' rumors, meant to make me run from Briarcliff with my tail between my legs and never come back."

Eden scoffs. "If seeing your best friend murdered in front of you didn't make you want to hightail it out of here, how could they think ... sorry. Too soon."

I pull my mouth out of the frown, peering closer at Eden. She may be talking about Ivy off-the-cuff, but the sheen of loss in her eyes tells me differently. "Did I miss anything while I was away?"

"Nothing to report." Eden shrugs, falling into step beside me as I shut my locker and make my way to class. "The place was deserted, though, which was a nice change. No student ... or Virtue ... in sight." She adds under her breath as we enter the crowded hallway, "No secret meetings, either. I'm guessing it's because Daniel Stone and Sabine stayed in New York for the holidays and couldn't be bothered planning a coup long distance."

I jerk to a stop, grabbing Eden's elbow to halt along with me. "I thought they went on some fancy, tropical vacation together?"

"My sources tell me otherwise," Eden says easily. "They holed up in their luxury penthouse in Manhattan. Chase and Emma were there, too. And that creepy-hot Tempest guy."

"But..." I think back to my rare, but necessary, public outings with Blair. In particular, Christmas Eve, when I saw Chase everywhere, but nowhere, at the same time. I didn't see his ghost at all after that, instead focusing on finishing my break on a high note and spending all my time with Lynda, Dad, and Blair. Lynda never mentioned her hot cocoa meltdown again, and I didn't bring it up, either. Perhaps I'm just as guilty as her, pretending everything's fine when it isn't, but I wasn't sure when I'd see them again. Or if. I *needed* us to be okay when I left.

Eden jolts, her eyes widening in sudden realization. "Shit, your parents run in the same circles as them. You didn't run into those assholes, did you?"

I shake my head. "We kept to ourselves, getting to know the baby as a family instead. Dad and Lynda went to some New Years' ball, but I stayed behind to watch Blair. They might've crossed paths then."

My eyes flit to the side as I work to recall New Years' Eve. Blair was asleep in her bassinet next to me as I watched the ball drop in Times Square from the comfort of the den's couch. I must've fallen asleep, because I don't remember said ball actually dropping and woke up to the sound of footsteps —Dad and Lynda wandering in well after midnight.

"How was it?" I'd mumbled, rubbing sleep from my eyes. Infomercials had replaced the live coverage of the revelry thirty blocks away.

"Good," Dad said at the same time Lynda trilled, "Great! Only one boob decided to leak. The other stayed painful and swollen but, oh my God, to be back in socialization again. I practically forgot it wasn't highbrow to whip a breast out in the middle of the dance floor and squeeze it for relief."

"She's had champagne," my dad said as explanation for her outburst, but I smiled, patting the couch next to me for Lynda to sit down.

"Squeeze away. I won't judge."

I try to remember if there was strain around Dad's eyes, or if Lynda's voice was higher than normal. Wouldn't a surprise confrontation with the Stones send them home stiff-backed and concerned? They don't know about Ivy, but they're well aware of the threat the Virtues pose. Lynda, especially.

I can't recall any tense moments when they got home. Just Lynda sagging in relief beside me and Dad making some dad joke about how badly I want him to order the new omelet maker on television.

After searching my face, Eden grows serious. "Do you think they're in any real danger?"

"I didn't think Ivy was in any danger," I say honestly.

Eden's lips press together.

"How lovely, the stank possum and her skank are back in business."

Rather than turn toward Falyn's familiar, grating voice, I say to Eden, "Let's go."

"Was last semester not enough for you?" Falyn's voice follows us down the halls. "Do you have some sort of sick craving to be humiliated and tossed aside by every guy at Briarcliff? So pathetic, Callie. Why couldn't you have taken the warning and gone back to your gutter?"

I whip around so fast and so hard, Falyn has to skid to a stop before barreling into me. She rights herself, smoothing her skirt, but can't smooth the tic of surprise in her expression when she meets my eye again.

"You were saying?" I say softly. When her chin trembles and she doesn't respond, I add, "Go on."

Falyn lifts her upper lip. "I was saying what a skank you were—"

My arm flies out and slams her against the wall, my forearm pressing against her throat. Gasps sound out, a few footsteps scampering back.

Falyn gurgles, her hands scrabbling against my arm. I

say, "I'd appreciate it, as a fellow sister, if you'd shut up about my slut status."

"I'm not your sister," she spits out, her voice strained.

I press harder. Violet yelps, and Willow steps forward, but one scathing look from me and Willow freezes.

"Callie 2.0 in the house," Eden sings under her breath, backing away, but her stare locks on me in fascination.

There must be something different in my eyes, I think offhand. *Enough to make these bitches step back.* Then I add idly, *I wonder what it could be?*

My gaze slides back to a squirming Falyn. "I beg to differ. Not only am I your sister, but I'm next in line for the throne." Falyn starts a garbled protest, but I press harder, adding loud enough for our audience to hear, "But I think you knew that. With that in mind, I'd appreciate you backing off Eden, Emma, and *me*. Understood?"

Falyn's nails, sharpened into manicured talons, dig into my skin, drawing blood. "You can't possibly still want to be with us."

I tip my head. "But I do."

"After ... after everything that's happened?"

A glint forms in Falyn's eyes—a shard of metal, a sharpened, cunning blade.

She knows the truth about Ivy.

Heat travels into my throat, and I snarl into her face, "I'm not going anywhere, you *fucking* bitch."

Heavy, unhurried footsteps sound out, amplified in a hall shocked into silence, until they stop at the base of my heels.

Breath skitters against my nape, goosebumps firing

along my jaw. I know without looking that if I spear my elbow back, I'll hit nothing but rock-solid abs.

"Screw off," I say through my teeth, though my focus remains on Falyn.

"I might, if she's worth it," Chase muses at my back. "Is she?"

Heat crackles at the base of my spine. Chase isn't close enough to touch, but he's near enough to awaken the atoms between us, rippling the air as they electrify and pop with every exhale he makes.

If he breathes extra-hard, he'll flutter pieces of my hair.

I keep my inhales steady. My eyes facing forward. "I don't need any *prince*, and neither does she."

Falyn cringes when I press my forearm harder into her neck.

Chase's arm crosses my vision, his gold cufflink shimmering as he grabs my wrist and pulls me off Falyn. I don't have time to cry out my indignation before he sends me into a twirl that has my back crashing against the wall, where Falyn's once was.

He boxes me in, his bronze stare bearing down. Falyn gasps and sputters beside us, clutching her neck and running to her friends for cover. He doesn't spare her a look.

"Causing quite the spectacle on your first day back," he says.

"So what?" I push at his barrel of a chest, but he doesn't move. "I'm sick of being pushed around by assholes like you."

His eyes narrow. "Looks like you can add pissing me off to your first day to-do list as well."

"It's clear you'd rather I cower, or run, or cry whenever I come near you, but you know what? Winter break taught me the opposite."

"And how's that?"

"You can't stay away from me."

A chilled waft of air hits me when he straightens. "Come again?"

"I saw you," I whisper through stiff lips. "Watching me. Stalking me. Unable to stay *away* from me in New York."

Something flickers in Chase's eyes, but he checks it, his nostrils flaring. "Are those paranoid delusions bothering you again, sweet possum?"

I ignore the internal blade slicing through my chest. "You lied to me. Your dad wasn't on some island vacation with Sabine. They were right here. In *my* city, likely watching me as much as you were."

"Is it somehow my fault you can't fly under the radar?"

"Stop it," I hiss. "Don't pretend you're not concerned for me. You wouldn't have tracked me down on Christmas Eve if you didn't still have feelings—"

Chase draws away, pouting as his eyelids give a derisive twitch. "Hmm. Poor thing. I hoped you would've figured out your place while on break, if you decided to come back here, that is. Hasn't enough been done to you? Run back to your fake uncle, or better yet, go live with your fake parents. Or, hey." He points to my stomach. "Go have a fake baby. A little thing like that might actually love you back."

My mouth trembles with the need to hurl insults. My eyes sear into his with the desperation to hurt him as much as he's killing me. I say in a low, unrecognizable voice, while keeping my eyes on him, "I chose the wrong person to save."

A muscle tics in Chase's cheek, yet his stare doesn't waver.

But I know I've hurt him. I know it, and I can't control it once it starts. "You're the last person to dole out love advice. Your mother wants nothing to do with you. Your sister despises you. Your father uses you like an object and can't wait to discard you once you've proven your worth. You're trying to tell me blood means family? None of them have affection for you. I can't even call it goodwill." Chase's lashes flutter close to a flinch. My stomach pitches at how hard he's working not to show emotion, but I forge through the nausea. "Look down on me and my lack of a blood relative all you want, but that only means I have people with no obligation to me who care anyway. You have no idea what that's like, and you never will."

I press my hand to my abdomen, noting the flutter there —butterfly wings of sentiment. *I mean what I'm saying.* Dad, Lynda, Ahmar, Blair ... they may not be tied to me through DNA, but we're something. We could be a family, if I at last opened that door instead of staying in the locked compartment of my mind with my dead mother.

But I can't leave her behind.

Brave hollers and applause echo to the arched ceilings. We've drawn even more of a crowd than I thought, but Chase doesn't acknowledge them. He simply stares in silence, assessing the few feet between us.

"Big words for a discarded orphan. You were shipped back here as soon as they could."

So much blood has collected in my cheeks that my ears ring. But I raise my chin. "I don't need your acceptance to keep going to this school. I certainly don't need it to claim my rightful place."

Chase's lips twitch. His eyes narrow. "If you do that, you'll be making a terrible mistake."

"Too late." I point to Falyn, now part of the audience, the murderous gleam of her teeth visible from here. "I've already sent in my request. It's done."

Chase scans the crowd. He can disparage me all he wants, but the Nobles' long-reaching gag order strangles him from voicing any displeasure at my continued role in the Virtues.

I latch onto that weakness and stand tall. "You tried to scare me away last semester and failed. I'm not going anywhere, Chase Stone. The only difference being, now I'm here for blood."

Spinning on my heel, I push to the exit, finding Eden in the outskirts of the still-forming crowd and pull her along with me.

"Holy shit, what's gotten into you?" she breathes out as she tries to keep up with my steps.

I don't trust myself to speak until we're well away and turning into the South Wing. Facing down Chase is too much. My heart is crumbling in my hands.

I hide it all when I say, "I've decided to no longer take any bullshit."

"Hey, I'm down with you beating up Falyn and putting Chase in his place—that was baller, by the way—but what was that whole thing with Falyn? Are you really—I mean, do you seriously still want to be a Virtue?"

"It's the only way," I say as we wander deeper into the South Wing. New semester, new classes. Philosophy is my first of the day.

"To show Sabine you're not afraid?"

"Not quite." We're approaching my classroom door, first period having started ten minutes ago, and I slow my steps. "To prove she killed my mother."

"Shit. Okay."

"Find Emma after first period and meet me in the gym bathrooms. We all need to talk."

"You don't say?" Eden says dryly, then splits off from me.

I watch her until she disappears into her classroom, then push into mine, beginning my morning of pretending to be a normal teenager living campus life, starting my last semester of freshmen year, dewy-faced and filled with revenge.

17

CALLIE

Normally, I'd be calling an emergency meeting with Ivy, popping open a bottle of wine, both of us sitting on my bed while I asked her to tell me everything about the Virtue robing ceremony and what I should expect.

She'd hug me with reassurance—I know that. Insist on standing beside me in support. And she'd do everything in her power to help me avoid any surprises ... except for that time she revealed herself as a Virtuous princess after I almost drowned, and then decimated our plans to break into the temple and steal Sabine's files...

On second thought, Ivy would be terrible to doomsday prep with, but the ache between my ribs every time I think about her makes me want her here more than ever.

I miss you, Ivy.

"Okay, so let's get back to the part where your mom was murdered because you're Rose Briar's missing great-great-

great-grandchild and stand to inherit the entire fucking society."

It also means I'm left with Emma as my ride-or-die.

"How didn't you know I'm a Briar descendant?" I ask her as we crowd into the handicap stall at the end of the girls' bathroom. After checking that all other stalls are vacant, Eden comes in and locks the door behind us.

"Ivy knew," I continue. "Chase was made aware God knows how long ago." I flick a hand in Eden's direction. "Eden's the one who clued me in. I thought I was the last to figure it out."

"It was obvious there was something special about you," Emma says, "considering how much Father and Sabine were focused on your every move, but no, I was never given that information."

I study Emma quizzically. It's safe to say that out of everyone, I expected her to possess the most information about me—well, her and Chase.

He pops into my mind without permission, and I squeeze my eyes shut to rid myself of the image. I don't need him now. I can't have him.

"If you're robed," Emma says, "that makes it official. You can show your copy of the birth certificate the Nobles have kept hidden and claim your position. Here, send it to me." She pulls out her phone at the same time I do, and I airdrop the photo to Emma and Eden. Safety in numbers, after all. Tempest can't rob all three of us without one of us finding out before he's finished. I've never proven it was him who stole all my evidence, but process of elimination isn't difficult.

"There's also this," I say, and pull the pendant of the raven's crest out from my collar.

Emma gasps.

Eden asks, "Where did you get *that?*"

"It was my mother's. Don't all the Virtues get one?"

Emma shakes her head, her attention locked on the pendant dangling softly from my fingers. "They stopped handing those out years ago. It prompted too many questions from outsiders, especially with the rise of social media and camera phones. Sabine's—I mean, Sabine and your mom's—class was probably the last to receive it. That's really special, Callie, but no one should see you wearing it."

Lifting the pendant to my eyeline, I say somberly, "My mom managed to keep this from me for sixteen years. I can do the same. I'm not taking it off."

"If you're sure." But Emma doesn't sound convinced.

It's because of her tone I don't mention the moment when I first saw the iron raven crest, hidden in the trophy case beside the Chancellor's office. The secret society marker was familiar somehow, meaning I must've seen this necklace hanging from my mother's neck at some point. I just can't—*won't*—remember.

Eden cuts into my thoughts. "That's cool and all, but we should probably get back to why Sabine let you get this far. She's not the type to just *allow* you to become a Virtue with this kind of power over her."

"Sabine's the one who tapped Callie as an initiate in the first place," Emma counters.

"So she could control her and show Callie who's boss,"

Eden says. "Callie coming back from break despite Ivy being killed pretty much splatters that whole plan."

Emma pushes her lips to the side, conceding Eden's point.

"You're quiet, Callie," Emma says after giving me the once-over. "Why?"

The bathroom door pushes open, brisk footsteps following suit. We clamp our mouths shut and freeze, all of us well aware that if whoever's in here so much as glances down, she'll see three pairs of feet and get curious.

But the girl goes about her business, the toilet flushing, then the faucet running, as she finishes up. I relax, remembering that this is Briarcliff University—three girls conducting a hush-hush meeting in the bathroom isn't exactly prime time news.

Her footsteps don't slow as she passes our stall and the main door shuts behind her.

"We better hurry," Eden mumbles. "There's three minutes before second period starts. The caffeine addicts are gonna need to pee before class."

"Well?" Emma asks me. "What's wrong with flashing the birth certificate around once you're robed?"

"I can't prove it," I say. Emma's chin jerks back. Eden makes a sound of unfortunate agreement. "Not until I have Sabine's files and prove she killed my mom to end the Briar line."

"She left you alive, though," Emma says. "The Briar line didn't end with your mom."

"Could've been an accident," Eden says. "Contrary to movies, it's difficult to order a hit and get away with it. You said you were supposed to be there for dinner, right?" Eden asks. I nod. "But you were late, and after all that planning, the hit had to go through—it's better to get one than none."

"And knowing Sabine," Emma adds, warming to Eden's argument, "she'd adapt immediately. Instead of killing you another time, which would look suspicious after your mom was just killed, she invited you to Briarcliff University, thinking it was better to have her enemy close than not at all."

I should shudder at such matter-of-fact talk regarding Mom's horrible death, but the truth is, I've been thinking the same thing. Maybe I wasn't meant to survive that night. Perhaps, despite Mom's best efforts, I was never meant to live my life free of Briarcliff.

But I can rip from the chains.

"I've always been told what to do, who to be," I say, drawing both of their attention. "I've felt out of control since Mom died, and now I'm finally getting answers. It's time for me to take charge and take away Sabine's power. If I can get back into the temple and into the princess's bedroom, I can get those files. Sabine's vain—if she succeeded in killing my mom, she'll have something to remember that by. I know it."

Emma nods. "We can start there."

"I'm not finished," I say.

Eden perks up. "I like this new Callie."

"I need both of you to go to the public library and steal some of Rose Briar's DNA."

"*Excuse* me?" Emma asks, at the same time Eden pumps her fist excitedly.

"Oh, come on," Eden says to her. "You willingly took a baseball bat to the face. You can open a compartment in an underfunded library and pocket a hairbrush."

Emma gives me a pointed look. I raise my hands, saying, "I didn't tell her."

"I'm not stupid," Eden says before Emma can respond. "In fact, I'm incredibly observant. It doesn't take a genius to connect the dots between Piper, you, and Callie."

"Actually, it does," Emma says, but her expression softens into one of respect. Maybe, after all this time, it's nice to be acknowledged for all the suffering she endured.

Eden shrugs it off. "I don't think those DNA kits online do these kinds of samples. Is there a way we can trace Rose's descendants?"

I say, "We can try, if we can find her baby, Delilah, and determine the children she had. I'll also call Ahmar, see if he can call in a favor to this forensics lady he used to date."

Emma raises her brows. "Do you think Ahmar would help you with this? You said he was … concerned … for your well-being after you confided in him."

I nod tightly. "He will." I hesitate. "If I lie and tell him it's related to finding my real father, he will. Ahmar wouldn't say no to something like that."

"Okay. Good," Emma says, and thankfully, leaves it at that.

"That'll take time, too. It's why I'll focus on pinning Sabine for Mom, first."

Both girls nod in agreement.

"So, we good?" Emma asks, hands on her hips.

"One other thing," I say.

They pause, waiting for me to continue.

"I, uh, I need you to teach me how to swim, Eden."

Eden crosses her arms and glances to the side. "I don't know if..."

"You have to," Emma cuts in, moving to stand next to me. "Callie nearly bit the dust once, and we don't know if that was a fluke or whether Sabine knew Callie couldn't swim. We can't let that happen again."

"Eden," I say softly, blinking away the image of Ivy wrestling me to the surface and saving my life. "I'm sorry. I'm asking you for a tall order, but out of everyone, you could teach me the fastest. You're a champion swimmer."

"Used to be," Eden says, working her jaw.

"You still are," I say.

"Besides, Callie would owe you one."

I cut a sharp look to Emma, who shrugs. "What? Eden does better with quid pro quos."

Sighing, I agree. "I would."

"Fine," Eden says, but directs her statement to the ground.

"Eden, if it's too much—" I start.

"I said fine. Meet me in the mornings at the indoor pool in the rec center. 4 AM." Eden flicks her eyes up. "I don't want anyone seeing us."

The early timing doesn't even register, and I'm not about to push the issue with Eden. "Cool. Thanks."

"Great," Emma says. "We've all got our assignments. But Callie ... there isn't anyone on the inside to protect you anymore. If you do the robing ceremony..."

"I'm on my own," I finish for her, but my voice is strong. "I'm good with that."

Eden angles her head, studying me carefully. "You don't seem the type to *want* to be alone, though."

"I do now."

My statement quiets both of them. After a beat of silence where it's clear I'm not backing down, Emma unlocks the stall, and we head to the exit.

"Hey," Emma says before we split off in the hallway. She squeezes my shoulder. "Good luck."

"You, too," I say. "And thank you."

Emma shakes her head. "You don't have to thank me. I'm finally getting justice, too."

"And me," Eden pipes in.

I smile at both of them, but it's wane and doesn't stretch into my cheeks. To cover it up, I stick my hand out, palm up. "Off with her head."

Both catch on and place their palms on top of mine.

"Off with her head," they echo, before our hands break apart.

18

CHASE

"She's *fucking* doing the robing ceremony," I spit, pacing around my room. "Is she *fucking* out of her mind? Does this chick want to *fucking* die?"

Tempest shrugs. "I doubt emphasizing 'fuck' with every question will get Callie to change her mind."

I run through all the possible reasons Callie has for continuing to step into a viper's nest. She's desperate to solve her mom's murder. Determined to avenge Ivy. Most of all, she wants to decimate the very thing that destroyed her mom: The Virtues.

But at the cost of her life?

"I did this to her."

"Quit jerking off to yourself." Tempest reclines on my bed, propping his hands under his head as he contemplates the ceiling. "Callie's making her decisions with or without your dick."

"No, I pushed her too far. She has no one now. Nothing to lose."

"What about her detective? Her stepparents? Her step*baby*?"

"She'll isolate them." I rub my index finger over my mouth as I contemplate. "Keep them out of it. And Ivy's dead. Now I've left her."

"Your sister hasn't. And that quiet one with the kind of hair that'll come out of an ancient hellhole and strangle you."

"Emma and Eden can only do so much. They're not allowed on societal grounds."

"Okay, then there's her fath—"

"Don't."

Tempest sighs. "It's not like I know his identity, but circumstances tell me it could be *quite* the important clue to help her."

"It won't."

"Whatever. So, what are you saying then?"

I point at him. "You."

"Me, what?"

"You're going to figure out why Sabine would allow Callie to be robed in the first place."

"How am I supposed to do that? She won't say shit to me."

"James might, if you talk to him. He's her latest lackey." I mull over the memory of that jackass tossing a pillowcase over my head, then clamping his hand over my fabric-covered mouth. My heart jackknifed into my throat. My lungs swelled until they squeezed my heart. I couldn't breathe. Couldn't. Breathe.

And one of my supposed best buddies was using my phobia against me. For *her*.

"Or torture it out of him," I growl. "I don't care."

Undeterred by the ominous death-wish in my voice, Tempest says, "It's common knowledge I'm your second-in-command. What makes you think—"

"Then go through Rio, I don't give a shit. Just get it done." I nail him with a look. "I'm ordering you as my second-in-command."

"Jesus. Fine." Tempest sits up. "And what about you? You're not gonna be able to stand back and let other people do your dirty work, despite your vow to keep Callie at arm's length."

My brows lower, shadowing my vision. "I'm going to the source. Sabine may have her reasons for allowing Callie into the Virtues, but my father's priority will always be the Nobles. He doesn't want them destroyed any more than I do."

"Ah." Tempest leans back. "And if Sabine has already conned him to her side?"

"I have another option," I answer. "If Callie tries to claim her rightful place, I'll stop her. Simple as that."

"Uh-huh. You're the boss."

"I am." Stopping in front of the mirror by the door, I take a good look at myself, arming my expression for what it will take to protect the new Nobles from whatever fuckery Callie's planning.

The Noble alumni may be far from her reach, but the initiates aren't. Briarcliff University isn't.

But Sabine can't win. She'll have to get through me if she wants to so much as flick a finger against Callie's nose. I have to somehow stop the Virtuous Queen from harming Callie, and yet I also have to stop Callie from reaching her truth and finding justice.

I have to save her and sabotage her, all at the same time.

The lake house is dim and deserted when I pull up the drive and shut off the engine. I slide out, my shoes crunching against the gravel, the noise amplified in the quiet, surrounding forest. It's so cold and blustery, not even the owls hoot.

Ice crackles in my periphery. I glance over on instinct, but it's the brittle tree branches weighed down by snow melted by the sun, then hardened by the moon.

Unlocking the door, I step into the warmth, our lake house kept at a warm 75 degrees despite the lack of residency most of the winter.

My father: the environmentalist.

I don't waste time on the main floor, though my stomach growls at the lack of sustenance I've given it since returning to Briarcliff. My crew practice suffers for it, my 2k completions on the erg becoming longer and longer stretches of time, but I can't bring myself to give a fuck.

Not when Sabine's treating the Virtues as a brothel, with

my sister as a victim and Callie's revenge on ultimate nuke level.

The Nobles are redeemable, I think on a determined frown as I take the stairs to the basement level. I wish Callie would simply focus on the destruction of the Virtues, but no, she wants all of us.

I was on her side until she admitted the Nobles had to suffer, too. Now we're at odds, and I've come to believe the rumbling in my stomach isn't solely due to hunger for food.

It's starvation for *her*.

I'm unable to fill myself on her scent, sink into her warmth, find gluttony in nipping and licking her skin. It's sent me into a spiral, where all I can see is her smile, such a rare thing, yet it's settled in my mind's eye as a soft-focus filter whenever I think of her.

I can't. She's the enemy now.

Because of this bullshit, instead of running my hands all over her naked body, she has me going through Father's things, proving her wrong, *showing* Callie there comes good with her Missing Heir status, not simply murder and mayhem.

Sabine has to go—I'll help her with that. But my brothers? *My* heir status? *No.*

I step back after punching in the code at Father's bookshelf, waiting impatiently for the hidden door to slide open, so I can access the Noble files.

There has to be something here to prove to Callie that the Nobles can be saved. A document, a hidden relic from the founders, *anything* to showcase their lack of support in Sabine's disgusting plans, or failing that, my ability to turn them around, *even* while they're still under my father's guidance.

Callie says—my *sister* proves—certain Noble alumni are signing forbidden agreements with Sabine to take advantage of Virtues enrolled at Briarcliff University. If I can find those men, kick their asses out, and hell, provide their names to Callie's NYPD detective, I can begin the cleansing process.

But if Father is part of those men? Not necessarily partaking in underage girls, but sanctioning it?

I step into the panic room, scanning the sterile area and the wall of gray cabinets, resembling more of a morgue than a Noble King's workspace.

... then I'll kick his ass out, too, and start my kingship early.

That has to be enough to convince Callie to leave us alone. Her focus can remain on dethroning Sabine. Then she can do whatever the fuck she wants with the Virtue society.

Something chews on the back of my mind as I pull open the nearest drawer, flicking through folders with the expertise of a person who's been locked in here and forced to study Noble rites and rituals for almost a decade.

Why is Sabine allowing Callie to get this far?

It doesn't sit easy with me. I'm in my father's study to sift through all known documents and records of the Nobles, pulling out folder after folder of members, adherence rules, rituals, prohibitions, but it's only now coming to light just how little I've learned of the Virtues.

Was it deliberate? It's unclear what my father was

taught, and his grandfather before him, though it makes sense that I learned the same.

Casting through my memories, I touch upon the Virtues' origins. Rose Briar created them soon after her husband established the Nobles, in an effort to educate women and provide them with benefits befitting a privileged woman at the time. Education, a perfect marriage match, a lifetime of wealth. When Rose committed suicide, Thorne Briar allowed the Virtues to continue under the auspices that they would always be second to the Nobles and, if ever overridden, to capitulate to the mens' demands. That was about the time the Harringtons took over.

Add in my self-imposed research of the Virtues and...

Sabine Moriarty became pregnant and married Paul Harrington not for wealth, as she didn't need it, or education, as she was already on track for Harvard, but to inherit the presumptive Harrington throne in the Virtues.

Paul didn't have any sisters. He was an only child. His mother—what was her name? Prudence, yes. The Virtue Queen, Prudence Harrington, was expected to hold the throne until Paul had daughters, otherwise—

Otherwise....

Frowning, I turn back to the files. What would've happened if Prudence Harrington died before Paul had any daughters, if he had any at all? That kind of loophole practically begs for a more cunning, opportune Virtue to step in.

Piper did say her grandmother and Sabine were close. Like true mother and daughter. I wonder if that relationship prospered before Paul came into the picture, and how much

Prudence supported Sabine not only getting pregnant but marrying her son.

That would take away any fears of losing the throne to a...

I frown again. To a what? A challenger?

My mind fires on all cylinders, and I flick through the files faster, desperation coating my fingertips. Incident reports, initiation prospects, background checks—all related to the Nobles.

Where are the Virtues? Is there anything in the Virtue handbook about challenges to the queen?

My hands freeze. I straighten, my stare boring into the opposite wall.

Fuck, how about challenges to the king? In all this time, since the Nobles' and Virtues' inception, there's never been a challenger. Thorne passed, and he bequeathed the society to his brother, Theodore. Theodore died, and without heirs or any remaining brothers, he performed the rite to pass it on to his best friend, my great-great-grandfather, Montague Stone.

It's been carte blanche ever since. No ripples, no waves, no angry rebellions...

Until Callie.

The last time I was in here, Callie and I discovered a hidden birth certificate of a child born to Rose Briar. Beside that single piece of paper were decades old records of Virtuous members. But *besides* that, there is nothing in here on the Virtues.

Growling, I slap the tops of the files and step back. How could I not see it before? I could search through every folder in this place and come up with the same questions I did when I broke in here.

A deliberate veil covers the Virtues, and I'm pretty fucking sure it's been in place since the first Harrington.

"What are you doing in here, boy?"

I don't jump. Any jolt of surprise I feel is pushed down into the dark place I reserve specifically for my father.

I slam the cabinet shut. The metal rattles under the vicious energy. "Searching for answers."

Father stands at the open archway, the eerie blue-black light of his office framing the backs of his shoulders despite the glaring halogens I stand under.

"Nonsense. You've read through these papers and gone through my computer since you were a young boy. There are no surprises in here."

"My point exactly."

Father crosses his arms. "Explain yourself."

"Where do we keep our checks on the Virtues?"

"Pardon?" He arches a brow.

"According to my teachings, thanks to you, Father, the Virtues are allowed to assemble, provided they report to us. Their meetings, their minutes, their prospects and *initiates* … where are all those records?"

Father chuckles, the sound grating against my spine. A muscle pulls at my jaw, but I keep myself in check.

He says, "Even you can admit times have changed since the nineteenth century. We don't require their every twitch and thought these days."

"Why not?" I counter. "We've preserved every single rule from the beginning—it's our law. Or so I thought."

"Are you saying you prefer your women subservient?" Father's lips pull into a thin smile. "It's lovely to see that my lessons continue to hold. If only you could put them into practice with Calla Lily Ryan."

I play to his assumption rather than give into my boiling rage. "I believe you like to call them accessories. So why give them independence? Free reign? Do you have any idea what my future stepmom is up to?"

"Please, boy." Father scoffs. "There is a reason I keep her near."

"So you know." It's my turn to cross my arms. "You know the truth about Ivara Alling."

Father tips his head, neither acknowledging nor denying.

"And Callie's bloodline." I let my father's controlled expression finish the rest of my explanation.

His lower eyelid tics. He sets his jaw. But he does nothing else.

I come toward him but fall back enough not to grab for his throat. "Tell me the truth, Father. What's Sabine playing at? What are you helping her hide?"

"It's none of your concern."

"Emma was made into a sex slave for Sabine," I deadpan. "How is that not my business?"

Father's eyes spark, flat gray rocks rubbing up against mine. "Get ahold of yourself, boy, before I have to do it for you."

His hands twitch at his sides, aching, I'm sure, for the times when he could put me in a stranglehold, and I'd stay there.

"Don't tell me you're in such denial, Father," I spit. "Your flesh and blood was used, torn open, her soul *eviscerated*, and you stand here before me like it's nothing."

"It isn't," my father snarls.

My cheeks go numb. Any blood anchored in my face is pulled to my fists, swelling them to levels where I need my knuckles to *burst* on my father's skin. "You are pathetic. Sad. A waste of a man who hides behind a woman's skirts while she does your dirty work. You hate us so much, why go through the pretenses of raising us, when we both know you'll never give up your leader status, because that's all you have, you fucking soulless bastard—"

The back of my head slams into a cabinet handle on my father's roar, his maneuver catching me by enough surprise that the sharp corner sinks into my nape and sets my neck on fire.

Father pushes his face into mine, gripping my lapels, spittle hanging onto his stubble as he snarls and spits like a rabid animal. "I don't give a damn about her because *she isn't mine!*"

Shock has me halting my struggle. Father takes advantage of it and swings for my face. I duck, and his fist crashes into the cabinet behind me.

Cursing, he stumbles back, holding his injured fist like he just lost a bar fight and didn't just go head-to-head with non-sentient metal.

"What did you just say?" I whisper while circling him, my breaths haggard.

He glares at me.

"*Answer me!*"

"Emma Loughrey is not mine," he repeats, holding steady. "Why do you think I was more than happy to allow her to take your mother's last name? She is the product of Marilee's weak heart."

"The fuck is that supposed to mean?" I respond, still whispering, still barely breathing.

"She's adopted. When you were two years old, your mother came across a young girl during her charity work. Lovely Marilee decided it was better to work in a homeless teen counseling center than go to college after marrying me—the heir to an empire who put a four-carat diamond on her finger. One of her female Cretans had an unwanted toddler—malnourished, dirty vermin. I blame it on the goddamn hormones, but Marilee wanted this child. She hemorrhaged after having you and was told she couldn't have another. She was desperate for you to have a sibling, and at the time, I wasn't around much—"

"Already fucking Sabine, I bet." But the words have no passion. I'm numb. Sucked dry.

"Watch your mouth, boy. I allowed it, didn't I? You got yourself a sister, Marilee decided to make you two twins, and I was blessed with two assholes instead of one."

"Father of the Year," I say through gritted teeth.

"I care about you," Father says in defense as he rises out of his hunch. "Educated you, taught you, made you the prince to all this." He sweeps his arm out. "Don't you dare be disrespectful in the house you stand in solely because of *my* efforts."

"How about the basement you kept Emma in, when all she wanted to do was escape you? Why didn't you let her? If you wanted nothing to do with her, why keep her after she tried so desperately to leave? All I'm hearing is that Emma was trash to you, so you allowed Sabine to do what she wanted with her. You *sanctioned* young Virtues to be made into pets for your Noble alumni. You betrayed your daughter—because yes, she is your daughter, legally and in all the ways that matter—you never told her she was unwanted, just made her believe it. We're nothing but objects to you, are we, Father? Profits and gains."

"There is nothing profitable about you," Father spits through a trembling jaw. "Your grandfather practically sewed into me the importance of preserving the Stone line, so much so, I impregnated a girl at the neighboring Dover Shores, so he'd shut the hell up. And when that girl found out she was having a boy? I'll admit, I aimed high when it came to my only son. Married her, accepted her goddamn bleeding heart of a baby girl, but here *you* are, flipping through old files instead of solidifying your rightful place as prince and taking control of our initiates, still trying to save Calla Lily. But now I'll say, go ahead." He waves at me in dismissal, but his lips twist into a sneer. "I can't do anything with a child who focuses so hard on saving other people because he's too broken to fix himself."

It takes a severe amount of effort to stay calm through his ruthlessness. It always has. "Doing what is right does not make me flawed."

"Thinking I needed a son to maintain my power over the Nobles is the flaw I'm most ashamed of," Father retorts. "Sabine has taught me just how unnecessary you are, as well as your sister and *Calla Lily*. You were meant to be my mirror image. Instead, you reflect the worst parts of me. You and Emma may not be blood-related, but you were raised as twins. You've inherited her knack for self-mutilation. Get out of here, boy, before I remind you what true anger looks like."

Shaking with wrath, I step toward the door.

Then shoot my arm out and go for his throat.

Father catches me mid-swipe, twisting my arm behind my back until I fold over, my throat clogged with pain.

"Try that again, son," Father mutters near my ear, "and your athletic status will be sorely wanting as you await your sports scholarship from Princeton."

"*Fuck* you," I hiss through the searing tendons gripping my shoulder, my neck, my jaw.

"Indeed."

Father releases his hold, and I stumble forward, my cheeks pulsing with indignation and rebellion.

When I jerk toward him, he throws up a hand. "As for the curiosity that brought you here, allow me to squash that as well."

He moves toward a lower cabinet. I eye him, holding my shoulder, as he pulls open a drawer, takes out the files, and lifts a false bottom, revealing a thick, brown leather book.

"The Virtues' original handbook. Written by Rose Briar, I believe, and revised by Prudence Harrington. Should be some quiet reading for you."

My stare pings from the drawer, to the book, to my father. "Why have you hidden it?"

"For the same reasons we kept the baby Briar birth certificate in my vault all these years, before you and your weak spot decided to weaponize it." He jerks his chin toward the door. "You'll soon discover where you fall, son. Until then, I highly recommend you allow Sabine to do as she pleases when it comes to Calla Lily Ryan."

"Never," I say, but Father shoves the book at me and stalks past me without another word.

I stay where I am, digging my fingers into my wounded shoulder while my slack hand holds onto the book, trying make sense of his revelations.

Twisting my world.

And forcing my hand when it comes to Callie.

19

CALLIE

T he letter strikes me as unceremonious.

You'd think, with all I've endured up to this point, the final communication from the Virtues would be accompanied by an obvious, robed Falyn, or heck, delivered by a live raven or the queen herself.

But no. A single piece of paper is propped in a standing fold on my desk, unimposing, the expensive cream stock a normal occurrence at this point, the white rose accompanying it expected.

I'm predicting the script on the inside flap before my backpack hits the floor and head toward my desk. My damp hair drips the last of the pool's rivulets down my shoulders, Eden's first swim lesson mainly consisting of me bobbing in the shallow end, the water hitting just above my chin.

My swim failure aside, I figure this note contains something along the lines of, *Your ritual rites are complete; thus, you shall be robed. That is, if you're prepared for a Virtuous future* or some other ominous language.

What I'm not prepared for is the addition of a black rose beside it.

Fingering the white satin ribbon, I lift the rose, bringing the ink-dipped petals to my nose and inhaling the sweet, slightly chemical scent. I haven't received one of these in so long, I'd forgotten they were a thing—but they must be how the Nobles communicate, too. I received a black rose when new furniture arrived in my dorm, along with an undamaged uniform. Another appeared on my bed after a particularly haggard day. These petals made an appearance whenever I needed a right amid such wrongs. Part of me assumed—okay, *hoped*—they were from Chase, his secret Noble communication assuring me he had my back, though he had never confirmed it.

But it couldn't be him, not this time. He's made his feelings on me becoming a Virtue clear. This must be their official acceptance of my robing, meaning they'll probably be attending as well.

Chase will be there.

The realization skitters along the edges of my skull, spreading goosebumps and inciting angst. He'll be watching me, and I'm positive I'll feel his disapproval all the way to my toes.

But it's not about him anymore, or us. This is about my mother and all the other girls who've been hurt, maimed, and killed by this so-called society of Virtuous women.

After carefully setting down the rose, I ignore the white

one and move to the letter, opening its crisp fold and reading the perfect calligraphy.

Dearest Initiate,

As you receive this letter, you've been granted the highest honor. Passing our trials is no small feat, and congratulations are in order. Please join us at our temple on the eve of Friday the 16th, where it will be my greatest pleasure to lay a Virtuous robe upon your shoulders.

- Your Queen

"Wow," I say under my breath as I close the letter. She actually signed it this time.

"So, it's official, then."

I turn to see Emma hovering in my doorway.

"Sabine's accepted you," she finishes.

Nodding, I set the letter back on the desk. "Am I supposed to pretend that you didn't read this while I was with Eden?"

"Nope, I totally snooped." Emma steps inside my room, then sits on the side of my bed. "Missed the drop-off, though."

"Everyone always does," I muse, then slide off my jacket and perch on the desk chair. "For all we know, there are secret corridors into all the dorm rooms, too."

Emma shudders. "Don't put that into the universe."

I respond with a commiserating grunt. "I can't stand the thought of Falyn watching me while I sleep, either."

"Are you ready for what's next?" she asks.

"As I'll ever be. Unless you have some last-minute wisdom to impart…?"

Emma pushes her lower lip out in thought. "I don't know much about robing a BU freshman. We're usually initiated high school freshman year, and it always occurs in the forest near Lover's Leap. The fact you're asked to come to the temple is already unusual."

"Yeah." Emma's words bring me back to my first day at Briarcliff when I stumbled blindly behind Richardson House and almost tripped over a Noble and Virtue initiate ceremony. Back then, I was stupid, thinking it was a creepy, witchy extra-curricular rich kids enjoyed dabbling in.

Now, there's a body count.

"We cast our invitations into the bonfire," Emma continues, "reciting the motto for our societies. Then, the Viscounts and Viscountesses—that's Chancellor Marron and Miss Lacey, by the way—

"Miss *Lacey* has been a Cloak this whole time?" I cut in, thinking of our small, innocent calculus teacher with a brain the size of Arkansas, and who Chase jokingly said he was screwing. I frown, a lick of jealousy gliding across my gut.

"They like to keep the mentors, or viscounts and countesses, in the faculty, since they're always around."

"I've never had a mentor, other than Ivy, maybe."

Emma gives me the side-eye. "You're a unique case."

"Fair enough. Go on."

"Okay, so, they ask us to pledge our loyalty, to put the societies above all else. We take an oath, sealing it with a blood vow—"

"Excuse me, blood?"

Emma heaves out an exasperated sigh at my constant interruptions. "With Thorne Briar's personal blade, yep."

My vision goes dark as I remember the opulent knife that killed Ivy. Could it be the same one? It was intricate enough. Old, precious, special. If I have to hold it, if I have to place it against my skin the way it pierced hers...

"Callie? You've gone pale. You okay?"

"Uh-huh." I nod, swallowing audibly. "Keep going."

"We hold our wrists over the fire, our blood mixing into the flames. Then, we recite the maxim again, line up in front of the queen and king, accept our robe, then go party in the Nobles' room. That's where our first introduction into the life of a secret society is—drugs, booze, served by almost-naked men and women. And you can take any of them to bed." Emma shrugs, as if throwing this in front of a fourteen-year-old is standard practice at Briarcliff. "Those who overindulge are taken in by Sabine or Daniel and cared for until they can come back to school."

"I'm not sure whether to find that unoriginal, creepy, or downright terrifying," I say, then nod as I come to a conclusion. "It's all of it."

"Yes. It starts off stereotypical. Six figures drop in a bank account they open especially for you, to be accessed when you enter Briarcliff U, earning interest and being invested on your behalf until then. Your wardrobe is updated when you get to your dorm room. A concierge number is put into your phone, who you can call and ask for anything. A pick-up, a clean-up, a cover-up. Your grades are suddenly switched to the higher tiers—except, to be one of them, you'd already have to excel in something, whether it be athletics, debate, English Lit ... They help you with your weaker subjects."

I prop my chin in my hands, fascinated. "Ivy didn't tell me any of this."

Emma exhales from the side of her mouth. "I said it starts off like that. Then you're asked to do things for them, small favors like allowing a fellow Virtue to cheat off your exam, or cleaning up small, undetermined blood splatters in certain classrooms. After that ... it becomes different from the Nobles. Sabine asks you to attend outside events, like hotel ballrooms with small orchestras, or attending box seats at the Metropolitan Opera one night, before being introduced to her 'friends.' This is probably why Ivy didn't tell you. She showcases her new initiates to her clientele. Sabine selects the girl with the most interest and begins the grooming process for the next princess."

"That's what gets me," I say, giving Emma a needed break. "Do you really think Sabine stops at just one girl? If she's as greedy and vain as I assume, I'd think she'd have a few, just in case one didn't work out."

I hate talking about my peers like this, girls who could be me, but it's necessary to get into Sabine's head. Think like her, before I confront her.

"It takes a lot of effort to turn a girl," Emma answers, then adds softly, "I should know. Sabine focuses all her energy on you. And it's kind, gentle, alluring. She becomes like a mother, and with many of us being so far away from home … a yearning starts, right here." She points to her chest. "Suddenly you're confessing all your insecurities to her, and she's bringing you tea and listening intently, offering advice and comfort. You start going to her more and more … she's the queen, after all. She's given you all these gifts, so many privileges. The least you could do is meet with her and confide all your sins and discomforts until she sees you as perfect and deserving of the Virtue title." Emma pauses, staring unblinkingly at the floor. Her lashes don't flutter. "Until the final time, when, after you finish your tea, you get tired. Heavy. Clumsy. Sabine's beautiful, concerned expression blurs in and out. It goes black. And you wake up in a strange room, on a strange bed, with an undressed man on top—" Emma chokes.

I rush over, grabbing her hand, pressing her head to my clavicle as I stand over her, shroud her. "You can stop. It's okay. It's over."

Her hair tangles in my fingers as she shakes her head back and forth. "That's the problem. It's only just beginning."

My lips turn hard and grim above the crown of her head as I stare off across from us. *This* is why I'm being robed. Precisely the reason I'm staying on the inside instead of skirting the edges and trying to destroy Sabine and the Virtues from afar. I wish, so badly, for Chase to understand that.

The Nobles are a part of this demonic underworld. Riches and unlimited power have turned these teens into rabid, unaccountable adults. Girls are destroyed. Rose's message is all but erased.

These societies *have* to go.

"I'm ending this," I say through my clenched jaw, so quietly I'm not sure Emma hears.

"I'll be nearby," Emma says, patting my arm and dragging me back into the present. "I've outlined the standard ceremonial robing process. That doesn't mean I have any idea how Sabine plans to approach yours."

I find a smile and aim it at her as I withdraw. "Sabine won't harm me in front of everyone. It'd ruin her whole image she has going. I think she enjoys being so clandestine and one-upping the Nobles without them even realizing she's pulling all the strings. She wouldn't be so blatant."

"While I agree, Eden and I will still stay close. You never know."

I press my lips together, knowing she's right. We *don't* know what Sabine will do next, even after I'm officially a Virtue. She has yet to even acknowledge my buried secret—my legacy—let alone act on it. Is she allowing me in because she has no other choice? Keeping me close because she killed my mother? To deny me entry would be to admit I *did* have power, enough for her to wantonly keep me out after being the person to ask me in. It would look confusing to her Virtues, maybe suspicious. After all, I don't have proof, merely a picture of an old birth certificate. There's nothing I can point to when it comes to my mother, either, other than conjecture. And she must be aware of that.

Keep playing her game, so you can start your own.

"When are you and Eden headed to town?" I ask.

"We both have a free period after lunch. We'll go then."

"Good."

"Have you called Ahmar about comparing old DNA to yours?"

Preferring to pick at my sweater's sleeve, I answer, "Not yet. I will."

Emma doesn't push it. "Okay. Well, I gotta go. Meeting Chase for breakfast."

"Oh, yeah?"

She hits me with a droll look as she rises. "Wanna come?"

"No."

"That was too quick an answer to be real. You sure you don't want me to tell him what we're doing? You two may be at odds now, but if he knows you're mainly after proving Sabine murdered your mother—"

"He already knows that. Chase'll be at the robing ceremony, anyway, so I have to prepare."

"Fair enough. Want me to figure out his plans for fucking up your ceremony instead?"

A genuine smile crosses my lips. "If you can. The guy's a vault."

"Tell me about it." Emma crosses the room to the door.

"Must be a genetic thing," I say wryly.

She responds with a closed-mouthed grin. "That's the one talent we don't regret inheriting from our father," she responds, then leaves my room.

I wait until she shuts the door, then stand and focus on keeping up pretenses by getting ready for another day at Briarcliff University.

Surprisingly, the week whizzes by, my mornings spent in swim lessons, and my evenings focused on homework assignments to the point where I don't have time to stress about the robing ceremony, except to idly wonder if I fail to hand in my homework, if I'll get an A anyway.

Do I even have to apply for colleges, or will the Virtues do that for me, too?

Despite my thoughts lingering on the question, I'm fairly certain the answer to that doesn't have worth, since I don't plan to stay a Virtue past this semester, thus, my studies remain with me.

None of that should be clogging up my mind right now, as I'm gazing at my closet, chewing on my thumbnail, and contemplating the best outfit to wear to tonight's ceremony.

Emma said first years wore something similar—and as important—to a prom dress, but the only gown I have of that nature was gifted by Sabine, and considering what happened the last time I wore it...

No. I won't be wearing that atrocity tonight.

This evening, I get to own my power, striding through the temple doors with the knowledge that I *own* the Virtues. Even if I can't claim it immediately, that hidden diamond glimmers within my soul, just waiting to be cut from the earth and unveiled to the societies.

I have to be smart, though. Sabine's nothing if not scrupulous with her multiple fail-safes, should her original plan falter. If I want to beat her, I have to think like her, and collecting evidence against her, silently and willfully, is the first step in succeeding.

Eden and Emma managed to snag—literally—strands from an old hairbrush of Rose Briar's, on display with other items from her bedroom vanity, carefully protected from the elements in a velvet box when not positioned for tourist's eyes, not that many frequent Briarcliff, never mind the library. Eden parroted that fact while attempting to dunk me in the swimming pool and push me into a front stroke, stating that Darla was only too eager to chat Eden's ear off about the Briarcliff items, while Emma subtly lifted the top of the display case, tweezered a few pieces of Rose's hair from the bristles, and placed it in a plastic baggie before they sat with Darla for another twenty minutes and listened to the founder brothers' scandals.

Once safely ensconced in my room, we put our heads together and searched on my phone whether 200-year-old hair could be viable for a DNA sample. Turns out, it can, since scientists have identified remains of a Woolly Mammoth by ancient pieces of hair. Even better if the hair follicle is attached. We squinted into the baggie, decided there were indeed clear bulbs attached to the ends of some pieces, and then it was up to me to call Ahmar and explain to him *why* I'd like 200-year-old hair DNA tested against mine.

It was an awkward conversation, both in my bringing up the mystery of my childhood (thinking I'd found Mom's great-great-grandma and how it would be an amazing history project to have my genealogy traced against all these other rich kids with vast resources at their fingertips) and his failed relationship with a forensic anthropologist. He'd also brought up that I'd not seen him for coffee when I was in town, and I was forced to use the baby card, stating I'd fallen in love with Blair and had wanted to spend as much time as I could with her before I went back to school.

It wasn't entirely a lie.

Fifteen minutes later, Ahmar reluctantly agreed, not that he believed shit. *An ancient grandma?* Ahmar had said. *Kid, please.* But I knew he felt guilty for the wedge that's transpired between us, and it didn't take long for him to give in, considering it wasn't doing any harm *and* gave him an excuse to converse with his ex again.

He warned it would take some time—maybe a long time, what with convincing his former lady love to do him a solid and get the results, but I wasn't in a rush. Not on this.

Lynda warned me to keep Ahmar out of society business, and I was. Sort of. I'm not asking him to investigate the societies and Mom's murder anymore. She can be content knowing he's helping me ace a so-called "history assignment."

With those ducks lined up, I could move on to more precarious items on my to-do list ... like choosing an outfit for the first time I'm seeing Sabine since Ivy died.

Ivy's name incites a swell of rage. I rip my thumb from my mouth and grab for the nearest dress, a deep-V black mini Ivy made me wear to Chase's party at his family's lake house.

It seems fitting that I'd wear this to a ceremony Ivy can't attend. It'll remind me of her, and I'll be the only one to know the tangible memories that float under my newly donned gold cloak.

As I'm pulling off my uniform, I glance out my bedroom doorway, searching for Emma. She's not back from class yet, but I figure I'll cook us a quick dinner before I head out, considering neither of us enjoy dining hall festivities.

I half-expect Chase to be traveling with her, though I know it's a fruitless thought. She hasn't seen him since their breakfast meeting a few days ago, and she told me he was distracted, subdued, and curt enough that she wasn't eager to meet up with him again.

Doesn't matter, anyway. Chase wouldn't be much help, even if he decided to communicate with multiple syllables. He chose his side, and I chose mine.

Now it's time to see who's won.

20

———

CALLIE

It's so cold that a layer of ice has sealed in the mounds of snow, and each time I slip and stumble off the path, despite my winter boots, it cracks under my weight and into the night.

My breath makes opaque shapes in front of me as I trudge on, my fur-lined hood pulled up to protect my face, but my bare knees knock together like a plastic skeleton prop each time I take a shaking step.

A cocktail dress might've been the wrong choice. Snow pants would've been better, whether or not they looked good under a golden cloak.

At last, small beams of light skimming the rooftop of the M.B.S. Library of Studies float into view, and I scurry the rest of the way, slipping only twice on the unsalted sections as I take the gradual hill to the front of the building.

I don't see any other Virtues or Nobles taking the path ahead of or behind me, but as Emma assured at dinner, they would've arrived early in anticipation of getting a prime spot for the rare robing of a BU freshman.

And what a freshman I am. A Briar heiress. The Missing Heiress.

Just the thought of throwing that title in Sabine's face makes me flash my teeth into the cold night.

Not yet, my mother's voice reasons. *You don't have enough to prove your legacy. Stay patient, Calla. Stay smart.*

The automatic doors smoothly open as soon as I step up to them, the library black with shadows on the other side.

I take one breath. Two.

Then step over the threshold, alone.

A silent Cloak, head covered in gold fabric and bowed, stands at the secret entrance into the Virtue Temple.

Once I'm close enough, I stop and clear my throat, but the person doesn't move, save for the hem of her Virtue cloak swaying at her ankles.

Unable to stand the silence in such a dark space, I say, "Um. Am I early for—?"

I'm cut off by a whisper. "Do you accept your elevated status, Initiate?"

"Yes," I draw out, clenching and unclenching my fingers as they tingle from the invasive warmth of the library. "It's why I've come."

"I'm tasked to remind you: this is your last chance to turn around."

This time, the whisper is familiar. I peer into the darkness of the hood. "Willow?"

The gold fabric jerks as the head beneath it swivels in my direction. "You are *forbidden* to refer to us by name until you are fully enrobed as a Virtue Baroness. One more mistake, *Calla*, and you'll pay dearly."

Her reference to my endearing nickname, used only by my mother and Ahmar, gives me invisible, painful hives.

"I've already paid the worst price in order to be here tonight," I say through cracked lips.

If Willow reacts, I can't see it. "Take off your jacket."

Deciding not to argue, I unzip my coat and pass it to her. Willow drapes it over one arm, my padded security blanket slumping uselessly in her grip.

I shiver, goosebumps pimpling my exposed arms and legs, colder now than I was outside.

Willow's golden cloak sweeps the floor as she spins, using her credentials to unlock the hidden door.

I wondered about that—if, in killing Ivy, Sabine also scrubbed my clearance into the temple until she deemed my access necessary again.

Denial into the temple would be a petty cherry to her vapid sundae, but I can't put anything past Sabine, from the simplest insults to the vilest deeds.

For you, Ivy, I think as I follow behind Willow. *And you, Mom.*

The circular temple is dark and cavernous, our hollow footsteps absorbing most of the noise. The sconces rimming the main arena create dimmed ovals of illumination on the walls, but they do nothing to highlight the figures I'm sure stand above me, staring down from the rafters as I take up position in the center.

"No one's on your side this time, possum," Willow mutters before she retreats, merging into the shadows.

Like I don't already know that.

With Willow's disappearance goes the only noise, other than my hitched, tentative breaths.

I count to one hundred in my head, refusing to be the first to speak. The chill of such an empty space seeps into my bones, crowding my thoughts, and I'm blinking rapidly even though I don't mean to.

Folding my arms into my chest, I squint into the shadows, searching for vague outlines, desperate for a certain one.

Chase is here. He must be. Where are you?

The darkness is overwhelming, disconcerting. I've spun in place, but I don't know if I've stopped where Willow originally left me.

Disorientation is so much worse when you know at least twenty people are watching you struggle.

"I did not assume you'd get this far, Initiate," comes a sinuous, beckoning voice.

Sabine.

I whip toward the sound. "Then your expectations were wrong."

"Clearly."

A sconce flares to life beside her, fire flickering against her flawless, sharp cheekbones. Her eyes remain eclipsed in shadow.

My heart lurches at the sight of her—my first glimpse

since Ivy. She's regal, standing high, so confident she's untouchable as she regards me from her balcony.

Her lips pull at my study, my incendiary wrath likely obvious with each scathing breath I take as I keep my eyes on her.

"You are not afraid?" she asks. "If I were to judge on your current behavior alone, I'd say you were terrified."

"I'm not frightened. I'm cold."

Sabine chuckles. Her cloak ripples with the movement. Something glints under the velvet, and my breaths pause.

The knife. Thorne's blade. Ivy's death.

Sabine casts her gaze up, her arms spreading to her sides. "You stand here before your prospective brothers and sisters, mentors, and rulers."

The second story sconces gleam alive, each one lighting before the next, until all the hoods—both light and dark, black and gold, their outlines taking shape with fiery auras until I'm surrounded by a circle of them on the upper level.

Their faces are unidentifiably black, but experience has taught me they stand according to their ranks. Next to Sabine, the tall man in a purplish-black robe—the sign of a royal—has to be Daniel Stone.

On the other side of Sabine would be the next princess. I squint. Falyn ... or Violet? I can't tell.

Dragging my gaze in the opposite direction, a magnet pulling at the same time it's repelling ... I know who I'll find next to Daniel. The prince.

The purest Noble.

Chase Stone.

My chest sinks with an exhale, almost as if my lungs

deflate of all oxygen when I set my eyes upon him. It hurts, just seeing his outline, blurry and obscured by a heavy velvet cloak.

It *burns*.

Swallowing, I tear my gaze away, skimming the red cloaks on either side of the monarchs—cloaks I noticed the older men wear during the Noble initiate's underground ceremony, like Chancellor Marron. They must be the viscounts. Including Miss Lacey, a teacher who could barely suppress her gag reflex at the sight of a used tampon on the ground of her classroom, now positioned ruthlessly beside her underground queen.

The marquis are next. Chase's buddies, Falyn's cronies. Then the rest of the barons and baronesses, because no one is an initiate now. Just me.

It's funny and a little sad how I'm coming to understand the rules of these societies so much clearer at the moment I must ruin them.

"Accept these men and women, boys and girls, into your fold, dearest Initiate," Sabine continues, "for they will be all you have once this night is over."

Hairs spike at the back of my neck. "Touch my family, touch one inch of them, and I'll kill you."

"Oh, my." Sabine feigns shock as she palms her chest. "We would never take it that far, dear one. You are our daughter now, but that does not mean your family will suffer. They will merely become second, for your priority now lies with me. Your every decision shall come up against my permission. Your clothing, your grades, your choice of university. All made with your best interests in mind, of course." Sabine defers to Daniel for a moment when a rumble emits from his hood. "But you are no longer independent, not until we deem it so. We are here to mold you into your better self, and you are to do as we ask with no question."

I clear my throat. Her speech is *mighty* different than the one Emma prepared me for, but all I have to do is remember Ivy, bleeding out on the very floor where I'm standing. And Mom with her throat slit all because of a hidden bloodline of which she had no interest in claiming.

All because of *this* bitch.

"I'm curious why you've allowed me to reenter your temple when I've proven, on multiple occasions, how unstable I am."

"Why, that only makes you a prime candidate," Sabine answers. "It's been so long since I've had the pleasure of breaking in an initiate. They all come so eager to please."

I don't expect even a rumble of discontent or insult to flow through the circle. When it comes to Sabine, no one ever protests.

Sabine continues, "I can understand how this might be difficult for you, but you are here. Capitulating before us despite my continuous reminders that you are no longer the girl who first entered Briarcliff University, and you never will be again."

"You took Ivy," I whisper, my lips puckered as I whisper the curse. "You took my mother. But I will take you before you ever get to me."

"What's that, Initiate?"

I jump at Daniel's booming voice, glancing up from the floor.

"I'm ... going over my options," I answer.

A snort comes from Daniel's right. Chase. Daniel's hood jerks at the sound, a profanity spat out.

"It's rather clear you're out of options, since you've shown up to become one of us, rather than heed any warnings, from me or my future stepmother," Chase's voice rings out. He lowers his hood, as if he knows his impact on me is better seen than heard.

His blond hair shimmers in the low light, his brown eyes darkened to black, held in place by chiseled, flawless skin and bone.

I hold my ground, notching my chin and meeting him breath for breath.

"You know why I'm here," I seethe, then blink myself out of the instant anger he sparks in me. "This is a privilege unlike any other."

Chase's mouth starts to move. Maybe one last warning or threat. Dare I think it could be a plea. He's so far into the shadows, it's difficult to make out his expressions, but his jaw appears sharper than normal, his cloak shimmering more than the others with his unseen twitches and tics of stress or frustration. With me? With the world?

I'm not supposed to care anymore.

"Then you will agree to my terms," Sabine cuts in. "You *will* stay quiet, now that you're aware how much authority I hold."

The hidden message is obvious, but only to me. Ivy's

quiet whimpers, the sounds of her drowning in her own blood, echo in my ears.

"You claim to be a legacy of this society, but that has yet to be proven, if ever," she says. "I have centuries of history behind my reign, and I've allowed you into this temple and order you to get on your knees, because by now you understand the depth of my abilities to mold you or erase you. I am here to be your queen, Calla Lily Ryan." She shifts, and her eyes come into the light, gleaming. "And I do so look forward to ruling you. On your *knees*, Initiate," Sabine repeats.

Every limb of mine rebels at the forced supplication, but I'm staring past Sabine, through the wall behind her and into her office, into the princess bedroom, and at the red binder.

Mine.

My mother's murder is in there. I'm sure of it. Accessing that evidence is more important to me than satisfying Sabine's hard-on at witnessing me kneel before her. Thinking she's won.

My knees bend—

"Wait," Chase says.

I freeze. Sabine frowns. Daniel throws back his hood. "Son, if you so much as—"

"As her chosen soulmate, I'm the one meant to go down there and take her blood vow," Chase says.

"Why, yes," Sabine answers. "Although you're referencing quite an old rule of the Virtues. Remind me, dear," Sabine says to Daniel. "Something along the lines of a Noble *choosing* a woman to become a Virtue through the soulmate rite. Hmm." She puts a finger to her mouth, innocent enough, yet I brace for impact. "That doesn't apply here, now does it? Callie was tapped before you two got together."

"Wrong, *Mom*," Chase answers. "Father asked me to get close to Callie well before she reached this school. And as prince, it is my right to withdraw any Noble attachment I've given to her. And I'm withdrawing it now."

I angle my head, my stomach swaying at what Chase's outburst could mean.

Chase looks down at me and doesn't speak until I raise my chin and lock eyes with him. "I refuse her as my soulmate."

Sabine freezes. Daniel glowers, and the rest of the Cloaks murmur their shock.

"Come again?" Sabine asks, those two words so stilted and spaced out, it's clear she's making every effort to remain calm.

"I'm rescinding her soulmate status. And as an unbound female who was not initiated as a child..."

"Oh, now you're *really* digging deep into outdated Virtuous rules."

Chase raises a brow at Sabine. "Yet they're still in effect."

"Daniel," Sabine hisses. "*Do* something."

"Son, it's much too late for this unrequited love business. Callie has made it through her three trials, and she's accepted her Virtuous status despite the multiple challenges laid out before her. There is nothing more you can do."

"An elder initiate with her soulmate status revoked can

no longer become a Virtue. It's made clear, in black and white, in Rose's original rulebook."

Chase pulls out a tattered leather handbook from beneath his cloak.

Something crushes against my chest like a vise. My ribs move with my breaths, but they're coming ever closer to spearing my heart. "Chase..."

I can't retaliate by arguing my rightful position. I have no evidence of my legacy. Not yet. And I can't retrieve proof relating to Sabine's duplicity without becoming a Virtue.

What is he doing?

What has Chase *done* to me?

He's putting his promise into action.

Chase doesn't blink, the rest of his expression an ambivalent marble carving showing no sorrow or shame. "Callie, as an initiate claiming a Noble soulmate, can't finalize her robing without her soulmate's approval."

He can't do this. I wasn't ignorant enough to believe he'd let this ceremony go on without a fight, but revoking his attachment to me? So officially and publicly? This is worse than being covered in garbage, than enduring public humiliation.

This is final.

"Then I claim another soulmate!" I shout.

Fabric rustles as everyone spins back to me.

Daniel says through downturned lips, "Well. I don't think you can." He turns to Sabine. "Can she?"

Sabine meets my eye with a wicked grin. I recoil, repulsed at the prospect of having something in common with her. Her reasons for keeping me a Virtue can't possibly be as important as mine, yet we're one with this goal, and it makes me sick inside.

Chase's eyes incorporate the flames of the sconces. "That's not possible."

"Isn't it?" Sabine asks sweetly. "I don't believe Rose's handbook touches on that subject. My great-great-grand-mother-in-law's, however, does. The Harringtons are about empowering women, not stifling them. Callie may have begun her trials bound to you, but she may choose another eligible Noble at her robing ceremony to assist her in her Virtuous transformation. If you need proof, dear boy, you may go into my study and read through the dusty chapters. The rest of us will see this exciting ceremony through."

"There aren't any *eligible* Nobles left," Chase forces out. His exposed hands clench into vengeful fists. "Our barons have chosen their soulmates. The upperclassmen have theirs. Callie's finished here. There's—" Chase cuts himself off. His eyes widen, his gaze swings to mine, the realization in them as obvious to me as shooting stars in a pitch-black sky.

I narrow my eyes and grin, emitting none of the shrieking pain in my heart. "Tempest," I say, the name echoing in the silent chamber. "I choose Tempest as my soulmate."

21

CHASE

S o few words come out of my mouth, yet the curses filling my head would make an undertaker hand over his scythe and slowly back away.

My palms slam against the stone railing, my grip begging for the rock to crumble as I match Callie's defiant stare and try not to strangle her with my mind alone.

The light in here is so dim, shadows claim it as their docile pet, but the scarlet color of her lips manages to cut through the gloom. They're swollen—she's been gnawing at them, chewing out her thoughts until she reached this moment, pitting me against her and the society.

"Tempest?" I ask her. His name cuts against my tongue in ways that make me uncomfortable.

"Yes," she responds. No hesitation. No shame.

My chest tightens, inhales and exhales shrinking into pinpricks of air. Blood rushes into my neck, heating my ears. Tendons harden where my skin should be soft, and I'm having trouble restraining myself where my best buddy is concerned.

"You've been summoned, Tempest Callahan." My father's rough voice lingers in my ears, overtaking the shuffling of his steps and rustle of his robe. "How do you answer?"

"Simple. He doesn't," I bite out.

A heavy hand hits my shoulder and digs under the bone in warning. "It's no longer your call, son."

"It's always my call!"

I'm aware I sound like a spoiled jackass, but see if I fucking care. This is Callie. She can't be one of us. There wasn't supposed to be any chance of her succeeding in becoming a Virtue. I'm protecting the Nobles by exiling her. Ensuring the Stone legacy. Why can't Father *see* this?

Because he's built his empire on lies. Callie isn't yours to direct any more than you believed Emma was your sister.

I growl at the unbidden retort, made by my own brain. This is in my control. It's all for the greater good.

Confusion over why Father gave me Rose's handbook in the first place, when he's seemingly taking his fiancée's side, shouldn't take up so much headspace. I invoked my privilege, cast Callie off as insignificant, yet she remains confident and unaffected at naming my most trusted friend as her Plan B.

A black hood slithering off ebony hair catches my attention, Tempest's light eyes, both in hue and in humor, reaching mine before drifting over to Callie. "I'm not sure I have a say in this, brother."

His assessment of her fuses my bones into weapons of destruction.

"You're my second-in-command," I growl, my throat growing hotter the longer I keep focus on a guy who's enjoying this way too much. "Which means, you *do* as I command."

"It's Callie's right as a Virtuous prospect," Sabine adds, capping her statement off with a coquettish wink. "Seeing as her initial soulmate rescinded."

Throwing Sabine off this balcony and breaking her neck in her own temple would be all too kind. Callie may be so blinded by hate, she doesn't see the danger in enfolding herself as a Virtue under Sabine's direction, but I do.

"I believe we've been forced into this conversation because of you, son," Father says. I lock my jaw against his constraining glare. *You're the one who gave me the option, Dad.* "We'd be well on our way to a celebratory party if it weren't for these added shenanigans."

Callie's annoyingly sweet, headstrong voice cuts through our tension. "Then allow me to expedite this part. Tempest? Would you mind?"

Tempest pushes off the railing.

I storm behind the half-circle of Nobles and Virtues and fly in front of him before he hits the stairs. "If you take so much as another goddamned step—"

"You'll what?" Tempest asks dryly but keeps his voice low. "Implode your entire scheme to preserve the Nobles and dropkick your dad and Sabine out the secret door? Let this happen, man." He grabs my wrist before I can cock my fist.

"Callie won this round. It doesn't mean she's beat you. So she turns into an insipid Virtue. Who cares? She has no evidence. There's no one on her side to believe her story of legacy and matricide, save for a few unreliable outcasts." He pauses, as if taking time to watch the simmering blood rise from my neck and into my face. "If you'll stop sucking your own balls for a minute, you'd see Callie's in less danger by going along with Sabine's wishes." He gives me a light push. "So, back off. You, me, and Callie are *alllll* aware who the true soulmate is."

"That's not—" I sputter. "Callie's not—I'm not pissed because you're her soulmate instead of me. This is about the brotherhood, and her coming between—"

"Uh-huh. Bye-bye now."

Tempest disappears down the stairs.

Rather than watch him descend, I whirl, then stalk toward the railing, but I'm stopped by a thin, boney hand—deceptively strong and sharp with manicured nails.

"You told me she wouldn't make it this far," Falyn whispers through her oversized, golden hood.

"I was wrong," I clip out, then glare down at her hand in a gesture of what I think as a polite way to say *get your fucking hand off me.*

"You're admitting played this wrong?" Falyn squeaks, then tempers her voice at my growl of warning. "What's wrong with you? She can't be a Virtue. Sabine won't choose me as the next princess if Callie—"

I yank out of her hold so abruptly, she stumbles forward, but I don't catch her. I leave Falyn to right herself.

Back at the railing, I press my forearms into the cold

stone and lean forward, pissed I've missed even seconds of Callie and Tempest's blood union.

Because that's what I'm allowing, aren't I? It should be *me* standing with her, cutting my wrist and pressing it to hers, then slipping the blade through the stain of my blood on her skin and mixing hers with mine.

Tempest is not the one for her. Whether in farce or for the preservation of my goal, he *is not the one for her.*

"Easy, son," my father murmurs beside me while staring ahead.

"You did this," I snarl through my clenched jaw. Tremors collect down my arms, in my thighs, desperate to launch my body over the balcony and drag Callie, kicking and screaming, through the temple doors. "According to Rose Briar's original rules, my revocation should've made Callie's ascension null and void. Yet here I stand, watching another guy claim *my* right—"

"That you revoked. Yes. I can't have you attached to her, boy, in any way, moving forward. She is unstable, volatile, and entirely Sabine's responsibility. We know enough about Calla Lily Ryan now. You're no longer needed as our messenger."

"You knew I'd choose this," I whisper harshly, my stare burning into the two people below. "An official, societal vow to separate myself from Callie was your final blow. That's why you gave me the original handbook."

"It's for your own good."

I whip in his direction. "Just like Emma? You seem to enjoy alternating your mindfucks between us. What's next for her?"

Father doesn't bother to shift in my direction. "My boy. Haven't you learned? I'm leaving that entirely up to you."

I prepare to leap. "You son of a—"

"Are you ready for the blade?" Sabine's melodious voice cuts in.

In the midst of our private, vicious conversation, a stone column rose from the floor between Callie and Tempest, high enough to become a table of sorts.

Or an altar.

Sabine reaches into her robe—

The knife flashing, arcing toward my chest—Callie leaping for Ivy—no, for me—the dagger sinking into Ivy's neck—

Closing my eyes, breathing deep, I dislodge the image.

The dagger shines as it did that night, cleaned and sharpened. Sabine tosses it over the railing, but I don't gasp like the rest of my brothers and sisters. I'm fully aware of Tempest's ability to catch sharp things and come out unscathed.

His hand whips up and catches the blade at its hilt. Callie's eyes widen, impressed, a hot exhale building in my mouth as I watch.

"Let the ritual commence," Sabine coos, ensuring one last look at me, smiling, before she continues conducting the robing ceremony of the Virtues' Missing Heir.

And Tempest's new soulmate.

22

CALLIE

When the lush, gold cloak hits my shoulders, I don't smile.

The weight of the heavy fabric anchors my shaking legs, and as Tempest moves to my front, tying the heavy rope at my neck, my throat hits his deft fingers as I swallow.

The balcony applauds as Sabine introduces me as the newest Virtue in her ranks.

"Relax, possum," Tempest says, his eyes lowered to the knot. "This is what you wanted, isn't it?"

"Yes," I whisper, but no amount of licking my lips will keep them moistened.

My wrist burns with his cut, the thin layer of Tempest's blood on the delicate area already stiffening my skin as it dries.

Droplets of my blood and his stain the circular stone

table that sinks back into the ground at the same time Tempest pulls up my hood.

My gaze flicks up—unbidden, yet necessary—to Chase, the movement of the table reminding me all too much of his time in the underground cage.

It's just a stupid ceremony, meaning nothing to me. Mixing Tempest's blood with my own—while unsanitary—doesn't say anything about how I feel or to whom my heart belongs.

And the dagger used to slice my flesh may have been used on Ivy, but it's nothing but steel. It doesn't contain Ivy's lost soul, nor is it responsible for her death. Sabine is. She always will be.

So why do I feel so desolate rather than smug? I got what I wanted. I'm a Virtue.

"We shall reconvene in the Nobles' ritual room to celebrate," Sabine continues, her teeth flashing as she pulls up her hood. "You are dismissed, my children. Viscounts and countesses, please come with us."

The elder members retreat from the railing, Sabine and Daniel leading the way until their forms disappear behind the stone carving of a sleeping raven—Sabine's study.

My vision sharpens on their backs, wishing I could run through them and steal Sabine's binder. Now. *Right now.*

"Ready to party?" Tempest asks beside me.

"I'm ready to hurt something."

"Already learning the decorum of a Virtue, I see." Tempest offers me his arm. "Allow me to escort you, *soulmate.*"

I wince but take his arm.

"You know, if you were any other girl, I'd be highly insulted by how clearly it pains you to put your hands on me."

"Why aren't I any other girl?" I ask, but it's distracted and without much feeling. I'm too busy spying Chase, his eyes, a glittering onyx, disappearing as his form merges with the other cloaks and he leaves the balcony.

"Simple. Because you're Chase's."

I turn to him sharply. "Not anymore, I'm not."

He chuckles. "That's what you think."

The temple's underground tunnels take us to the Nobles' ritual room without having to deal with the frigid air outside. Before losing signal, I sent a message to Emma and Eden, telling them it was done. I'm a Virtue.

Eden replied with a thumb's up emoji, and Emma's answer popped up as dancing dots, then disappeared, nothing left in its wake.

I shove my phone in my jacket, the coat being proffered to me by a reluctant Willow as soon as the members started dispersing. Tempest pushes open the final heavy, wooden door and accepts a flute of champagne from a tray and offers it to me, calling me the "martyr of honor." I recall the last time I accepted a glass of champagne within these walls, during the Societal Ball when Chase was buried even deeper in Briarcliff's underground than I am.

He's not helpless this time, instead making it here before me, his shoulders hunched as he feigns interest in what a crowd of Nobles around him are saying as they swig their liquor and stand pretty in their privileged status. He's shed his robe, an expertly cut, two-piece charcoal suit taking its place, and he holds his champagne as if he's drinking it, but I know him well enough that he won't take a sip.

"These peeps are all here for you," Tempest muses, "to celebrate your induction. Try to smile, pretty possum, since all attention's on you."

"I have to figure out a way to get back to the temple."

"Come again?"

I jolt, not realizing I said it out loud. Covering up my blunder by bringing the flute to my lips doesn't do much to sway Tempest's interest. He cocks a brow, regarding me idly. "Whatever could you want to go back there for? To clean up our blood?"

To avenge Ivy's blood is the retort at the tip of my tongue, but I swallow it.

"My, what a murderous look you have," Tempest observes, then squeezes my hand as he draws me deeper into the crowd. "Try not to make it so obvious, not among this crowd of opportunists and savages."

"And what are you?" I ask, submitting to his tug and feeling less like a faulty beacon as I enter the fray of other cocktail dresses, gowns, and suits, now that everyone has shed their cloaks. "An opportunist or a savage?"

"A survivor," Tempest quips before withdrawing his hand, sending a wink—not my way, but behind me, before he meanders away.

Spinning, I nearly smack into the Chase's unforgiving chest.

"Excuse me," I say, side-stepping.

He clasps me by the waist, stalling my movements. "Happy now?" he growls.

I lift my chin to meet his eyes. "Not in the least."

"Good. Neither am I."

"*Good.*" The word comes out more emotional than scathing, but I use that energy to rip out of his hold and stalk around him.

I can't have him so near, hurt and want swirling so close to my heart they threaten to stop its beats. Chase can't be my distraction when I've come so far. My mother's justice is within reach, if only I stick to what's important, and that's *not* Chase Stone.

Music starts, at first mellow in tone, then picks up haunting beats as the DJ, set up under the carving of the Nobles' crest, spins his dials and flicks on otherworldly, neon lights.

The younger members cheer, lifting their drinks up high as they undulate with the admittedly addictive notes, twirling and hopping, twisting and writhing, until they've created a makeshift dance floor, and I'm desperate for escape.

They say it's for me, this celebration of a new member, but it's not difficult to grasp how distant my importance has become with the endless champagne, the private DJ, and the permission to act without boundaries underneath the constraints of Briarcliff University.

Falyn separates herself from Willow and Violet, her arms raised as she trots into the fray, her hair wild and her kaleidoscope dress strikingly familiar to the one Sabine gifted me for Winter Formal. When she catches my eye, her carefree smile drops from her face and her arms smack against her sides. She parts her lips and mouths something, but I don't need a translator to understand it's a message along the lines of, "*You don't belong here. Fuck off out of my party.*"

I send her a wink in answer, letting her know I'm just as aware of my place in the Virtues as she is.

"Callie, there you are."

The voice tickles at my nape, spiking the hairs there, sending ice picks under my skin.

Reluctantly, I turn. "Sabine."

"I believe, as a Virtue, you are to refer to me as your queen." She steps up beside me, pretending as much interest in the figures on the dance floor as I am. "I wonder if I could speak with you in private for a moment."

"Not on your life."

"That's fair." Sabine's lips quirk. "Perhaps you'll be willing to join me on the fringes instead. There's much we have to discuss."

"I don't negotiate with murderers."

"Aren't you curious as to why I've allowed you to come this far?"

"*Allowed,*" I echo. Unable to contain myself, I turn to her. "What's that supposed to mean? That you could've killed me at any time up until this moment?"

"Well, yes." Sabine smiles, her eyes lighting up with the malicious intent behind her grin. "But that's not what I'm referring to. I'll ask you one more time. Join me."

She tips her head, motioning toward the far wall. I

debate for a few seconds, well aware of my penchant for needing answers, then follow her to the far reaches of the room.

I look over my shoulder just once, in time to catch Chase clocking my movements. His focus makes me feel better, knowing, despite our differences, he cares about my outcome.

Or merely waits for another chance to sabotage me.

"There now," Sabine says once we've settled against the wall. Both of us hold flutes of champagne. Neither of us drink from them. "I trust you enjoyed the robing ceremony."

I stare at the shallow cut on my wrist, sliced diagonally and now clotted with dried blood. It still smarts. "I wouldn't call it a happy experience."

"You would have preferred Chase to be the one to welcome you," Sabine surmises, a confident curve to her mouth. "Alas, he is of his own mind and is determined to prevent you from reaching your full potential."

Frowning, I spin the flute's stem between my fingers. "And you *want* me to be at my fullest potential?"

"Indeed, I do. I realize how unconvincing that may seem, what with Ivy's short life so fresh in your mind."

She speaks of ending Ivy's life like she'd ask for a second glass of champagne, and I'm reminded of how dangerous she is, even while in public, mingling with her own kind. There's nothing to stop her from unsheathing the same dagger and stabbing me between the ribs, in front of everyone, their coveted membership to the Nobles and Virtues swearing them into painful silence.

But how excruciating would it be for them? The benefits of the Cloaks are extraordinary. Surreal. Limitless and empowering.

My life—Ivy's life—seems paltry compared to all that.

Shit, what am I doing?

"You may also be wondering why I haven't harmed you," Sabine continues, choosing to run her finger along the rim of her glass rather than look at me. "It's simple, really. I feel like you and I can still reach an agreement. I'd rather have enemies on my side rather than just dispose of them."

My grip tightens dangerously around the crystal stem. "I'll never team up with you for anything. Ever."

"Think wisely, my dear. You have the bloodline to run the Virtues, but no clue how to invoke that right. There's no family tree to point to, no physical evidence to showcase in front of our members."

That's what you think. Give me time, bitch.

"In any case, there's your pesky medical history, which discredits anything you might bring to the table."

I stiffen.

"I want to work with you, Callie. Ivy was a warning, it's true, and Chase would've been a better lesson, but with my hold over the Nobles tiring, new blood needs to step in and keep up the strength of the Virtues. We're better than the Nobles. Quieter, deadlier, smarter. If only you could see that and understand that all I wanted from your mother, from *you*, is cooperation to keep our strength going."

"Strength and power don't include rape," I spit. "Which is exactly what you're doing to your so-called princesses.

Harming them, fucking up their psyches, and for what? Money?"

"No, dear. It's true we've only known each other a short while, but surely I've left enough of a powerful impression for you to realize my true nature."

"Manipulation. Extortion. Blackmail."

"Quite right." Sabine brightens. "The girls I choose realize the importance of their position, for it is because of them I'm able to call in favors, for these men who visit them show their weakness, their penchant for the forbidden. Take Ivy, for instance. She was desperate to give her father back his stellar reputation. Once she became princess, we were able to do that, for the Noble who visited her was the CEO of her father's company, and he received a promotion soon after."

I scrunch my eyes shut at the image of what Ivy was forced to do in order to save her family in the only way she thought possible. I can't believe I'm talking to the woman responsible for Ivy's suffering, holding a conversation with her like we would at a reception. "And the princess before that?"

"Emma?" Sabine leans against the wall, pursing her lips in thought. "Before she rebelled, the man I chose for her would've opened the kinds of doors for her that she needed. Finding her father and knowing her mother, for one."

My lips pucker in minor confusion, but I keep on track. "I'm not talking about her. I'm referring to Piper."

Sabine meets my gaze. "Piper wasn't a popular choice when it came to the Nobles who frequent our territory."

"Why? Because she's your daughter, and you can play

favorites like that? Use the poor girls, the desperate ones who need something, to do your bidding instead of your own blood?"

Sabine laughs, the champagne flute catching the light as her movements reflect her mirth. "No, child. Piper couldn't be trusted to keep her mouth shut. She was willful, that girl, but when Emma ceded her position—quite permanently, as you know—I was forced to put my daughter in her place before the Nobles started asking questions about Emma's demise. You and I both know my preference would've been Violet, but the amount of trust and grooming it takes to create the ideal princess ... well, there simply wasn't time. To keep up appearances, I chose my daughter, but with that decision came the consequence of losing business."

Business. She calls sex trafficking a business. I'm going to be sick.

"Then I guess her dying opened you up for business again," I deadpan.

I expect Sabine's quiet laughter in response, but shadows cross over her expression instead. "She was never meant do die. And my youngest was never meant to be her killer."

"I guess that's what happens when they get a mother like you."

Sabine's eyes sharpen, then drill into mine. "My girls were strong. Intelligent. And in one case, lethal. I may not be proud of their actions, but I'll always honor their spirits. Unlike your mother, who couldn't stomach the idea of being pregnant with you. She wanted to abort you; do you know that?"

I ignore the jab, but it's difficult. "Is that why you killed her?"

Sabine lifts her chin, the neon lights from the dance floor cresting over her cheeks. "Meredith ran from greatness. Avoided her potential and squirreled you away in a janitor's closet. She was a coward."

"She *saved* me." I peel my lips back on a snarl.

Sabine doesn't twitch. "Did she? You're here, aren't you? Despite her better efforts."

"I'm here to—" *destroy you*, but I don't allow myself to get that far. Just as Sabine wants me under her wing to gain a closer watch on me, so do I want to keep her at a distance to maintain the element of surprise. "I'm here to claim my rightful place. The Virtues are mine, not yours."

"You can't have them without me, just as I can't keep them without you. Do you finally understand why you're still alive, dear child? We need each other. Keep in mind, do you really want me to stop considering you necessary? Reflect on what happened to your dear friend..."

A slithering, sickening feeling uncoils in my gut, realization mixed with stubborn refusal. I can't resist the next words that peel out of my mouth, "I don't need *you* to take this entire institution down."

"Oh, my, is that why you and that boy are at such odds?" Sabine squints against her new perception. "Sweet child, *now* I understand why you're both so bull-headed about each other. Chase Stone will never allow you to hurt us. His entire life revolves around these societies." Sabine pauses, pushing her lips to the side as she feigns contemplation. "I'd wager he'd rather see *you* destroyed than his brotherhood."

"You overestimate my feelings for him. He doesn't influence my decisions, and I don't affect his." I push off the wall, done with this conversation.

"I'd rather think I've hit them spot on," Sabine murmurs at my back, but I hear the arrogance, the certainty that she can't be wrong.

"Don't forget your first dance with Tempest!" she calls soon after, but I'm pushing through the crowd, searching for the nearest exit. "Your most recent decision notwithstanding of course."

My exposed skin tingles as I pass through the dance floor, the too-tight dress constricting my movements at the same time it's putting them on display. My eyes skim over heads until I land on the second source of my unease.

Chase stands at the opposite wall, his chin lowered, his drink dangling at his side. Yet, in all his languidness, his stare is fervent and on fire, as if he's eager to incinerate me on the spot.

He watches me mumble to Tempest that I'm not feeling well and need to leave. Stares me down as I take the stairs up and out of the Nobles' hidden room.

And I feel him long after I exit into the Wolf's Den and creep along Briarcliff University's pathways, searching for warmth.

23

CALLIE

Emma's waiting up for me when I step into our room, the under-cabinet lights in our kitchen slinking across her hunched form as she perches on a stool near our countertop.

"Glad you made it," she says, straightening as I shut the door softly behind me.

"There were a few unexpected twists."

"I figured, since a BU freshman's—"

"Never been initiated before. I know," I finish for her on a sigh.

Emma responds with a laugh that surprises me. "You're done. I get it. Go rest, and we'll talk about next steps tomorrow."

She shocks me again when her heavy arm lands on my shoulder. She gives a squeeze so minute I have to concentrate to feel it, then drops it to her side. "Well done, Callie. You did great."

I offer her a slanted smile, then slide my jacket off my shoulders, kick off my shoes, then drag my beaten ass to bed.

"Wait." Emma catches me by the wrist—my wounded one. "This is deeper than normal."

I respond dryly, "Ever heard of a *soulmate* blood vow?"

"The mixing of blood? Shit," Emma hisses. "That kind of thing hasn't been used since, like, the Dark Ages. I can't believe my idiot brother agreed to this."

"He didn't."

"Huh?"

I'm reluctant to get into it, but this is Emma, one of the only friends I've kept. "Tempest did the blood oath with me."

"You did *what* with *who*?" Emma's eyes pop wide.

"Remember a few seconds ago when you said we'd get into the next steps tomorrow? I'd like to play that card again..."

"Nuh-*uh*, Callie Ryan. Explain to me how Tempest is now your soulmate and my brother is not."

I do it in a rush, unwilling to dwell on the devastating moment Chase officially scorned me, yet Emma's astonishment won't fade. "What's the big deal? It's not like we're in a forced marriage or anything. In fact, I'd argue Tempest is the best soulmate to have. He's the human equivalent of a cold-hearted vampire. He has no feelings and doesn't give a damn what I do. I can still break into the temple and get the binder."

"Assuming it's still there."

My lips tighten at Emma's decision to voice what I've been afraid to dwell on. "If it isn't, we'll find out where she put it and grab it from there. I *will* avenge my mother, Emma."

"If you're looking for someone to understand your passion," Emma says softly, "you know I'm your girl. But don't disregard their rules. Sabine will make good on the debt you've created with Tempest. Some way, she will."

"There's nothing more she can do to me that could break me."

Emma gives a sad, slow shake of her head. "Don't be so sure. I mutilated myself to get away from their rules. Think about that."

I open my mouth—

"And there's always my brother."

My jaw hangs silent, caught in the grip of her argument, before I clamp it shut.

"We won't have to worry about him." I shake my head resolutely. "By the time I'm done, there won't be enough Virtues or Nobles remaining to make good on a blood vow *or* a threat to a prince."

"I hope you're right."

"I am." It comes out more clipped than intended, but I can't take it back.

Emma and I war with our eyes for a few more seconds, until her shoulders slope and she motions in the direction of my room. "Go on, then. Catch some sleep."

I nod grimly, tempted to crush her into a sudden, meaningful hug. *We're on the same side. We can do this.*

But we don't do that kind of thing. I wave good night and step into my room, shutting the door.

Then choke on a scream as I'm backed into the wall.

24

CALLIE

A familiar freshwater scent envelops me, even as I squirm and bare my teeth.

The room is dark—pitch black—yet Chase's opaque outline, darker than shadows, more languid than shade, overtakes what little vision I have.

The backs of my hands hit the wall behind me, his unyielding grip on my wrists driving them hard into the plaster.

"The *fuck* do you think you're doing?" he snarls, his teeth snapping near my nose.

I don't flinch. "I'd be quiet if I were you. Your sister's one scream away."

Chase growls in answer. My wrists flop onto the top of my head at his sudden release, his footsteps clomping away.

He flings my door open, the shaft of light caressing his twisted, aggravated features.

"Emma!" he barks. "Go to the lake house."

"What?" comes her addled reply. I don't think she expected him here anymore than I did. The fridge door shuts. "Why?"

"Because I said so. Now."

"You're not my keeper, Chase."

"If you don't leave in the next minute, all you'll hear is Callie's constant orgasms and my pounding—"

"*Ew!* Don't go any further!"

"Uh, how about don't do it at all?" I cut in.

Chase whips his head toward me, his finger cutting through the air as he points. "If I were you, I'd shut the fuck up at this moment. I can't promise I'll be a gentleman any more than you can promise not to betray me."

My mouth drops open. "That's not—"

"Callie. Fucking zip it. Emma, get the fuck out."

Chase's entire body tightens at each jerky move he throws out, gesturing to his sister, pointing at me. His thighs bulge in his pants, primed to leap, while his torso ripples beneath his thin white shirt, begging for release.

I'm not sure what concerns me more. The fact that he's cursing at us like he's *never* done before, or that he looks about to explode, *or* that Chase has been here long enough to strip down to his undershirt and slacks without Emma or I noticing.

I squint at him. This can't possibly all be due to Tempest, can it? "Chase, what's going on?"

He doesn't bother to look my way. "Go," he says to his sister through the doorway. "Unless you want me to make you."

"You had me at 'pounding,' dear brother. I'm outta here."

I push off the wall. "Emma, wait—" but, my voice cuts off as soon as I note Chase's flinch at Emma's use of "brother," the lamplight bathing his expression in golden pain.

"Unless," Emma quantifies, "Callie wants me to stay. Do you, Callie?"

My palms press into the wall in an automatic retreat to Chase's expression. He glares at me under his brows, allowing my response, but his nostrils flare impatiently.

"It's okay," I say, keeping my eyes on Chase. "I'll be fine."

"Good," I hear Emma mumble as her footsteps near the front door. "It's about time you two figure your shit out."

I don't respond, instead licking my lips as I wait for the apartment door to shut.

My lips part. "I—"

Chase rounds on me, cutting off anything I was about to say—what *was* I about to say? I can't think clearly when he's this close. Can't form enough obstinance to rip my forearm out of his hand when he lifts my arm and brings my cut into the light.

Chase's nostrils, still flaring, don't compare to the utter, vengeful twist to his lips. "You let him brand you."

I test my strength against his, yanking my arm. It doesn't budge from his hold.

Fine. Plan B. "What did you expect me to do?" I hiss. "After you publicly disavowed me to the entire society?"

His eyes slide from my inner wrist to my face, the action seeming to pain him. "I expected you to walk out of the temple and never look back, like I've asked you to do repeatedly."

"Then you should invest in a better crystal ball," I retort, "if you can't even predict I'd throw your commands back in your *face*."

My back presses against the wall when he steps forward, his forehead almost touching mine as his exhale billows out, spearmint mixing with rage.

"I only wish I'd had a trashcan to toss at you, too," I risk continuing. "And maybe a used tampon or two."

He snarls, slamming my wounded arm back into the wall. "When are you going to figure out what you're dealing with?"

"Depends what you're referring to." I press forward, the front of my body molding to his so well, I can feel his heartbeats against my own. "Are you talking about your possessive, asshole self, or the Nobles and Virtues?"

His voice lowers to a growl. "All of it. You won't get what you want if you continue to walk your insolent ass onto their turf, thinking you have the upper hand. Binding yourself to Tempest hasn't given you any advantages. It only deepens your obligations to them and enters you into a contract you have no hope of escaping."

"I'm not alone," I reply, deeply affected by the flare to his eyes but refusing to show it. "I have Eden helping me. And your sister."

Again, he winces.

"What is that?" I ask. "Your reaction to Emma's name. I noticed it before, too."

Chase lowers his head, and against my better judgment,

I lift my free hand and risk tracing a finger along his jaw. "Chase? Talk to me."

His shoulders rise and fall. Chase fixes his gaze to the floor, and I swear, despite the death grip he has on my wrist, he's about to confide in me.

Until his eyes flick up and his snarl reaches my lips, his mouth brushing over mine while his eyes bore rivulets of fire into my gaze.

"You're *mine*," he breathes into my mouth. "Do you understand me?"

"I'm not anybody's—"

He smothers my urge to rebel by yanking my arm forward and forcing my wrist between us. "This means *nothing*. Tempest may cut into you, you may have recited overdone, emotionless, and bloody vows, but this skin is mine. Your body is mine. Your soul?" He angles his head. "Mine."

"*Fuck* you," I spit, trying to wrestle out of his hold. "What makes you think you can come in here and lay a claim on me when you've spent the last few weeks doing everything in your power to push me away? I'm *not* yours. I'll never *be* yours. You lost that chance."

"Everything I do is to protect you."

I roll my eyes, until I'm jerked to a stop with his fingers digging into my cheeks. His fervent stare captures mine, fearless yet exposed, drilling into me with a depth that's almost crazed.

"I kept my distance to prevent Sabine and my father taking further interest in you. I've kept secrets for them involving you not for their benefit, but for yours. You can't know how much they've fucked with you, and how much more they will. I'm acting like your buffer, keeping you away from the worst. But how can I do that when you claim my best friend as your soulmate? Your Noble protector? How can I push at my parents and push at you, thinking I won't fucking snap in two? No. It ends here." He shakes his head. "You aren't anyone else's. I'm staying with you, and I *refuse* to let you do more stupid things."

"Stupid?" I guffaw, uselessly shoving at his chest again. "I've gotten myself this far, no thanks to you. Learned about my mom, kept my promise to Ivy, and I *will* avenge them both, whether or not you decide to be my fair-weather boyfriend. So, go on, come in here and piss on my furniture all you want, but my mind will always belong to *me*."

I expect him to snarl, bark, maybe even spit and swipe, considering he's acting like an animal. What I don't expect is for him to pull my inner wrist up to his lips and bite down hard around my wound.

"*Jeez*—what? Ow! *Ow!*" I scream.

He releases my arm. I inspect the teeth marks around the cut—just indents, he didn't break skin—then hold it close to my chest. "What the hell is wrong with you?"

"Everything. Everything is wrong with me."

"You need to leave."

"Well, I'm not going to."

"Chase, I've had it. With you, with these societies, with this goddamned *school*. Leave me the hell alone and let me—"

He walls me in, his hands slamming on either side of my head. "Mine."

"You don't—"

"What?" he pauses, reading my expression. "I don't know what it's like? To have someone ripped away like they didn't have meaning in your life? All because someone *else* decided to make them disappear just because they could? I know what it's like, Callie. It may not be the same, but that burning inside you because something vital was torn out of your skin..." His voice tightens. "It's been taken from me, too. *I know what it's like.*"

I search his eyes, finding nothing but a shimmering onyx reflecting back at me. "Who?" I manage to whisper. "Who was taken from you?"

Chase glances at the open doorway, then cuts to me. After a few seconds, he growls. "My teeth marks surround Tempest's cut. But if that's not enough for you, I'll use another blade to erase his mark, too."

Breathing heavy, though I've taken no steps, I retort, "You've lost your mind."

"How nice of you to notice."

"Tell me what's going on. Why you're acting like this. You've never been so possessive. Territorial and ... frightening. Tempest and I aren't anything to be jealous of."

Chase's face comes close to mine. "Don't ever use him and you in the same sentence again."

I exhale a loud sigh. "Chase, I'm not about to become some sort of property dispute between you and your friend."

"Then agree with me."

"No."

"Admit you're with me."

"Never."

"You can keep your mind. Save your soul, even. But confess that your heart belongs to a Stone, and I'll let you go."

"N—" I falter. Damn him, he has it. He's always had it, since the moment I walked into Briarcliff, glanced up into the Wolf's Den, and found his eyes clashing with mine.

A distracting flicker of pleasure resonates in my brain, shockwaves of it coming from my core. I glance down in the small space between us, noticing his hand grazing my thigh and moving under my dress.

"Chase—"

His fingers push my underwear aside, and he slips into my folds, his thumb pressing down on my clit. Circling. Massaging. Coaxing.

Moaning.

"Chase, I mean it…"

His nose grazes my jawline when I lift my chin, the back of my head clonking against the wall. Chase nips at my chin, then draws my lower lip into his mouth, sucking on it then biting down.

He catches my yelp of pain, groaning as he savors it and pulls me into a deeper kiss. I sink into his commands as his expert fingers play along my clit, pinching and tugging, creating zips of pleasure that tighten my body as I await delicious release.

My hips take up his rhythm, moving in his circles, angling for his fingers to go deeper, curl more, flick often.

He must hear my wishes, because his fingers do just that.

I lift my leg and curve it over his, widening my pleasure center and forcing his own hand to brush against his bulging erection as well as become soaked in my juices.

Chase groans, angling our kiss until his tongue dances in my mouth, my jaw relaxing at the same time I'm coiling for a salacious orgasm.

"Just ... just..." I pant, breaking off our kiss to better angle myself for his hand. I grip his wrist in much the same way he grabbed mine, but push his hand deeper, his fingers sinking into my folds, first one, then two, three, four....

My head falls back, the tips of my hair tangling in his other hand as he holds the small of my back.

He starts pumping, his thumb still managing to massage my clit as he pushes in roughly, retreating only half a second before diving deep again.

The movements are possessive, mirroring his current, concerning attitude, but my mind merely flits against the similarity, then flutters away, because he's spreading me wide and pushing as much of his hand to the point that I feel stretched and full.

I have to use both hands now to hold his wrist as I ride him, the one leg I have around his torso digging into his back once I reach my climax and...

Oh.

Oh.

OH.

A hand shouldn't be able to do this. His fingers can't produce as much ecstasy as his dick, but here I am, holding onto his arm like a rodeo cowgirl and flying into the air like he's just bucked me.

Spent, I flop into his arms. Chase catches me effortlessly, and instead of wiping my juices on his slacks or doing anything to clean us up, he shifts me against his chest then carries me to bed.

I expect to be laid down, and he does just that, but then he starts pushing my tight mini-dress up my hips, then to my stomach—out of the way.

"You better still have energy for my cock," he says, his gaze meeting mine briefly before he goes back to taking his fill of my half-naked body. "Because I'm two seconds away from creaming my pants, and I'd rather be fucking you while I come."

"Yes," I say, still panting. I glance down, realizing one breast has escaped the deep V of my dress, but I don't bother fixing myself.

I like looking messy.

I love looking roughed up from sex because of *him*.

The whys can be sorted out later. Right now, all I want is his naked body and big, thick dick. I'm swollen for him, aching for his fill, and I hope that's all in my eyes when I look at him and bite down on my lip.

"Ah, fuck me," he whispers, then tears off his shirt and pants.

25

CHASE

"What did you lose?" Callie murmurs beside me.

"Hmm?" I let my head fall to the side, catching her in a midnight glow, the moon passing pale white beams across her skin from her window.

I buried myself inside her, losing myself and giving into her heat, her skin, *her*, but the afterglow is wearing thin, and I'm starting to realize I revealed too much when I confronted her.

Tempest's touch upon her body blinded me to the consequences, his nearness and ownership of her, in front of both societies, instantly became too much. I lost control, refusing to believe that on top of having my sister taken away, I have to lose her, too...

I've ended up in Callie's dorm without quite knowing how I got here. The red was too blinding, the possession too complete, for me to realize that I could be hurting Callie more than I was saving her by being here and branding her.

Because that's what I did, didn't I? I bit into her skin just as easily as Tempest's blade, marking her as he did, but not stopping there. No, I had to fuck her, show my weakness, explain that she was mine and mine alone, and in doing so...

I offered her my hurt.

Goddammit, I can't hurt. Emma's heritage isn't my concern, the Nobles' future is. Emma's adoption, Callie's bloodline—they can't take up my thoughts like this and pulverize my brain, when I have to put all focus on my father and his operations. I *have* to inherit the Nobles.

"Who was it?" she repeats, her voice a note above a whisper.

Callie rolls to her side, her hand sliding over my naked torso, her pinky brushing against my nipple and sending a *zing* of renewed vigor.

Perhaps if I fuck her again...

"No one," I answer, but it comes out guttural, unsure.

"You can try to fool me, but you'll fail." Callie rises up on her elbow, her long hair flipped over one side and cascading down her arm.

The urge to bury my face in it, throw her on her back, and lose myself in her is almost unbearable.

"I recognized it in your voice," she continues. "The rawness. The pain. What has Sabine done to you?"

"It wasn't Sabine." My answer is out before I can control it.

Callie scrunches her brows. "Then who?" When I don't

answer right away, her forehead smooths. "Your father."

Her eyes, so liquid they melt into gold when they're on me, won't leave my face. I reach up, tucking errant strands behind her ear, then cup her jaw, tracing the line there. "It's about Emma."

I'm not sure what makes me say it. Perhaps it's her undivided attention, or her soft voice, or the simple understanding of what it's like to live a lie.

"What about her?"

"She's not really my sister."

I leave the bomb between us, unwilling to trigger it further by admitting, *she's not my real twin.* The idea Emma and I don't share the same birthday, never mind the same womb, remains so mind-boggling and heart-wrenching, I can't stand to give it voice.

Callie's hand curls against my chest, her nails scraping my skin. "Wait, what?"

"My father admitted it to me a few nights ago. Emma was some charity case of my mother's, an unwanted pregnancy ... I don't know all the details, but I'm starting to think I don't need to. She's not my blood. She's an imposter and doesn't even know it."

"My god. Chase." Callie sits up. "This will *kill* her. Is this for real?"

I catch Callie's wrist before she lifts it from my chest. "You're not telling her. You can't."

She jerks her chin to me, her eyes widening. "I can't keep something like this to myself! She's my friend, Chase. My best—"

"And I'm her twin." I cut her off, cursing at the easy use

of a title that's not mine anymore. Rising, I catch Callie's chin between my fingers. "Think of what you're trying to do. If you admit this to her, you're right, it will kill her. You won't have a comrade anymore. Emma will turn into herself, run, escape, fly back to our mother. In essence, she'll leave you. Us."

"She'd have every right to. You're telling me everything she knows is a lie."

"You know what that's like." I level Callie with a look. "As do I. Your plans to take down Sabine will be null and void."

"I can't..." Callie shakes her head, then digs her fingers into her hair. "So, I use Emma to get Sabine's binder, squeeze her dry until Sabine's named for Ivy's murder and my mother's, and then I tell her? I'm not going to keep this from Emma until she stops being useful to me. I *can't*."

"What's more important to you?"

I ask her the question knowing the answer and hate myself for the added knowledge that it's killing her. All Callie wants is to prove that her mother was a good woman who was wrongfully killed, and Ivy an innocent caught in the crossfire. This additional information about Emma? It's an aggravating twist, a serrated knife to an already too-deep wound. I know it and must use it against her.

"What about you? Why don't you want to tell her?" Callie asks. The sheets have fallen from her chest, her breasts heaving with her aggravated breaths, but I can't bring myself to admire the sheer beauty of her while so much turmoil surrounds us. I shouldn't have taken advantage of her in the first place.

But she's *mine*, damnit.

"Because she's my twin," I say after a beat. "She'll always be my twin, blood or not. And I can't rip something like this away from her—rip *me* from her—when so much hangs in the balance already. She wants Sabine to pay for her sins as much as you do. Wants the Virtues destroyed as desperately as you. To hear this on top of it all ... Emma's been through enough these past few years. I would reduce her to insanity if I told her this without giving her anything in return, like Sabine's head on a platter."

Callie takes a breath, her focus shifting to the wall across from us. "But you want to save the Virtues and the Nobles. You don't want to risk their safety by telling Emma the truth, do you?"

I study her, Callie Ryan, my weakness and my strength. "What would you do if I said my priorities have changed?"

Her stare whips to mine. "Not possible."

"My father can't be saved. The Virtues created under his idleness and Sabine's rule are unsalvageable. What he's done to my *sister*—" I hiss out a breath, collecting myself. "I'll help you with the Virtues and Sabine. But the Nobles? You leave them to me."

Callie stares back silently, her plush lips a hairsbreadth away from gawking. "I can't keep up with your mood swings."

"You don't have to if you simply accept that you're my girl, the Virtues are yours to fuck with, and I retain control of the Nobles." I rest my forearms on my raised knees. "Does that sound good to you?"

To my surprise, Callie breaks out into a genuine smile.

She rushes me with her arms, crashing us back to the bed. "You have no idea how much I've wanted you to … to…"

"Simply be there for you?" I murmur into her ear. "Calla Lily Ryan, it killed me to be away from you."

She finds my lips, sucking them between her teeth, then flicking out her tongue and making that adorable purr I can't resist. Unfortunately, she pulls away soon after. "I wish this could be the end of our fairy tale. But your sister. And Sabine…"

"Are you sure you want that binder?"

Callie nods fervently, her small body pressed against mine.

"You've tried once and failed," I add, my brows weighing heavy above my eyes. "And it's so explicit. Sabine's shown us her knack for predicting our next move." I angle my head and peer at Callie. "What if we approach it from a different angle instead? Like, a more psychological one, and beat Sabine at her own game?"

Callie pulls in her lower lip, sucking on it thoughtfully. In the shadows and moonlight, she looks like a tentative goddess. "If we could somehow make her question the amount of power she has over the girls, plant seeds of doubt…"

"Exactly." I wrap my arms around the small of her back, delighted she's catching my wave of thought. "The way to push Sabine off-balance is to go after her insecurities, and that lies with her false claim as the true queen of the Virtues."

Callie responds, "I don't know if… what if it's not

enough? Mom's murder won't be solved. Ivy's death won't have closure..."

I grunt, acknowledging her worry. Sabine and my father always seem to plan for all contingencies, my poor sister included. There must be a reason Father revealed Emma's adoption to me, same as the reasons Sabine allowed Callie to find her hidden folders on Meredith Ryan in the first place. I just haven't figured out why yet.

"We need more believers," I say.

Callie raises her brows.

"The Nobles." I clarify, "The younger initiates, you could probably talk them onto your side, especially with your claim to the Virtue throne. And through that, we could tell them about Sabine's treatment of the princesses. Enough games. No more behind the scenes. We could tell them the truth." I move my gaze to the ceiling. "I'm sick of all the lies."

"Me, too." Callie shifts with me. "Sabine's gotten away with so much because she's kept so many people ignorant. Maybe, if we had numbers on our side. But ... all I have is my word."

I run my finger along her cheek, thinking of my father gleefully admitting my twin is not my twin. Or Sabine, allowing Callie into the Virtues for dangerous reasons that escape me. "Maybe that's enough."

Callie thinks for a moment. "With you beside me, I can try." She raises her eyes to mine. "Will you be? On my side?"

"Sweet possum," I say, "Yes. You're the only good thing I have left."

26

CALLIE

It doesn't take long for Chase to fall into dreams, but I can't seem to catch up with him.

I love watching him sleep. It's like my favorite parts of him float up to the surface of his skin. Chase's relaxed brows, his soft lips, his thick lashes becoming crescents against his golden skin. It all points to his hidden sweetness, that section of him he works so hard to bury and keep at bay.

I run a hand through his thick, unkempt hair, and he purrs in his sleep, angling toward the touch.

If you were to ask Chase, he'd say he's weakened in slumber, all his vulnerabilities exposed to any enemies creeping closer. He's too soft, he'd argue. His lips would never tilt so serenely, his body would never become so relaxed and floppy if he were awake. But I'd argue he's at peace.

Reluctant to rouse him any further, I withdraw my hand

and slide out of bed, in need of a hot coffee so I can sit and think.

Chase gave me a lot of himself tonight—more than he's ever allowed. Now I carry his secrets, and my stomach turns at the thought of what I must keep from Emma.

Darkness eats away at all of us, but I had no idea how it infiltrates even those who think they've overcome it.

My door doesn't creak as I open it, and I close it with just as much silence, aware that the slightest *snick* of sound would wake Chase and ruin any dream state he finds calm in.

That plan is nearly derailed when I catch sight of a shadow in front of me and choke on a scream.

I fumble for the light switch, then release the gasp when I realize it's Emma. "You scared the shit out of me," I say. "I thought you were gone."

Emma doesn't shift or flinch at the sudden glare of light. That should've been my first clue. "I never left."

My hand falls from the switch. "What are you doing standing here in the dark?"

"I left the lake house keys here. I came back to get them."

"Then..." I check her empty hands, dangling near her sides. "Where are they?"

"I stopped mid-grab," she answers tonelessly. "Since they were on our coffee table. Right near your door."

Her lower lip trembles, and she blinks rapidly against shining, welling eyes.

"Emma." I don't think I've ever seen her cry before, and I rush to her.

She pushes against my arms as soon as I raise them for comfort. "Get *away* from me!"

Stumbling back, I glance toward my shut door, conscious of Chase's nearby presence. "Emma, what's wrong? What can I do?"

"Were you really going to keep it from me?" she asks, her voice raw and broken.

I stall on the question of what she could be talking about, because I know. *Oh God, I know.*

Emma mistakes my frozen silence as an answer. "So you were. You and my brother weren't going to tell me—" Her voice falters as she meets my eyes with the most crestfallen, defeated expression. "But he's not my brother, is he?"

"Emma, I can explain."

"No. You can't. You were supposed to be my *friend*, Callie!"

"I am! I've only just learned the truth about your family." Even as I say it, I'm aware of how terrible an excuse it is. My heart sinks. "I came out here to process it, to figure out what to do. I didn't want to keep it from you any more than Chase would."

"Don't defend him." Emma sneers, but she's too heartbroken to give it any force. "How long has he known about this? How *long* has he known I'm an unwanted *mistake*?"

"That's not true," I whisper. "You're not a—"

"Four days."

The roughened voice comes from behind me, and I twist to Chase, hovering in my doorframe.

His dark stare rises from the floor to Emma. "I've known for four days."

"And how long were you going to keep this to yourself? Wait—stupid me. You confided in Callie. *She* was more important than enlightening me, whose life has been fucked over for years! *Years!*" Emma cries. "And for so long I wondered why! Why was it always me being punished? Why didn't Father ever compliment me for my good grades, or make our birthday parties equal instead of always defer to your preference for a theme? Why, when we turned sixteen, did you get the fancy car when you failed your driving test and I passed? Why why *why*? And now I know." Tears streak down Emma's face, the rivulets curving and pooling against her scars. "Even when I was hurt, mutilated, *raped*, beaten, and lost, Father still wouldn't come to me."

"I did," Chase cuts in, his voice a rasp as he peels from the doorframe and approaches his sister. "I cared. I was there for you. Good grades? I made sure you got the same credit as me and gave you half of whatever Father awarded. Birthdays? I made sure to choose some godawful theme that was neutral for both of us. Pirates and princesses, donuts and sprinkles, goddamned fairy dust and gun powder, whatever the fuck. And that fancy car? You can drive it whenever you want, use my things, stay in my room, sleep in my bed when you were too afraid of your shadow. But it's not enough," he adds as Emma opens her mouth to argue. "I'm aware it'll never be enough, not after what you endured, what Father put you through—what he *locked* you in to change you back into a good, supplicant, docile Virtue. I'm sorry. I'm so sorry and that won't change the truth, either, but Emma..." He lets out an explosive breath. "I didn't want to keep hurting you. I kept this from you because I couldn't be responsible for breaking you, too."

"I'm not a doll who rips or shatters," Emma says, her eyes on fire. "I'd prefer my real story over the hell my life has been any day. You don't get to make that choice for me, Chase. Or Callie, for that matter, who should know what it's like to be protected and shrouded when all you want to do is rebel." She shifts her glare to me. "Yet the people closest to you, the ones who supposedly care about you the most, won't let you."

I step forward. "Emma, I—"

"No. You don't get to change your ways now that I've discovered this secret before you were ready to 'process' it. This is *my* life. *My* choices. *My* family and friendships on the line. And you know what? I don't need either of you."

"Emma, wait," I say.

"Waiting is the worst advice I can take," she bites out. "Just look how far it's gotten you."

I reel back, but Chase storms forward. "Emma, sit down. I love you. I'll always love you regardless of what blood is in your veins. You're my sister. My *twin*."

"I'm not any of those things," she whispers fiercely, her cheeks rising with color. "And it's high time I find out who I am without you, or Father, or the cursed Virtues."

She spins, and I catch Chase's arm before he tries to run her down and keep her here.

He whirls on me, ready for a fight.

"Let her go," I say.

"Never," he snarls.

"Let. Her. Go." My grip tightens on his inner elbow, well

aware that if he wanted to rip from my hold, he would've shaken me off like a horsefly by now. "She needs time. We all do."

"This has gone too far." Chase pulls away, raking his hand through his hair and pacing the room. "Murder. Sex. Blackmail. Stolen privilege. Broken families. Callie, I'm fucking done."

I stay where I am, watching him carefully. "So am I."

"We need to do something. Emma's right—waiting is the worst thing we could do right now."

"Biding our time is never a mistake, especially when it comes to Sabine and your father."

"Then our moments of pondering are finished as of now."

"I agree."

Chase pauses in his movements, eyeing me suspiciously. "You never agree with me."

"Maybe that's the problem." I sigh, bone-weary and desolate. "Everyone around me always gets hurt. Destroyed. Killed. I want it to end, too."

Chase checks his watch, but I don't need the time to understand the pinkish gray skies in the window behind him. He looks up and says, "I'll set up a meeting with the Nobles tonight. We'll finish this."

"We'll get your sister back."

He nods resolutely. "And cause enough questions and instability in the ranks to fracture the societies."

"Are you sure that's what you want?" I study him, aware of the Noble Chase simmering under his skin, the one that's desperate to save a society he wants redeemed.

Chase's shoulders rise and fall with deep, angry breaths. "They've involved my family. My sister. I made a promise to her years ago, when she was recovering from her injuries: she would never be fucked with again. And if she was, I would bring down Hell to protect her. Never again would she be hurt on my watch." His black stare lands on mine. "I refuse to fail a second time. When it comes to choosing between my family and the societies, my family wins every time."

My lips pull into a tentative smile. "I'm glad to hear that."

"Callie. My sweet, misdirected possum." Chase comes up to me, his hands landing on my shoulders and pulling me into a deep, heartfelt kiss. He pulls away, but his lingering study keeps the warmth from the kiss. "That includes you, too."

Emma doesn't return before classes, and I don't expect her to.

Chase left shortly after the confrontation, hoping to catch her at the lake house and succeed in the heart-to-heart I don't think either of them ever allowed themselves to have in all these years of forced distance and inequality.

It's what I hope for, and I check my phone constantly for a text from him, but the only *ping* I get is from Eden, reminding me of our 4:30 AM swim lesson at the rec center, which, if I'm already up and zinging with adrenaline, would be a shame to miss.

I pull on a simple black one-piece bathing suit, then dress in Briarcliff sweats. After burrowing into my winter coat, I shove my uniform into my duffel and leave the silent apartment behind, taking the stairs to the bottom floor, the eerie, red, EXIT lights the only source of illumination for my trip down.

I don't mind, since this type of lighting better reflects my thoughts.

The trek to Briarcliff University's recreational center goes by fast, mostly because I'm immersed in Chase's and my conversation, and the student pathways are deserted. It's chilly, though, frigid and windy, and I'm thankful to hit the heated confines of one of Briarcliff's more modern buildings on the other side of campus.

Motion lights flash on as I head through the single hall-way, making me think Eden either got here much earlier than me or hasn't made it yet. I'm not concerned as I push into the girls' locker room, finding the nearest bench and dumping my bag on it before I strip off my coat.

"What's up, sister?"

My hands freeze at my zipper.

Falyn chills at the end of the row of gym lockers, her arms crossed and her smile wide.

"What are you doing here?" is out before I can tell myself not to ask the obvious question.

"Enjoying the thought of you splashing around like a belly-flopping fish while you try to learn how to swim."

"What makes you think I'm here for that?" I unfreeze, casually stripping my jacket.

"Nice try, possum. Eden and I had a lovely chat." Falyn

uncrosses her arms and strides forward. "She mentioned your ... disability. It all makes sense now, that whole Marco Polo thing you and Ivy had going at the lake when I—"

"—pushed me?"

"I was going to say expedited your initiation. You should thank me. If it weren't for that, we wouldn't be here. Aren't you *proud* of being here?"

Falyn strolls ever closer until she's in my personal space, taking up my viewpoint and assaulting my nose with her powdery, fragrant scent. "Why are you taking swimming lessons, possum? Afraid of another drowning?"

"Ivy was killed in front of my face, so yeah, I'm preparing myself."

Falyn laughs, tucking her hair behind her ear as she draws back. "It's amazing how hard you work to cover your ass, when our princess is dead because of you."

I ignore the jab and respond with a croak, "Ivy didn't deserve to die."

"Your avoidance skills need work. You might as well admit blame."

"Maybe I do," I say hoarsely, "but so should you and every other Virtue who stood by or enabled Sabine to gain so much power over you. You're nothing but a pawn, Falyn, just like I am, and Ivy was. The only difference between you and me is that I know it."

Falyn's eyes grow small. "You think you're so much better? It's because of *you* we're all in this position. You've forced your way into a membership, killed people, *hurt* your closest friends, trash Chase, and yet you're standing here trying to tell me you're the good one? All you do is take and take and *take*. You don't care what happens to me, Violet, Willow, the rest of the Virtues, or even Eden and Emma. All you care about is *you*. You're fine with destroying our livelihoods so long as your dead mom gets some justice. So what? She's a rotten carcass, Callie. She doesn't give a shit what you—"

The slap rings out in the empty locker room.

I stare at my hand, appalled, until I tear my gaze away and notice the blooming red stain on Falyn's cheek. Narrowing my eyes, I close the distance between us. "Don't you talk about my mother."

"You fucking mad bitch!" Falyn spits, holding her cheek and stumbling into the wall of lockers. She keeps her back pressed to the maroon metal, hissing, "You deserve everything that comes your way. And *I* deserve everything I've worked for. I'm not going to let you steal it the way you stole Ivy's life or Chase's future. I'm the princess. *I'm* the future of the Virtues. And when Sabine retires and gives the crown to *me* and not you, I'll make sure you pay for every single mistake you've made by coming here."

I stare at her aghast. "You really believe all this, don't you? That Sabine has your back."

"More so than anybody on *your* side, Callie. Say, why don't you go check on Eden. She might need your help."

I stop my stalk toward her and veer to the entrance of the indoor pool, drowning Falyn's laughter with my heavy, panicked breaths. "Don't ever forget who has the upper hand, Calla Lily Ryan! Sabine will always choose me!"

Bursting through the doors, I scan for Eden, my mind concocting images of her floating face-down in the pool, her black hair twisting and twirling with the mirage of life as her body doesn't breathe.

"Eden?" I call. "*Eden!*"

"I'm here," comes the quiet reply.

I race to the shadowed corner of the rectangular room, the pool's lights reflecting soft ripples across the walls and Eden's slumped form at the bottom of the bleachers.

"Thank God," I breathe when I reach her, plop down next to her. "Are you hurt? Did Falyn do something to you?"

"No." Eden won't turn to me. She hides between the curtains of her hair. "We just talked."

"About what? What did she say, Eden? She's as ambitious as Sabine. I can already tell you anything she said is a lie, a power-play designed to mislead you—"

"Did you really choose Tempest as your soulmate?"

I wasn't expecting that. Pushing my brows together, I answer, "Yeah, but—"

"Really?" Eden raises her head and stares at me head-on. "Chase wasn't enough for you? Getting the most popular guy in school to notice you and ... and have *sex* with you wasn't what you wanted? You had to take him, too?"

"Eden, what are you talking about. I didn't take Tempest, and Chase's attention has hardly been wanted or kind..."

"But it turned you on enough to fuck him. Made *him* interested enough to drop every other girl and pledge himself to you, even when he was pretending to hate you— everyone knew it was a lie, including me. *Especially* me. You know why? Because I notice things. Observing is my special skill, and I can tell when you're depressed, or Emma's anxious, or Ivy is—was—upset. I can read you so well because you're my friend and you've been kind to me when no one else was. But it was all an act, wasn't it? To avenge your mom and now Ivy, to ruin the Virtues ... have you ever really wanted to be my friend?"

"Of course, Eden!" Shock and hurt reverberates in my tone, but Eden doesn't take notice.

"You're lying. If you really were my friend, you'd be able to read me, too. Like when every time Tempest entered the room, I'd freeze and duck my head because I had to hide the blood rushing to my cheeks. Or how overly thankful I was that he deleted all traces of my naked photo. Or that every time you mentioned his name, my breaths would come faster, and I latched onto every word you said about him."

"Eden," I whisper, reaching for her hands, but she pulls them from her lap. "I didn't know. I had no idea you had a crush on him."

"*Crush*." Eden laughs tonelessly. "Is that what you and Chase have? How you define it? I'm in love with him, Callie, and you didn't even notice!"

Straightening, I try to bring feeling back into my face, but it's so numbed, so devoid of blood, I can't tell it to move. *How could I have missed this?* "What I did at the ritual, it means nothing. Chase revoked his soulmate claim in order to sabotage my admission. The only way I could salvage it was to claim another soulmate, and Tempest doesn't have one."

"Neither does James. Why didn't you call out his name?"

I aim for a smile, because that idea is ludicrous. "James

is a masochist who gets off on pain. I couldn't tie myself to someone like that."

"So, you tied yourself to the one guy who's ever been nice to me in the entire school. The *only* guy I've ever noticed and have been working so hard to get him to notice me. How can I do that when he has you now? You don't see it, Callie, but you're beautiful. You're ... you're everything I'm not and you could have anything you wanted, even being a part of Falyn and her crew. Instead, you shackled yourself to me and Emma, the outsiders, the loners. It's starting to come together, now. Why you did that. You were using us."

"No," I practically shout. "You've got it wrong. I love you two. You've been there and helped me, and we've all become closer, because we *like* each other, Eden. I'd never use you and I'd never do this to you on purpose."

"You chose Tempest!" Eden screams. "When I wanted him! He's all I want. That's it. Nothing else. Why would you take that away?"

"Because I didn't know!"

"You never asked!"

I take a breath, trying not to flinch under her fury. I say, softer, "His was the first name that popped into my head, so I spoke it. But that's it, Eden. I swear. There's *nothing* going on between us."

Eden's silent for a time, and I allow the pregnant pause, understanding that the more I try to pry, the further I'll push her away. Because I *do* know her. She *is* my friend, and while I've neglected her in favor of gutting Sabine, I would never take her for granted.

I'm about to tell her that, but she speaks first.

"There's nothing going on between you and me, either."

"Wh ... Eden." I reach for her when she stands but miss. "Please. I don't want you to leave. I am your friend. We need to talk about this."

"Try floating without the pool noodle this time," she barks as she storms barefoot back to the locker room. "With any luck, you'll sink to the bottom."

"Eden!" I cry, horrified, but she's already walked into the locker room and shut the door on our friendship.

27

CALLIE

"They should be here soon," Chase says as he finishes helping me button my shirt. His is a lost cause and he's thrown his blazer over his open white shirt.

It's the next evening, and while Chase and I waited in the Nobles' crypt, we couldn't take our hands off each other. It was a nice reprieve, as selfish as it was, to lose myself in him and pretend my friendships weren't hanging on by a thread.

I'm not a complete asshole, however, and I asked Chase about Emma before he distracted me with his scent and prowess, but he refused to say much, and Emma won't answer my texts or calls. I'm determined to speak to both her *and* Eden tonight, and asked them to meet us at the lake house after this meeting. I need them, and not simply because Chase and I are implementing a new plan. I also miss them. I love them.

Chase strokes my hair back from my face. "While I can appreciate the brain fog I've given you, the Nobles are meeting us here any minute. You might want to find your underwear."

"How many?" I ask as I duck under the pews, spotting my pink thong in the cobwebs. I dig it out.

"The initiates and our barons. As well as Tempest, James, and Rio."

The mention of Tempest makes me flinch, but Chase doesn't see it as I shimmy my underwear back on.

"Don't shake your ass," Chase warns on a growl, "unless you want me to part it and slam into you again."

"Such a Romeo," I mumble, but my core sparks with joy. I manage to temper it with the reminder of how screwed up my life and the life of the people around me have become.

"There's not enough time to approach this gently," I say, turning to face him. "While we wait, Sabine and your father have figured out a thousand different ways to defy us. It's better to amass an army *now*, outnumbering the king and queen and ultimately, outvoting them. They can't kill them all, and even if they tried for ruin, my email is still relevant and out there."

Chase voices his agreement. "The Viscounts don't know about this meeting. The Nobles that are coming, they can be reasoned with. Informed. Their minds changed."

The implications sink in. "How confident are you that they won't betray us?"

"Callie." Chase places his hands on my cheeks. "Your email blast didn't work because you weren't writing to the people who could handle that kind of warped reality, especially if nobody but an anonymous sender was behind it. These new Nobles? They'll listen to you. Hear what you have to say. And then we can decide what to do about Sabine and how best to protect you."

I search his eyes. "I can't ask for something like that. You could lose your position in the society because of this. A society that, if you're not around, won't see how damaged and ignorant they've become."

"Seriously? Callie, what's going on with you? You were so confident the other night."

"That was before…" I close my eyes. "I'm realizing how selfish I've become, asking people to sacrifice so much for me. They shouldn't have to. *You* shouldn't have to."

"Crazy-talk," he says, stroking my cheek. "What other choice do we have, other than you breaking into the temple and finding the binder, Sabine's supposed murder book? Or waiting weeks for DNA results? If I'm not mistaken, these require wide enough gaps of time while we research and wait that could epically fuck us over."

I frown at his opinion so expertly tossed in my face, but his point sticks. "You win. We'll give it a shot. But I'd like you to come with me to your lake house after where I'm meeting Emma and Eden. We all need to talk."

"Hashing out our differences." He squeezes my shoulder with a pained expression. "How grand. Emma still wants to kill us, you know."

"I know," I say on a forlorn exhale.

Shuffling turns our attention to the small corridor

leading into the room, and Tempest appears first. He nods at Chase, but I brace for when his eyes shift to me, unsure of what I'll find there.

Those unwavering, sharp green eyes of his pin me to the floor, but they're steadying. Encouraging. "'Sup, soulmate," he says before draping over one of the pews, both legs spread, and his hands folded between them expectantly.

I flick a glance up at Chase, rigid and immobile beside me. His stare could melt volcanoes, but Tempest isn't affected. I wonder if he has any idea about Eden's feelings for him and what he'd do about it if he did. As much as Eden thinks I wouldn't, I'd shove his balls into his throat if he hurt her.

Chase moves to greet each boy who follows by name. James is next, then Riordan, and a handful of others whose names I don't catch, because of my fixation on Riordan.

His brown eyes don't contain the mysterious depths of Chase's. No, he shows emotion as easily as dropping a towel from his naked form. And he's glaring at me.

My focus skitters to the side as I try to sort through the reasons he would want to throw so much hate at me.

"Gentlemen," Chase says once everybody's seated. Nobody chatted or slapped each other's backs on their way in. And not one commented on Chase's unbuttoned shirt. "I assume you all know why we're here."

"Where's our king?" someone calls from the last pew.

Tempest slams a fist against the wood and stands. "Your prince is here, the king's legacy. That should be enough."

"And what about *her*?" the guy retorts. "Your ex and

Tempest's sloppy seconds. Do you have the same explanation for this chick entering our sacred crypt?"

"In any other circumstance," I say before Chase can decapitate anyone, "it'd be both hilarious and eye-rolling to listen to a freshman whine over cooties in his secret clubhouse, but the fact that you have a flaccid dick and I don't doesn't really help you out here."

A few guys hoot at my gall. I kind of enjoy clapping back. But I still shiver in front of these boys—tapped and initiated to become manipulative, powerful men—and it takes a lot of will-power not to shuffle behind Chase's back and peer around his protective form.

"There's no need for the king to be here," Chase adds, giving me an encouraging smile, "because what we have to say doesn't involve the Nobles of the past."

A few boys tap their feet. Some cross their arms. Chase isn't winning over the room, which is a disconcerting turn of events considering his charismatic air usually commands any space he steps into.

"Get on with it then," someone else says.

Chase's jawline juts out. He narrows his eyes at the idiot who dared to speak, and I wonder if I'm about to witness a vicious Noble punishment.

No. Chase wants to change things.

"I wrote the email," I pipe up, shifting a tiny bit forward, away from the hearth of skulls and towards some very alive, gnashing teeth.

"We know," James drawls. "It wasn't too difficult to put two-and-two together, possum. We didn't come down here for that big reveal. What we're truly interested in is *why* you fucking outed us to the entire school, and everyone associated with it, and now expect us to listen to your cunty mouth—"

"Then you might be surprised to know I was standing behind her the entire time she wrote it," Chase says, but it's a whisper. A purred warning for James to close his mouth before Chase fists it closed.

James shuts up.

I give a small, meaningful smile to Chase, then turn back to the room. "Chase shouldn't have to defend me. You've all read the email, and yeah, you're pissed I gave a public name to all the inexplicable *shit* that goes on at Briarcliff. I'll tell you my reasons. These secrets have turned some of you into accomplices. Ignorant bystanders. Killers. Your counterparts, these soulmates of yours, are being abused under—"

"You said she's dead, you fucking liar."

My speech shrivels in my throat. It doesn't take me long to locate the source of the spiteful voice. Riordan.

Chase raises his hand to his friend. "Let her speak."

Riordan stands, shoving his hands into his slacks' pockets, but it does nothing to relax his posture. "How am I supposed to sit here and listen to you parrot the same lies you wrote when I know for a fact Ivy isn't dead?"

"Riordan," I plead. "She is. I saw it."

"We saw it," Chase adds quietly. "I'm sorry, buddy. She died in Callie's arms."

"*Not true*," Riordan spits. He pulls out his phone. "I have a message from her last night. She went home because her mom's sick, and you assholes are standing up there with this propaganda *bull*shit because you want the society for your-selves." Riordan focuses on Chase. "It's easy to read the room when you saunter in, bro. You despise your father, laugh at our rules, and defy our nature like you're some kind of lost rebel here to expose the relics of this member-ship. *We* are not artifacts. The Noble maxim isn't some lost language you have to re-translate and sell to new members. I don't want to listen to you spout off about changing our brand when, you know what? It's really fucking awesome already. I'm graduating with Ivy. I'm marrying my soulmate and taking the position the king has offered me as soon as I finish at Yale, which I'm gonna fucking sail through, too. Using the tools the Nobles have given me—"

"Like advanced copies to the exams?" I cut in, unable to listen to his false tirade. "Fake grades? A doctored GPA? How very deserving you are."

Riordan loudly blows air through his nose. "Leave, bitch, before I—"

"Touch her, and I'll smack your head against that bench and taxidermy it for our fireplace over there while you're still fucking screaming at me to stop."

A few boys nearby gulp. I, for one, hold steady, but I don't enjoy the look on Chase's face that accompanies his statement. This is getting way out of control.

I rest a hand on Chase's arm, and say softly into the silent room, "Ivy's dead, Riordan. Sabine killed her. Every-thing I wrote in that email is true. And if you don't believe me, believe Chase. He's never lied to you, has he?"

"I have her voicemail," Riordan defends instead of

answering. But his voice grates. His chin trembles.

"Then you hear the fear in her when she talked about her mom," I say. "Her voice shook, didn't it? Her sentences trailed off, her words turned to whispers ... the Ivy I know bursts with sound and talks so fast, she has trouble catching her breath. She speaks before thinking and shares information because she genuinely thinks she's doing Briarcliff a favor when she gives in to gossip and spreads the latest."

Riordan's brows shadow his eyes, but he doesn't interrupt.

"And when it comes to her family, she confides to her closest friends. And before me, there was you. She was forced to keep a lot from me because of the societies, but she'd never keep anything from you. Would she?"

"She said she'd just heard the news about her mom," Riordan says, his tone rough. "In her voicemail. She said she was surprised by it."

"Then you should find her message suspicious, because when she's truly upset, when something *really* shakes her up and takes her by surprise, she swears. She cusses like a goddamned sailor." My voice shakes. My hands tremble at my sides. "She didn't do any of that in her message to you, did she? Riordan, she was coerced into saying those lies to you."

A deep line forms between Riordan's brows. His mouth drops open, then goes slack before his keening roar disrupts the room.

"Jesus!" James shouts before he grabs his friend, helping him sit down. "C'mon man, you can't honestly believe the possum. Sack up. Ivy's chilling with her parents. These are more lies crafted by a bored prince who doesn't want to be a prince anymore."

"James," Chase grinds out. "What the fuck are you doing?"

James lifts his head. "Putting it out there that you have your own motives in play and don't give a fuck about the rest of us."

"You're a fucking douchebag. You know how much I've sacrificed to stand where I am today."

"Yeah? And I know the spoiled legacy living inside you that loves to create nonsense and chaos—"

"I believe him," Riordan chokes out.

All eyes turn to him.

"I believe Chase. Our prince. My friend. And I believe the possum. Ivy liked her. Trusted her."

"I'm with him, too," another boy pipes in.

"Me, too," says another.

"Oh, yeah." Tempest raises a wry hand, as if his opinion was ever in question. "Then there's me. The soulmate."

"Guys." James drifts away from Riordan and appeals to the room. "Come on. You're taking the word of some chick who hasn't been here two semesters over my suspicions?"

"About that," I say, and this time, my step forward is sure. "One thing I left out in the email, and a fact I'm positive your *suspicious nature* will be interested in. Sabine isn't the true heir of the Virtues. None of the Harringtons are ... or were." I arch a brow. "But I bet you knew that, didn't you?"

James rears back and sneers, "I don't care to know shit about you, possum."

"Listen to her, cocksucker," Chase warns, then gestures for me to continue.

"You're looking at your true queen." I keep walking, my steps loud among the new, shocked hush befalling the room, until I'm all the way in James's face. "My murdered mother was the last descendent of Rose Briar before I came along. Then, when she was nineteen, well, I *came along*. I'm the last living bloodline of the original Virtue queen, so how about you sit the fuck down and listen to your future royals?"

"That was exhilarating," I say as we tumble into the lake house. "Do you think we swayed enough of them?"

He strips off his coat, tossing it on the couch, his open shirttails fluttering with his movements as he strides into the kitchen.

"We've introduced important questions," he says. "Next time Sabine and my father address them, the subject of her legitimacy will come up. The key is not giving her enough time to formulate a plan. When she meets with the Virtues tomorrow, I'll have the Nobles that are with us accompany them. We'll out her. No more secrets. The new generation will want answers."

As he heads to the coffee maker, I ask, "The rules of monarchy are steadfast in the Nobles, but I don't think they ever were in the Virtues. Maybe at face value, to keep the Nobles in the dark, but that's it. Are questions enough to kick her out?" I gesture absently. "We're waiting on DNA results, but that could take a while, and until I can prove Mom's murder..."

"Sabine's ensured a mindfuck kind of loyalty from her Virtues," Chase agrees, "who were left out of this meeting for a reason. But my Nobles still have influence. They can convince a few girls."

"That's looking way too far in the future," I counter, then collapse on the couch.

Chase tips his face to the ceiling, showcasing the purple hollows under his eyes. "All we want right now is uncertainty. Like any unrest, there will be factions—those for you and those for Sabine, but that's where Ivy becomes the tipping point in this war."

"Her death shouldn't be like this." Changing my mind, I push of the couch and go to him. "Used as a wager. Are you sure I can't just steal the binder, involve the police, and arrest Sabine for murder? We *saw* her do it, Chase."

"Your hospital transcripts." Chase lays a hand on my arm when I reach him, but thankfully doesn't expand on the matter. He doesn't have to. I'm the least credible eyewitness there is, and Chase has proven his bias when it comes to me. "The societies have operated underground for centuries. Let me try to fuck her over underground, too. It might cause Sabine to make a public mistake."

I fold my hand on his. "Us. Let *us* try."

"Yes." He squeezes. "Together."

"We did all we could in there," I say. Chase places two steaming mugs in our hands before we head into the den. "I gave them my version of events. Did you see their faces when I told them about Noble alumni sneaking onto the university to have sex with the Virtuous princesses and countless other girls? They didn't know. I can't *believe* none of them knew."

Chase goes rigid beside me. His teeth must be cracking under the pressure, but by some miracle, he restrains himself from lashing out with what he must understand is a pointless, too-late temper. He sits.

I nestle closer, holding my mug with two hands while I attempt to soften him with my presence and a reminder that it's in the past. "We won't allow Sabine to hurt Emma anymore," I say to Chase. "When Emma gets here, we'll lay it all out. We haven't been communicating well with our friends, you and me. It's taken too long to realize that. It has to be rectified tonight." I sip my coffee, my teeth clanking against the ceramic. "I won't let them leave until we work through this."

Chase barely blinks in response.

"This is why," I say, moving to squeeze his free hand. When I find it unresponsive, I repeat, "*This* is why we need the new generation of Nobles on our side. I'm hoping we did that tonight, and the next time Sabine tries to walk into a room with them, they'll confront her. Throw Baby Briar's birth certificate in her face. Demand she give them reasons. Maybe even tonight, they'll go to their Virtue soulmates and tell them everything they've learned."

"It's a damn good start," Chase grits out. "And farther

than I've ever gotten in changing their views. Listening to you..." Chase rasps but stares vacantly at a spot in front of him. "Hearing it from your lips, it was an entirely new level. And Father ... Father *knowing* about this and marrying the bitch anyway, I—fuck, I need to hit something. Kill something. If this scheme we've started doesn't work, I'll strangle her myself. She's not collecting any more girls. She's not touching my sister again."

I believe him. I'm so confident in his vow, my grip on his wrist turns solid. "There's been enough murder. Let's see where tonight goes, first. And the press could still get involved. My email was opened by enough outsiders that it could get things rolling, too. We haven't given it a whole lot of time. Sabine could be fucked already, inside and out. Can't we pour some whiskey in these coffees to celebrate?" I smile, though it's tight at the edges. "I think I saw a bar cart in your dad's study."

Chase raises his mug in a dry salute and pushes off the couch.

I stand with him. "You said it yourself. Confronting her doesn't work. And Sabine plans for betrayal too much to ever take her by surprise. But creating uncertainty? Having the future Noble society turn against her and demand she abdicate? That's something. They know about the trafficking now, the prostitution and grooming of little girls— that besmirches every single value even Thorne Briar originally created."

I follow Chase down the stairs, ruminating on my words and well aware I've started to ramble. I'm too nervous about Emma and Eden to sit and wait for them to arrive. "Sabine's one true fear is losing control of the Virtues. Each drop of uncertainty counts."

"We've planted seeds of doubt," Chase says, and I stare at a spot between his coiled shoulder blades as we descend. "But there might not be enough time to let it fester."

We reach the bottom, and Chase spins and takes me by surprise when I'm enveloped in a crushing embrace. "I don't know if what we did will keep you safe."

"Sabine wouldn't touch me. Not with the email, and now the Nobles. The old men in that brotherhood have a lot to answer for, too."

"You're staying at the lake house until I'm sure Sabine will stand down."

I lift my head. "Don't you think that's overkill? Sabine hasn't touched me since ... since Ivy. She's even made me a Virtue."

He sighs, then kisses my forehead. "It makes me all the more suspicious. I hate that you have to suffer."

I squeeze his waist. "You and your sister have been suffering under her rule long before I came along."

Chase turns his head to stare down the long, dark hall-way. Curious, I follow his gaze. "What's down there?"

"Nothing important," he murmurs, then takes my hand. "Come on."

We step into Daniel Stone's office, that eerie, blue aquarium light traveling over my skin the farther he draws me in. Bottles rattle as Chase sorts through the bar cart, but I can't take my eyes off those white, lethal specks traveling silently through ultra-violet water.

"Got it." An amber bottle catches the preternatural

shine as he holds it up. He turns, saying, "Father's best Macallan."

I tear my gaze off the floating creatures in time to see Chase's eyes sharpen. He shoots forward. *"Callie—!"*

Rough, thick fabric covers my head. Air goes stagnant in my mouth before I can scream.

28

CALLIE

Blinded, I can only feel it when arms wrap around me, so tight it's like being squeezed by a python. I gasp, but only manage to suck in cloth.

I choke on Chase's name.

"Get your *fucking* hands off her!" Chase roars.

Ethereal, purple light flickers through the bag—no, it's soft and thick like a cloak—thrown over my head. Daniel Stone's office barely gave me enough light when I had 20/20 vision. Now, I'm certifiably blind.

But I can struggle.

I throw a leg back, aiming for a crotch, but my captor pitches me to the side, and I slam into the wall with a *thump* of impact.

"*You motherfucker!*" Chase yells. A rip of fabric follows. The smack of a fist on skin. A yelp of pain. "You want to take her? I dare you."

"Follow the rules, you asshole!"

James?

My vision's scattered, but my hearing's on point when I sit, my hands immediately going to the cloak wrapped around my face.

A cold, boney vise stops me.

I work up to a scream—

"One sound," a voice whispers into my ear. *Falyn.* "Just one, and I won't hesitate to toss you into the lake again."

I stiffen under her hold on both my wrists, but don't so much as whimper when she pulls me to stand, the blinding cloak still in place.

The fight continues somewhere to my right, Chase and James, arguing, cursing, slamming each other into furniture.

"It was you!" Chase roars.

Scant light, then ripples of shadow, seep into the fabric over my eyes as Chase shouts, "You knocked me out, dragged me from my room, and brought me to Sabine. Why? Did you know she was going to kill Ivy that night? You want to betray me, fine. But Rio? The guy you love like a fucking *brother*? You let his soulmate *die*."

"Sabine has the right idea," James retorts. A muffled grunt follows his words, buffered by another swipe from Chase. "She learns weaknesses and exploits them until her chicks do whatever she says. Then, she deploys her little dollies out into the world, willing to do her every bidding. Why wouldn't I want to support that? I wish the Nobles would follow suit. They were, actually, until you decided to find a voice and side with that bitch possum over there. Do you have any idea what we could've accomplished?"

"And what do you think Sabine's succeeded in?" Chase's response comes out as a dangerous whisper.

"A First Lady, for one," James spits. "When Sabine calls, that chick does whatever Sabine wants."

"Because she was probably abused, molested, and blackmailed for years, you son of a bitch."

"Sabine has these girls tying themselves to men of influence, and those men turn into their asshole goons. So, we either gotta join her, or become the puppets to her dolls. And I ain't turning into one of those. I'm giving you one last chance, bro."

"She left my sister to die! She murdered Ivy, and had Callie's mom killed!" Chase shouts. "Sabine is a fucking psychopath. We need to stop her, not join her!"

"Suit yourself," James says, and a sickening, wet *crunch* follows.

"What was that?" I cry out, stepping forward, but Falyn holds me back. "Chase? *Chase?*"

James says offhand, "Knock the bitch out, too."

I don't hear the *thwack* when it comes to the side of my head.

But I do see the black.

⁂

I'm enveloped in a dark, warm, velvet blanket, and a gentle caress brushes my cheek.

I smile.

"Chase?" I murmur, arching toward the tickle of sweetness.

A gentle lapping drifts into my ears, its lulling tune allowing me to drift away into a relaxing, calming dream, where I do nothing but float...

Wait, float?

I'm floating.

My eyes pop wide, and I spear up, but the motion sends the surface I'm lying on tipping violently to the left, then to the right, every sharp dive causing a dangerous wetness to creep into the hollows of the—boat.

"Oh my God."

My desperate whisper doesn't reach the shore.

I lift my head, scanning and blinking wildly, but any small movement unbalances the boat in a way that makes my heart thump, thud, *crash* into my ears.

And my hands are tied behind my back.

My legs shoot straight out, stuck in a type of foot harness that keeps rowers stable.

Rowers. I'm in a scull. It's nothing but a thin strip of white in the black of the lake, and I bob helplessly along with it, my butt fitted into the rower's seat with tiny wheels underneath that move with my every tremble.

I'm not stable. I'm not safe.

True fear grips my insides.

"There you are. Our newest Virtue. Over here!"

Sabine's voice floats from the docks of the boathouse, and my eyes dart toward the sound. She's not far, maybe two yards away, but for a person who's had only a handful of swimming lessons?

It's an impossible distance.

Her smile under the single lamplight crosses the space

between us, seeping into my very airways. "How was your nap, darling?"

Every movement in my expression brings a shot of pain to my right temple. A feeling like dry, cracked paint sticks to every pore.

The dried blood cracks into a million tiny fractures on my face when I voice a guttural, angry scream at her in response.

"Now, now," Sabine trills, her long, golden cloak sparking against the night like a beacon I will never drift toward. "Don't lose your voice so early on in our game."

"Murderer!" I scream, my voice echoing through the quiet bank of trees. "You can kill me, drown me if you want to, but that won't change what I've already done. Everyone knows, Sabine," I bluff. "You tried to make me a Virtue to silence me, but the Virtues who broke from your rule won't stand for your deceit. The Nobles you haven't managed to stick in your pockets will talk to their parents and friends. Then those parents and friends will talk to the *press*. The police. You'll make national news by the weekend."

Sabine chuckles. "Please. You think I'm worried about your little team of avengers and your pathetic attempts at out-maneuvering me? Both Emma and Eden tried before and failed. Dear Emma was willing to lose her life, and her family, for her cause. What makes you think you'll succeed in her place?"

"Because I have the blood you're desperate for," I seethe. "And the legacy prince who will lead the Nobles. You may have manipulated his father, but you failed at bringing him to your side."

"On that, you and I agree." Sabine lifts a hand, gesturing behind her to the boat bay. "James, dear, can you bring out our second problem? I believe Callie needs a slight push in the right direction."

Sabine turns back to me, her face an expressionless mask, her beauty both wasted and wanton as she stands on the Briarcliff dock in the dead of winter as she guides the teenagers she's worked years to coerce into her waiting hands.

"You killed my best friend," I continue. "For *nothing*. I'll never bend to your wishes or do your bidding. Ever!"

"Hold that thought, dear." Sabine clucks her tongue into the shadows, as if calling her most trustful canine, and in a way, she is.

James comes out of the darkness, dragging a furious, struggling Chase down to the end of the dock.

My heart hurls itself into my throat when Chase comes under the paltry light, his black, Noble cloak billowing behind him. A breeze hits the hem, throwing it up into the air, and I notice his hands bound behind his back, just like me.

But unlike me, he's gagged. As he comes closer, I make out the Briarcliff colors on the tie shoved between his teeth.

His eyes are frantic when they land on mine. Stretched and urgent.

Violent shivers overtake my body, as if the fear upon seeing him adds to the cold of being left out at sea, but I keep my back straight. My hands clenched.

I'm confident if Chase is pushed into the lake as some

kind of threat to me, he'll untie himself. He'll hold his breath and break the surface easily.

This is his lake. He has to.

"I'm feeling rather benevolent after losing another princess so suddenly," Sabine says, her voice soft but her gaze hard as she follows Chase's reluctant path to the edge. "I'm giving you one last opening, Calla Lily. You're one of us now, so you have a rare choice. Stand by my side. Join me in my efforts to continue my Virtue reign, or..." Sabine glances at the water surrounding me. She shrugs.

"You wouldn't," I say.

Sabine smiles. "Are you still underestimating me, child? I'm fully aware you can't swim."

I keep the shock from rippling across my face. "You can't hurt me—my accusations are too public. If anything happens to me, it'll all point to you."

"Yes, well, you're very distraught, dear girl. After writing an unsubstantiated email of that nature, then being threatened with expulsion by your Chancellor, goodness. You've about reached the end of your rope. And with your past... do you know I have a camera recording of you in a New York City intersection with Lynda Meyer's newborn? You rushed into traffic, Calla Lily. You tried to *kill* that baby. If it weren't for that man behind you..." Sabine *tsks*. "There were so many warnings, yet the guardians in your life refused to see them. They wanted you to be good. They were desperate for you to be okay. You'd suffered so much already, what with walking in on your dead mother. Yet, they really should've known you were a danger to Blair. I have eyewitness accounts, too."

"I never tried to hurt Blair! You'll answer for my mother!" I scream, jerking forward, her accusations swirling into a wrathful tornado in my head, my words collapsing into fragments, the people I love breaking to pieces.

The boat tips dangerously, and I freeze.

My mind tells me it's over—I'm restrained in a boat, and Chase is slammed to his knees by his supposed friend. Sabine's won. I'll die here tonight as the villain, the source for all the wrong seeping into Briarcliff University, yet it will fester long after I'm gone.

Except, my heart won't concede.

"You need me!" I shout, my voice amplified by the lake. "You can't let me die."

"I killed your mother, didn't I? Blood heirs didn't matter to me then. Why should it matter now? Falyn, dear, go out and assist our poor Callie."

Falyn appears from the second boat bay, her tall, honed body clad in Briarcliff's unisuit. Her rower's knee socks pad silently while holding a scull above her shoulders, its shadow above her head doing nothing to obscure the enticement in her eyes as she locks them with mine.

"Think about this," I say to her, aiming for calm. "Falyn, think about what you're about to do."

Falyn replies, "You're not the queen of the Virtues. I'm here to ensure you never will be."

Chase moans something under his gag, guttural and violent. Falyn tosses a smile James's way but ignores the struggling beast he restrains.

The scull lands in the water. Falyn sets up her oars, then

slips in. She pushes off the dock with a silent, deadly curve. Aiming for me.

My eyes dart from her to Sabine. "You can't! You won't. There's no one left for you. If you end my bloodline, you'll end yours, too. Piper's dead. Addisyn isn't eligible to inherit the society because of her crime against her sister. You're left vulnerable, aren't you? You need me. You need me on your side to keep your influence!"

Sabine stills, the water lapping underneath the dock amplifying in the silence.

"The societies follow monarchy rules," I continue. "As much as you've tried to break them. You're out in the open, without daughters, without heirs. Without me, you'll have no claim to the Virtues. *None.*"

Sabine's lips part on my last sentence. "My Virtuous girls will never go against me."

"It doesn't matter what they do." I break off to track Falyn's oars swishing into the water, gaining on me. I go back to Sabine. "The Virtues didn't write the original oaths. The Nobles did. *They* will take control once they find out what you've done to me and their prince. And they'll dispose of you as easily as Daniel Stone will."

"My dear, have you not been listening? It isn't *me* who will end the Noble legacy." She tips her head and smiles. "It's you."

My face grows stiff. Stone cold. I whisper, through numbed lips, "No."

Sabine lowers her chin. Falyn's scull knocks against mine. She takes hold of my hull.

"Don't do this—" I plead with Falyn, but a sharp movement brings my attention back to the dock.

Sabine laughs. "You're beside yourself. I can understand, after what your broken mind has made you endure. Ranting about secret societies. Scaring the children with the myth of a sex ring on school grounds. Traumatizing parents with your hallucinations. This time, it's not merely your stepfather you've made suffer. Your delusions have become too much. You're *hurting* people, dear child. Blair. Sylvie. Ivy. You've experienced so much grief, have ruined too many lives, and you're desperate to end your time here on Earth and join your mother. However..." She pauses. "Your selfish nature won't let you die alone, now will it? You'd never leave Chase, your true soulmate, behind."

My breaths stutter out of my mouth. Tempest. *Where's Tempest?* And Eden and Emma? They could've been upstairs in the lake house when Chase and I were taken...

"Where are my friends? What did you do to Eden and Emma?"

My frantic exhales are the only sound in this cold, quiet lake. Even Falyn is motionless, her spindly fingers curled against my scull in wait.

"You kill the poor boy first," Sabine continues, ignoring my question. "Then, you row out to the middle of the lake and capsize your boat." Sabine's eyes widen. "That's the kind of news that will overshadow a fragile, broken girl's paranoid rambling, don't you agree?"

My breathing turns into hyperventilating. "Ivy's pretend vacation will have to end soon. When she doesn't show—"

"Oh, you killed her, too, and buried her body in the

woods. A sad little text message from your phone will admit to all that."

"Monster," I whisper, but Sabine hears, because she slowly, methodically, grins.

Sabine reaches into her cloak, and a silver shine catches against the moonlight.

She holds the dagger high. "I believe your DNA is already on this."

"*NO!*" My terrorized yell grows in sound, shattering like moonlit shards across the rippling lake.

A sickening hurricane builds in my chest, ready to burst out of my lungs—

"Callie!"

My terrified gaze turns to Chase. He's wrestled out of the gag, the tie hanging around his neck like a noose. "Howard Mason! Howard Mason is your father!"

Sabine freezes mid-arc.

"Wh-wh—?" I try to respond, but I'm absorbing the winter cold, my words coming out in shivers of sound.

"Security's bound to check the boathouse soon." Sabine jerks her chin at Falyn. "Tip her over, and the title of princess is yours, along with Tempest Callahan as your new soulmate. You'll be the most idolized couple on campus and beyond, sweet girl."

Falyn reaches behind me and pulls the knot holding my wrists, then pulls my feet from the shoes.

"Don't do this—she's manipulating you!" I gasp, wrestling my arms free to try and grab Falyn. She ducks, and I'm too off balance to try again. "She did it to Ivy, to Emma, to her own daughter, and she's disposed of them all.

What makes you think you aren't disposable, too? Falyn, please. Please! *Don't*—"

Nothing else I want to say matters, because the last thing I see is the swing of Sabine's knife into Chase's chest before lake water drowns my screams.

29

CALLIE

*L*et yourself sink a little lower into the water, Callie. Then *spread out your arms, your legs. That's it. Relax...*
  Float.

Float up....

Eden's wry, unhurried teachings whistle in my ears as my eyes bulge open, searching my watery grave.

Her voice comes back. *There's no time to schedule you in for a second drowning. So, hold on to that boat and KICK.*

My arms shoot up and swipe for the capsized scull, my knuckles knocking against the moving seat on the way back down. I only have time for a second attempt before I sink too deep, and I put all my effort, all my frantic kicks, into stretching my body and curling my hands around the wooden seat inside the hull.

Then, in one death-defying, most important push-up of my life, my face breaks through the water, but beneath the upturned boat.

Holding onto the seat pulls the scull in deeper and it slams against my head. In a desperate maneuver, I change my grip to the outer edges of the boat, my feet flailing.

I'm cold. It feels like my blood is solidifying under my skin.

This isn't like my Thanksgiving dunk. This is so, so, *so* much worse.

It's impossible to last very long in these temperatures. Yet, somehow, I have to move.

Kick. Kick. KICK, Eden screams in my head.

I do.

My iced-over legs spear out and in, but I have no idea if I'm moving. I have to get out from under. I have to get to Chase.

No. I have to stay where I am until I'm sure Sabine, Falyn, and James are gone.

A trembling whimper leaves my throat, but I count to five, then ten. After that, I convince myself that dunking my head one more time—just *one more time*—won't be so bad. I'll hold my breath and come out on the other side. It's that easy.

Eden, Ivy, Emma, please be with me.

I take a deep breath and sink.

My fingers slip against the scull, screeching against the fiberglass. I cry out underwater when I have to loosen a hand, then splash through the surface on a gasping breath that escapes my mouth in clouds.

But there can only be clouds where there's air.

I've made it! I'm on the other side!

I start curving my arms around the smooth curve of the

boat before scanning for Sabine. I slip twice, lose my grip once, but at last, I crawl up enough so only a third of my body is still in the water.

And I stare straight ahead.

The dock is deserted, the tall lamps at the end casting fading, golden halos over a slumped, still form.

"Chase," I whisper, then, "CHASE!"

I paddle furiously, using numbed, stiff fingers that no longer listen to commands, but my arms sure do. I kick uselessly, then finally find the clumsy rhythm Eden had me practice with a pool noodle that gets me moving in the direction I need, with the help of the lake's gentle current.

I have no sense of time but know that I'm cold. Covered in winter water. Growing snowflakes that give off frostbitten sparkles under the sleepy, lowering moon, but Chase is dying.

Dying. Not dead. He can't be dead.

"Chase!" I try again, but he doesn't twitch or make a sound.

I kick up enough water that it arcs over my body and into my eyes, but I get closer. Time ticks down, but picturing Chase's blood spilling onto the wood acts as the perfect impetus to keep my exhausted limbs submerged and kicking.

When the scull bumps against the dock, I slide back into the water, clinging to the dock and shuffling to the ladder with a shaking, trembling grip.

The instant I'm on the dock, I launch myself at Chase and drop to my knees beside him.

"Chase," I whisper through bloodless, frozen lips. "Can you hear me?"

He doesn't respond. I don't waste time searching his face, instead looking for the wound. My hands are white—too white—and I can't feel anything. I have to squint. My jaw slams shut with the amount of effort I'm putting into moving him onto his back, lifting fabric and probing skin.

Move. *Move, damn it!*

Blood seeps through the gaps between my fingers when I reach his stomach. Gasping, crying, I press into it, staunching the flow.

"What the...?"

I whip my head to the sound. *"Call 9-1-1!"*

The boy, dressed in his rowing training gear, gapes from the boat house.

"*Move*, damn it!" I scream. "Call an ambulance, or I will throw this oar like a javelin into your face!"

His duffel drops to his feet. He scampers into the boathouse.

I turn back to Chase, droplets from the tips of my hair becoming teardrops on his pale, bloodless face. "You're okay. We're going to be okay."

My jaw won't stop shaking. My body won't stop shivering.

But I won't stop.

I bend my forehead to his, and I hold on.

30

CALLIE

S oft *beeps* follow the tread of footsteps and gentle hands lift my arm, turn it, then set it delicately on my stomach.

My eyes slowly open, a burst of white solidifying into walls, a door, and someone snoozing in a chair.

I cough at the sudden dryness in my throat and attempt to lift onto my elbows.

The person—Eden—cracks an eye open, then shoots awake and rushes to my side.

"You're okay," I mumble. "I thought Sabine..."

Eden rolls her eyes as she grabs my hand. "Willow and Violet make awful bodyguards, and are even worse at researching their victims. They shoved us into this basement room in the lake house that Emma is all-too-familiar with. She showed me the key she'd hidden away when she was ... stuck there ... to sneak out."

While relief sinks wonderfully into my bones at the

news that Emma's okay, too, my short-term memory warps into a nightmare, and my heart picks up an erratic, panicked beat.

"Where...?" I succumb to another fit of coughs.

A plastic cup with a straw appears in front of me. "Drink this. But slowly."

Grateful, I clutch at the cup and bring it to my lips but pause after the first sip.

Tubes hang out of my left hand, and I stare at them in confusion.

"You're in the hospital," Eden explains. "EMTs found you and Chase at the boathouse docks unconscious. You were severely hypothermic. Any longer and..." Eden drags her gaze from mine. "Anyway, you're gonna be okay. You just need to rest."

Eden's explanation brings vivid snapshots of Chase lying at the end of the dock, blood pooling at his middle. Of me, bending over him, screaming.

I lift my hands, looking for his blood on my fingers, dried into my cuticles, but there's none. "What—is he—is Chase—?" I can't say it. I can't.

"He's here." But Eden chews on her lower lip and doesn't elaborate.

I push the water cup at Eden, then fumble for my sheets.

"Nope. No way, Callie. You're staying here." She presses a hand against my shoulder, keeping me down.

"I need to see him."

"I know, but you can't."

"I'm *going* to see him." My voice scratches against the

vowels, but I want to be by Chase's side more than I want water.

"You can't, Callie."

"I *will.*"

"They won't let you!" Eden cries, using both hands to pin me down. Her face is inches from mine. "Emma said she'd come up to see you as soon as you were awake. I'll go get her. You can ask her about Chase."

"But—"

"I mean it, Callie. Keep your ass in that bed or else I'll explain your hysterics to the nurses and have you restrained."

My eyes widen.

"I'm sorry," Eden says, softer. "But it's for your own good. You can't be with him."

Eden steps back from the bed, her form fading as she moves to the door, but I don't think it's from distance. My blinks are heavier, the periods of blindness longer, and soon, I succumb to a medically induced sleep.

***

"Callie? Can you wake up for me?"

I stir at the soft, masculine tone, turning my head toward the sound. Ahmar's kind brown eyes flicker through my slitted vision.

"Hey, kiddo. Nice to see you," he says, slipping his hand under mine and squeezing.

I smack my lips together, trying to speak.

Ahmar's answer is to shove a straw between my lips, and

I suck in the cool water on instinct. Then I shove the straw out with my tongue. "Chase."

"He's alive," he supplies. "Not doing well but breathing. His family is with him now."

"Sabine ... she can't—don't let her see him."

Ahmar's lips turn down. "She's not with them. She didn't think it'd be proper, under the ... circumstances."

Though my mind is foggy with cotton clouds, I don't miss the undercurrent in his tone. "Does everyone think it was me? That I hurt him?"

He gives a tight nod. "Sabine and Daniel Stone have given statements that your obsession with Sabine after her daughter was killed rose to concerning levels. You accused her of—being a queen of the Virtues? Do I have that right? And tried to take away her title by ... killing her future stepson? Calla, is any of this resonating with you?"

"Fuck," I whisper, my eyes going damp. My restraints don't let me wipe the building tears away.

Ahmar stares so hard at me, I can feel his desperate study within the deep trenches of my heart. As if the answers for what happened last night are written on my skin.

He hesitates, then says, "I'm gonna say this quick, because I—it's difficult. There was a note in your room, written by you, explaining how your obsession was too much for you to bear, and you couldn't handle it anymore. The same people who got to your mom were coming for you. Secret societies want to murder you just like they killed your mom. Chancellor Marron is one of their leaders, in cahoots with Sabine Harrington and Daniel Stone, and they all want you dead. You also drew a map where police could find Ivy's unmarked grave. You killed her to spare her suffering at the hands of the same society that's torturing you—"

"Stop," I whisper.

"I can't." Ahmar's voice cracks. "The police are outside waiting for you to be lucid enough for questioning. Your father and I are doing everything we can to explain you'd never write such a thing, never mind hurt your best friend, but they have all this evidence, all this documentation, proving you're mentally unsound. And this Daniel Stone guy is hellbent on pinning his son's attack on you. He's involved every top official he can think of to bring you down. I ... Jesus, Callie. He's leveraging his kid's near-death to give his accusations extra ammo. It's sickening."

"It'll be okay. When Chase wakes up, he'll explain—"

"*If*, Callie. It's a very real *if*." Ahmar's eyes go damp. He squeezes my hand.

"I tried to stop it," I choke out. "I couldn't—I tried to swim to him in time, but I was so scared. I hid under the boat for too long. He's bleeding out on the docks, and I'm floating three feet away, and I *still* couldn't get there—"

"Sweetie. Shh." Ahmar rests his forearms on the bed, cupping my hand in both of his.

I blink. "This isn't making sense to you, is it? I'm trying to explain, but I'm frightening you."

"This whole fucking thing is frightening to me, which is why this is how it's gonna go: I'll go out there and tell the cops you're still out of it. I have a lawyer friend on her way, and your dad and Lynda are coming, too."

I lift my head from the pillow. "Dad? Lynda? That's good! They know all about the Nobles and Virtues. They can help explain."

"They've already told me everything."

My neck strains as I try to raise myself higher, but my hands and feet are tied securely. "They have? You know?"

Ahmar offers another squeeze. He says somberly, "I do. Yes."

"Then the police can stop looking at me. They can turn to Sabine and Daniel instead. There's an entire underground worth of lies and deceit—I can give you names. I'll give you all of them, if it means—"

"Baby girl." I'm suddenly subjected to Ahmar's sorrowful, defeated gaze. "Lynda won't go on the record. She and Pete confessed to me because I was out of my mind. I thought you'd lost it, that this was the end for you. And I didn't do enough to help you, to stop this. That I failed your momma."

I try to rise again. "Ahmar, no."

"I'm educated, now." Ahmar sniffs hard, swallowing his emotion. "About this place and the players. And once you're given the physical okay, you're coming home with me and I'm going to fight for you until the Stones' Armageddon ends. Kiddo, I believe you. I believe you, and I'm sorry that we can't do more to prove it."

"They're pinning Ivy's murder on me."

Ahmar bows his head. "They're doing a lot more than that, sweetie."

"Then Dad has to speak the truth. He won't let me rot in prison. He can't. I'm—"

When Ahmar angles his head to meet my stare, my words die in my throat.

There's me, and then there's Blair and Lynda.

And the small detail of me accusing him and allowing *him* to rot in prison.

The squeamishness returns, the nausea and slime of not being blood-related to any of them. Of not being needed.

Except, there's Ahmar. No blood exists between us, yet he's my uncle, no question.

At the thought of him, an idea pops into my head regarding the blood I *do* share. "Check my DNA."

Ahmar frowns. "Huh?"

"My DNA," I repeat. "Check it against Chancellor Marron's."

"What are you talking about...?" Realization hits, his forehead smoothing. "No fucking way."

"He was a teacher when Mom went here. They had an affair. I..." I take a breath, weighing my options. "Last night, at the boathouse, the final words Chase spoke were that Howard Mason was my real father. That's Chancellor Marron. I was confused when he shouted it. It was so unexpected that *that* was what he chose to say when Sabine was holding a knife to his throat, but—now I understand why. There's no evidence left. Everything I've learned, all I've collected, was taken by the societies." I look down at my inner elbow, where an IV drips steady fluids into my body. "All except for this. Me."

"I'm ... I think I'm following you, but I need more information."

"Marron is my real father. Is that enough evidence to

show some credibility that what I'm saying is true? Marron is a high-ranking official of the Nobles. He works for Daniel Stone. And he's aware of everything Sabine's done for the Virtues. He sanctions it. I have no idea if he knows I exist, but being his secret love child while he was a teacher..." I think of Dr. Luke. "It would disgrace him. He might do anything to keep it from coming out. Including turning into a credible witness for me, explaining to police that I'm not a killer and admitting to them the society exists and Sabine's been trafficking girls. He'd be heralded as a hero if Sabine goes down, can take all the credit for all I care. This could work. It's not much, but it's something."

Ahmar slow-blinks. Licks his lips. "Calla. You're scaring me. Think this through. If this is your father, can you be okay using him this way? It would ruin any chance you have to get to know someone you thought you'd never meet."

I shake my head, my mouth thinning. "He's not my father. He lost that right when he left my mother to fend for herself. He's my sperm donor, nothing more."

"Kiddo."

"I mean it, Ahmar."

"Okay. I won't push it." Ahmar pauses, studying my heart monitor, then comes back to me. "So, this boy. This Chase. You trust what he has to say?"

Marron being my father is yet another secret Chase kept hidden, and while it's crushing, it makes a sick kind of sense that Chase held it back. It's not the proud moment of finding my real father I'd always envisioned. It's a sickening blow of news against my head, and if Marron knew, all this time, yet sicced his actual daughter and her friends on me anyway ... Willow. *My half-sister.*

"Yes," I say. "I believe Chase."

"Jesus, fuck." Ahmar rubs the top of his balding head. "Meredith never said a word."

"Just that he was a random one-night stand," I supply. "I received the same story."

"I gotta believe, with all my heart, she was protecting you." Ahmar leans back. "Considering what you've said, what Pete's told me..."

"She was. Mom didn't want me to know my father, or for me to be at Briarcliff, because I'm a threat to what Sabine and Daniel have built. Tell Detective Haskins. He may not believe it, coming from me. But he might respect your opinion."

Ahmar shakes his head. "I'm trying, kiddo. This whole business about a secret bloodline and you being some kind of rightful heir, though ... it's a hard sell."

"Don't forget sex-trafficking, rigged exams and grades, and tax evasion." I smile wanly.

"Uh-huh." Ahmar sets his jaw, thinking. "Haskins is suspicious, but he's a good man. A smart one, too. These families see him as a small town bumfuck who can be buried alive with enough Benjamins, but—not to get your hopes up—there was a sparkle in his eye when I explained this Noble and Virtue business that Pete threw on me. Haskins wasn't surprised. I'll give him this info about Marron. Testing your DNA against his will take a much shorter time than whatever hair you had me pass over to my ex, but Callie..."

"Be prepared for the worst. I know."

"And I hate that you do."

Ahmar leans down and kisses me on the forehead. "I'm going back out there. And I'll make sure Haskins is the only cop that comes in here to question you. We'll get to the bottom of this, baby girl."

When he pulls back, I read between the lines in his face. Determination and resolve creep into the cracks, but grief remains the deepest crevice.

Frustration at losing my mother. Not being able to save her.

Desperation to save me, instead.

"I love you, Ahmar."

"Ah." Ahmar swipes the back of his hand against his eyes. "Don't do this to me. I'll see you in a few hours. I'll be back *after* I become a goddamned tick on Haskins's back and never leave him alone."

I lift my restrained wrists as much as I can. A light clink of the belt loops follows. "I'll be here."

He stares at the leather cuffs. "I'm sorry."

"Me too," I whisper, and I don't close my eyes until Ahmar disappears from view.

31

CALLIE

"Up and at 'em, night possum!"

The voice, too lighthearted to be real, tinkles against my ear, and I swat at it like a mosquito.

"I'm asking nicely, but seriously. I'm not a nice guy. Wake the fuck up."

I pry my eyes open, heavy with a drugged, gritty sleep the nurses keep forcing on me. But once I focus on the form looming above me, I croak out, "Tempest?"

"Yes, your beard is here to save the day."

"My what?"

"Your fake soulmate. You know, the disguise you wear to cover up all your smushy feely feels for Chasey-poo."

"Whatever." My roll to my side is halted by his rude grip on my wrists.

"Let go!" I complain.

"I'm not touching you."

I glance down and give a small grunt when I notice the

shackles on my wrist through the greenish light of my room.

A hospital room. With beeps and blips of machines chugging along softly beside me.

It all comes back in a *whoosh*.

"Chase!" I fight against my restraints. "I need to see him."

"Do *not* fight, scream, or flail, or else I'll be forced to gag you with a latex glove." He waggles his brows. "And I do love my foreplay."

"Are you joking? Your best friend is in critical condition, and you're here making fun of me."

"I'm not kidding around. I'm merely passing the time it's taking for you to have a breakthrough moment where you figure out I'm here to bust you through those doors and take you on a mad escape spree through the halls."

I stare at him.

"Well, why didn't you just say so?" I jangle my chains as permission.

Tempest glides to one side of my bed but pauses with his hands hovering over my arm. He arches a brow. "This is gonna hurt."

"What?—*fuck*, Tempest!" My whispered, wet curses fall on deaf ears as Tempest yanks at my IVs and pulls the needles out of my skin without so much as a testing pull.

Tempest moves to unlock the belts at my hands and ankles with surprising dexterity, then helps me sit up until my feet dangle over the bed. But my fingers tangle in the sheets, stopping him from lifting me to a stand.

"What is it?" he asks.

"My hospital gown. I'm..."

"No need to be modest. You have an excellent ass. For a rodent, anyway. And," he adds when I fumble to close my gown at the back, "there's not much time, so grab your shit and let's hustle."

"I need clothes. Did Ahmar...?" I scan the small, private room for any kind of bag, and find a small sports duffel on the single visitor's chair.

I stumble over to it on weak legs, pretending Tempest isn't judging my body as I turn my back to him, my gown puddling to the floor, then throw on a long-sleeve shirt, jeans, and a winter coat.

His silent presence tells me that's exactly what he's doing.

I spin to the clear, plastic bag beside the duffel, containing my soaked clothes. Ripping it open, I search for one item in particular. When a sharp point hits my fingers, I smile.

Tempest is still too quiet, so I distract him while clasping the raven necklace around my neck by saying, "Ahmar has this under control. He believes us and is willing to help reveal the truth to Haskins."

"Oh, yeah? And what happened the last time you trusted the process, little possum?"

I drop the pendant underneath my shirt, zip up my jacket, and turn. "Tell me another option, then, because after becoming a popsicle in a lake while I watched Chase bleed out in front of me, I'm out of ideas."

"There's your problem." Tempest points at me. "You're a no optimism possum."

He hooks my arm and pulls me to the door, using his other hand to put a finger to his mouth.

"Police are stationed at my door," I whisper. "I sure hope you have a plan other than to tip-toe out of here."

Tempest cracks the door open, peers through, then, seemingly satisfied, pushes it all the way open. "The nurses are changing shifts. We'll cut through the hallway and slip through the exit over there. And we're talking small-town cops, babe, not super-duper detectives." After he ushers us all the way out, he gestures to the slumped over cop on the chair. "Slipped him some of James's Ambien in his decaf. He's out."

I study Tempest for some sort of reaction after mentioning a friend who so utterly betrayed him by offering Chase up to Sabine on a platter, but Tempest's face is predictably blank as he scoots me past the snoring guard and through the exit.

He grabs my hand to pull me downstairs, but I hold onto the banister to stop the descent.

Tempest's shoulders slump on a sigh. "Have I not reasonably explained the dire need to run at this point of our escape plan?"

"I thought you were bringing me to Chase."

His lips pop on another exhale. "Babe, I hate to tell ya, but he's the least of your worries."

"Ahmar's dealing with the police. He'll add enough doubt that Haskins'll look at more than just me when it comes to Ivy or Chase's attack."

Another sardonic brow arch. "How is any of this relevant to me right now?"

"You don't have to break me out of the hospital. I trust my uncle. He's the *only* person I'm certain has my back."

"Shit." Tempest tucks his hands in his pockets, then tilts against the wall to better see me. "You're assuming your uncle got out of this hospital unscathed, aren't you?"

Every part of me goes cold. "Why wouldn't he? He has nothing to do with secret societies or Briarcliff. He's an outsider."

"He's yours." Tempest eyes me steadily. "And he's important to you and willing to hear your opinion. All things Sabine doesn't enjoy hanging out in the open."

My chapped lips peel apart. "Sabine has Ahmar?"

Tempest's mouth turns grim. "No, she has Ahmar, Emma, and Eden."

32

CALLIE

"How am I supposed to believe what you're saying?" I ask Tempest, but my tone wobbles. My question is frantic. "You're one of them. You could be leading me right into Sabine's clutches."

"Well, I *am* leading you to her, but not for her dinner *appertif*. Chase is my boy." Tempest pushes off the wall. "My ride-or-die. I played no part in what happened tonight, and I fucking wish I did."

Tempest halts at the step below mine. We're almost eye-to-eye, and there, right there, is the emotion I was searching for when it came to discovering one of your best friends is a traitor.

"If I'd known, I would've told Chase not to go near you. If I'd had any *inkling* of what runs in your blood, I would've done everything in my power to harass you, terrify you, get you to quit and have you running back to your uncle-daddy with your tail between your possum pussy—and I promise you, while I might've fucked you like Chase, I wouldn't have left you whole the way he has."

I swallow against the vicious, streaming sentences, but hold his stare. "My mother did her damnedest to keep me away from this hellhole. If *I'd* had any inkling, I would've gladly gone through life without ever going to this school, seeing your face, knowing my real father, and figuring out that all secret societies are good for is protecting murderers and pedophiles."

Tempest tilts his head, a modicum of respect flashing in his eyes. "Not all of us. It's why I find myself in this position, where my boy can't. Chase wants all that shit to end, and so do I. We may be freshmen at Briarcliff University, but we hold a lot of fucking clout within our Noble circle.

"Sabine's presenting your uncle, Emma, and Eden to the entire societal membership. That's right," he says when he registers my wince. "Every. Single. One. She's there to solidify her position as well as your garbage dump of a reputation. She's likely blackmailed, coerced, and threatened your only remaining allies into backing up her story and will have them announce to her entire audience that you are no longer eligible to run the Virtues, even if your DNA results come back and you have Rose Briar's blood. Of course, her speech was meant to occur while you were cuffed, interrogated, and arrested in the nearby hospital, except now I've arrived to seriously fuck her shit up. No bitch who tries to kill my buddy will earn herself a centuries-old society for her efforts." He pauses, then angles his head at me. "So, are you in, or do you want me to assist in buckling you back into your hospital bed and leaving you there to trust your *process*?"

I match his unflinching stare. "I'm in."

"Good." He whips around and flies down the stairs. With my heart beating in my ears, I rush to catch up to him.

Tempest roars through the small town of Briarcliff with the smooth rumbling of a sleek luxury car, and I brace for his abrupt turns with a clenched, whitened grip against the door.

We don't speak during the trip back to the university, Tempest's foreboding last words as he pushed me into his vehicle being, "By the time the nurses figure out you're gone, we'll be buried underground," before whipping out of the hospital parking garage.

He pulls up to the M.B.S. Library of Studies, and I push my door open without hesitation. Tempest meets me at the front of the car, then takes some of my weight as we stride to the doors, my breaths a lot harsher than his.

"Should I have given you a Gatorade or something?" he asks, side-eyeing me as I hunch into him. "Basic care of another person isn't my strong suit. Chase was better at that shit."

"Is better," I correct.

Tempest holds the door open for me and studies me through the glass.

"*Is*," I repeat. "He's going to be fine, and when I'm done with that cunt in there, I'm going to tell him so myself."

Tempest makes an approving sound at my back. "I kept wondering why Chase decided to keep you instead of scare you off. Now I'm getting it."

We reach the back wall, and when I make noises that my fingerprints may not work anymore—last night's events pretty much exiled me—Tempest waves me off. He bends to the floor, his fingers bringing up a strange screen on the touchpad, then working furiously. After a few minutes, a soft *beep* sounds, and the hidden door slides open.

33

CALLIE

I probably should've braced for the moment when the hidden door would slide open to reveal Sabine, standing at the center of the circular room brimming with hooded Nobles and Virtues.

Her mouth is open mid-speech, and when she turns toward the sudden disturbance, her red-rimmed lips part further.

"Are we late to the party?" Tempest calls as he saunters in, hauling me against his side. "Apologies. My plus one had such a complex about coming to a soiree straight out of a hospital bed."

Pure, vile fury runs through Sabine's expression, paling it to such a degree that her lips turn into swatches of fresh blood. Her hateful stare burrows into my skin, my veins popping and thriving with her putrid death wishes, but just as quickly, she covers her surprise behind a serene, confident mask.

"Just as well," she simpers, then glances up to include the rows of Nobles and Virtues. "You're now able to match a face to the girl who's put our societies at so much risk. She writes about us in a mass email to parents, students, and faculty. And if that's not enough..." Sabine chuckles under her breath. "She accuses us of *murder*. This child has gone so far as to accuse us of tracking down her mother and killing her in cold blood. She's gathered so much hatred, so much misdirected anger, that Calla Lily Ryan can no longer tell reality from fiction." Sabine eyes me dryly. "Her very public accusations of her stepfather and resulting psychosis proves that."

I peel my lips from my teeth. "You sociopathic bitch."

"Callie is so traumatized, so unstable, she almost overdoses an innocent girl. But, largely due to her connections in the NYPD, she's able to escape accountability and came to Briarcliff with no charges, no soul. Her lack of empathy—or her succumbing to her demons, however you choose to see it, my lords—coupled with her lax supervision, allowed her to come onto our soil, desecrate our traditions, and *kill* our Virtuous Princess through a misguided sense of protecting the princess from me, her queen."

Sabine's mask falls when she includes me, her eyes stretching so wide that hollows deepen around them, giving her the face of a skull with stripped-back skin. "You rancid street rat, you have *forsaken* the Virtues." She twists, her scarlet dress billowing with her movements. "Bring them out!"

Noise hits my left ear, and I'm forced to watch my

friends, my *uncle*, being dragged out of the same corridor I'd used to follow Chase into an unbearable darkness.

Though their hands are untied and their footsteps free, Emma, Eden, and Ahmar's faces all tell me an emotionless story.

I frantically scan their forms for injuries or torture, but all walk with a natural, albeit hesitant, gait. And none of them look in my direction.

"How has this become a tribunal? I'm not the one needing to face judgment!" I cry out to the crowd.

Even Ahmar. *Even Ahmar* takes his place in the light like he's part of a police line-up. My breath hitches at what they could've done to make this born-and-raised Bronx man so placid. "Sabine's desperate to keep a throne where everything in her life has disintegrated. Yes, she has Daniel Stone, but he's just as colluding as she is. And when he finds out what she did to his son, I very much doubt he'll stick by her side."

I say this loud enough for the entire room to hear. My voice echoes throughout the hushed temple, but the thickened atmosphere, the stone-cold quiet, indicates I have much further to go before any of these people believe me.

"If you're quite done," Sabine quips, "allow your pseudo-uncle to speak. Ahmar Kazmi, is it?"

Ahmar lifts his head, but his eyes are so hollow, his warm brown skin so gray, that my stomach sinks before he utters a word.

"My beloved niece needs help," he croaks out. "She hasn't been right since Mer—my friend's death, and her recent escape from the hospital proves it." Ahmar turns in my direction but keeps his focus on the floor. "These people only wanted to help, honey. You're ruining lives. You've already destroyed so many. Don't bring anyone else down with you."

Tears brim at the edges of my vision. "You don't mean that."

"Emma?" Sabine croons. "How about you, dear?"

"My brother wanted nothing but the best for you." Emma's dulled voice carries across the attentive room. "And you stabbed him for it."

"Eden?" Sabine asks. "Anything to add?"

Eden's quiet voice comes through her curtain of hair. "You sent naked pictures of me to the entire school after I confided in you how much pictures like that destroyed me in ninth grade."

"I don't—Eden, I would never," I say. "Whatever Sabine's done to you ... it can't account for Ivy's death. Sabine *killed* her." My voice breaks. "Please remember that. And she put Chase in critical condition."

"No, dear, *you* did all that."

"No." But it comes out hoarse. "I didn't."

"Oh, but you did. I've called this emergency meeting precisely because you are a danger to our societies, our school, and yourself. Your uncle has kindly offered to put you into psychiatric care as soon as you recover from your ... failed attempt at suicide, which, since you're here, I assume you have."

I find Ahmar through the haze, and he lifts his head without hesitation. The skin around his eyes tightens, as if in a desperate effort to drill his thoughts into mine. I can practically hear them through his closed, tense mouth. *Do as she says, kiddo. Let's escape in one piece, all right? We'll deal with them when we're long gone.*

Or is that even what he's saying? I can't tell anymore. What he said aloud doesn't match these internal thoughts. He stated I was ruining lives. That I'd already hurt my dad. Sylvie.

Did I hurt Ivy and Chase, too?

My hands go to my head, my knuckles digging into my temples.

"Ahmar," I cry, scrunching my eyes shut.

"He can't help you anymore, child." Sabine's heels click against the marble. "In my opinion, he's helped you too much. Falyn? Come down here, please."

Falyn appears after taking the hidden stairs, her golden cloak floating around her ankles as she walks. She smiles when she spies me, then digs into a side pocket of her cloak and pulls out a sheaf of papers she then gives to Sabine.

"No!" Ahmar cries out. Then, his brows draw in. His back goes up. "Lady, I've done everything you've asked. That was the deal. You promised you wouldn't show her."

"What, this old report?" Sabine calls, with a look over her shoulder. "I'll keep my promise. I won't show her. But I *will* tell her."

Ahmar roars, stampeding forward, but is held back by a taller, broader Cloak—the type of stature I didn't think existed above Ahmar, gifted with height and breadth.

But I don't tell the Cloak to release him. I'm too fixated on what Sabine holds in her hands. "What is that?"

"It's a police report, darling, on your mother's death. Oh

—I stand corrected," she adds when Ahmar lets loose a string of threats. "A *forged* police report. One your uncle worked very hard to legitimize. And it would've worked, too, had I not done the digging necessary to unveil the true document he buried."

My stomach pitches. "That's not—Ahmar?"

He trembles beneath the Cloak's solid grip, muscles bulging from his neck, his cheeks, and a bulbous vein trailing along his forehead. "Baby girl, don't listen to what comes next."

"Why shouldn't she?" Sabine asks, gesturing to the balcony above. "Everyone else gets to."

Cloaks, a black and gold chessboard of iniquity, lean over the railings, their hoods dangling eagerly.

"Damn it, lady, *no*—"

Sabine turns to me and smiles, her teeth gleaming. She doesn't need fangs. She harbors so much dark energy her grin might as well contain venom dripping from her canines. "Calla Lily, I regret to inform you that it was you who held the knife. Your killing spree didn't begin with Ivara Alling. It began with your mother. *You* murdered her."

34

CALLIE

The marbled flooring lurches beneath my feet. My vision shrinks to a pinprick, Sabine's face at the helm. Chills pass along my skin, ants marching in single file until they reach their hill, apexed at the core of my heart.

"You had your mother's blood on your hands when Mr. Kazmi found you that night," Sabine continues, her voice a soft lullaby trailing across the hard stone walls. "Along with bruises around your neck, consistent with your mother defending herself. Your uncle covered it up as best he could —even allowed you to accuse your stepfather of your crime."

Breath lies ragged in my throat. "That's not true!"

"Mr. Kazmi?" This time, Sabine cuts her attention in his direction. "Care to provide some background information?"

Ahmar's throat bobs. He finds me in the small crowd,

where even Tempest takes a step back, his brows arched in surprise.

Ahmar rasps, "Kiddo..."

"Oh my God," I whisper. My legs ache to run, but there's nowhere to hide. I'm blocked in, by marble and stone, by people, by guilt. "I refuse to believe it. I *won't!*"

"He'd do anything for you, that man," Sabine says, clucking her tongue. "You were the last remnant of Meredith Ryan, a woman he was terribly in love with."

"Don't," I say, but my eyes *ping* to Ahmar's, and they won't leave.

She continues, the pain in my plea fueling her next words. "He saved you because he loved you like a daughter. Couldn't bear to see you rotting away in prison. It's not something Meredith would've wanted. Knowing that idiot whore, she likely would want you free, despite you slitting her throat. Because you're sick, darling. Your delusions started well before your mother's untimely demise."

"I tried to help you, Calla," Ahmar says. The words seem like they're choking him. "I convinced your dad to put you in a psychiatric hold. I'd hoped they'd diagnose you and work with you to get you better, but all they did was release you. And I couldn't ... I didn't..."

"Ahmar, I didn't kill her!" I'm so resolute, my voice strikes through the room like a whip. "I'd remember something like that. I'd *know* if I hurt her. She was my best friend. My favorite person. My *mom*." Shaking my head, I retreat, uncaring if my back hits the wall. It would feel more solid than the ground right now.

Ahmar drags his eyes to the report, still clenched between Sabine's long, taloned fingers. "It's all there, baby girl. I did everything I could to stop this from happening, but this place, these people ... they dredge up the worst in us."

"Our lies all have to catch up with us sometime," Sabine says. "And time is up for you. If you leave this temple, I will send this report directly to the NYPD. You will be arrested, and so will your uncle. Therefore, it's in your best interest to remain Virtuous. Stay by my side, do as I say, and this evidence will never leave the lips of a member." She looks up to the rafters. "Are we in agreement?"

A chorus of voices ring out, "*altum volare in tenebris.*"
Fly high in the dark.

Sabine lowers her stare to mine. "You see, child, we live off the dark collateral of others. It's how we keep everyone in such pristine alignment."

My mind pendulums through the possibilities—*did I really kill her, or am I making up the image of cornering my mother in her bedroom, wielding a chef's knife in my hands, and piercing her skin?*—

My shoulder slams into the wall, and I slide down into a crouch, covering my face, moaning the denial even as remembered rivulets of blood seep between my fingers, staining my clothes and puddling at my feet.

Sabine's faraway voice circles my head like a vise. "I think I've proven my point, my noblemen. My dear Virtues, even if she is who she claims to be and has the Briar bloodline..."

This is what they do. They use your greatest fear against you.

An inner voice speaks over Sabine, poking at my conscience, prodding me awake. Chase's cadence echoes into my soul, the very words he used when trapped in a dark cage coming into the light of my eyes.

I blink.

Sabine's using what I'm most afraid of. My fear of madness.

Because *I did not kill my mother.*

The certainty is etched into my bones.

Slowly, I stand. Push off the wall and stalk to the center of the temple, where Sabine, with her back turned, continues her propaganda.

"You're the elite!" I scream at the balcony, cutting her off. "Faculty. Senators. CEOs. *Parents.* And you allow this woman to use your children for the sexual pleasure of men who are standing right *next* to you. My own father—Chancellor Marron—seduced my mother when she was a student and he was a teacher. This club of yours isn't about rising high, it's about using sex and getting away with scandal, and allowing your children to suffer at the hands of your so-called members. You're all twisted and sick, the way you let her get away with this."

"You're forgetting an important piece of the truth you're building," Tempest adds, striding up next to me. He'd walked deeper into the temple but hadn't donned his robe. Nor has the fire died out in his otherworldly green eyes. "Calla Lily Ryan is a descendent of Rose Briar."

A rush of voices hit the air at Tempest's endorsement. Hoods bow together, arms gesticulate, and my chin notches higher. I step farther into the room. Closer to *her.*

"Don't believe me?" Tempest continues. "Ask your queen. Her family has hidden the birth certificate of the baby born from Rose Briar and *Theodore* Briar for well over a century. That's a decent piece of history she's kept from Noble discovery, and all because the Harringtons wanted the throne. Fuck, her eldest daughter dies and the other is arrested for murder—leaving *no chick* to inherit, and the bitch *still* won't admit that she's kept the true heir from you all this time."

Hoods murmur, but Sabine seethes. "Shut your mouth, boy, and join your ranks. You betray everything you've worked for, all you've earned, by defending this girl and helping to spread her lies."

"Am I a fibber?" Tempest looks up at the balcony, spreading his arms. "Guys? Am I known to have my pants on fire—ah, shit. *Fire.* Right." Tempest wags his index finger at Sabine. "You trapped a Virtue princess and the Noble legacy who rushed to save her in a fire and left them to die. Let's take bets on who's been a bad girl, 'cause I don't think it's Callie."

Sabine lashes out her arm and screams, "Take him! Tempest Callahan has no proof other than the word of a girl too mute with hallucinations to lend credence to a single word in her defense."

"I'm not suffering from anything," I say, "other than your lethal attempts to ruin me so you can continue your reign of terror on these girls. You traffic them. You make them have sex." I glance up at the balcony, shouting, "Too many of you know this to be true, because you're the ones who trap these girls in white sheets and pretend they want you to take their purity."

"Here we are, gentlemen," Sabine says through the increased mutterings, "solidified proof that this girl succumbs to nothing but her own fancies."

"Your Noble prince knew the truth!" I yell. "And Sabine stabbed him for it!"

"Lies!" a male voice cries.

A litany of "here, here," agreements follow.

"Then ask him," I counter. "When Chase Stone wakes up, hear it from his mouth. He doesn't suffer from 'hallucinations.' His credibility is tied to your reputations. You wouldn't dare go against—"

"*If* he wakes up," Sabine cuts in, "and indeed, agrees with your statements, it is only because you seduced him." Sabine's lips peel back in a grin. "The same way your mother seduced all the boys when she was here. Meredith Ryan was nothing but a slut, and you've inherited the same genes."

"I've inherited the Virtues!" I yell, stepping closer.

Sabine, not expecting the outburst, hobbles back in her heels but quickly composes herself.

I add in a softer voice, "Say what you want about me, but utter another word about my mother, and I will not regret putting real blood on your lips."

"My, my. Is that the guilt talking?"

My chest heaves. My vision skews with fury, but I don't

look away from her. "You're a liar, a killer, and a terrible mother. Rot in hell."

Sabine's chest concaves, her clavicles poking out like weapons forged from bone. "Do not force me to teach you another lesson."

I bare my teeth at her, but say to the room, "If you're all so proud, so willing to be a part of her madness, *show your faces*! Look upon your queen as your true selves and study your neighbors, while asking yourself if they've touched your daughter."

Voices pitch in horror, and to my amazement, some draw back their hoods. Others grab the shoulders of their neighbors and demand they reveal themselves.

Tempest sidles up to me, a smile plastered across his face. "My boy would be proud of you."

"Stop! All of you!" Sabine howls. Veins pulse as she strains her neck. "The girl is delusional! I have a *report*!" She smacks her hand on the abused paper, then flaps it around.

"And they have a birth certificate," a female voice calls down. "Tempest Callahan backs her up. I can't discount that."

"You very well *will*, Alexandra," Sabine spits. "*My* word is final, not a child's."

"Virtues!" I cry. "Speak up. Please. Tell these people what you've endured." I search the upper floor, aiming for a face, one that will, if pushed, speak the truth. She has to.

"Violet!" I call out, but I can't find her. So, I plead with her instead. "Please. I know you hate what the Virtues have become. You shied away every time I was beaten, or humiliated, or harassed. You've come to hate what the Virtues represent. You didn't accept their invitation to watch your friends be charmed, manipulated, then coerced. You've lost Piper. Addisyn is gone. And Ivy—Ivy was cast aside in an unmarked grave, all because Sabine covets power over human lives. Come out here and tell your story. I know you have one." My voice lowers. "You're the only one left who can speak the truth."

I hear a whispered *yes* behind me. I whirl, thinking Violet's appeared from the shadows, but it was Emma who spoke, her side resting against Eden's as they raise their bowed heads and give me an affirming nod.

"Our stories were told and ignored," Emma says. "Spun by Sabine into necessary lies. My torture, my burns, my *life,* couldn't fall on her, because she's not the one who lit the match or swung the bat. But she didn't have to. Her intimidations start when we're young. Her promises ingrained in us before we hit puberty. She hides the truth about as well as Piper hid her true self from her mother. So, if you can't listen to me—if you refuse to read my scars—then listen to a present Virtue. Violet, I'm begging you, give me, Eden, Piper, Ivy, and Callie, a voice."

Tears frame my vision. I give Emma a resolute nod in return.

"You sorry girls, I warned you of the consequences of rebelling in this temple. Emma Loughrey, the fake, adopted, *unwanted* child of Daniel Stone and false sister of Chase." Sabine says, only loud enough for us to hear, as she stalks toward me. Emma winces. "And Eden, an overweight, pathetic, useless vision of the swim champion she used to be. You swore to represent me, not Callie, in exchange for my assistance in giving you back everything you'd lost. Yet here you are, betraying not me, but yourselves."

"That's your problem," Eden says. "You're so up your own ass, you can't believe we'd choose a friend over vanity. An orphaned girl over a queen."

"It's so impossible for you to fathom I'd prefer being an adopted Loughrey over a Stone," Emma chimes in, then looks at me. "We would never let it get so far, Callie. We just had to play the game to get in here. But we're on your side. Thanks for the signal, Tempest. And for getting her here like you promised."

Tempest nods, crossing his arms on a grin. I narrow my eyes at him, wondering just what my Scooby crew had gotten up to while I was unconscious.

"Violet is not like any of you liars," Sabine sputters, her eyes glancing over Tempest, Eden, Emma, me. She's counting the growing number against her. "She is the loveliest of my Virtues. She would never, *ever*—"

"I'm here," a small voice says.

The scuffling, the accusations, the robe-tearing, halts at those two, whispered words.

Violet pushes past Falyn and ignores Willow's imploring hand as she moves to stand by my side.

She lowers her arm, catches my hand in hers, and squeezes. "Callie speaks the truth."

I jolt at the volume, unused to Violet emitting such echoing certainty. "Piper admitted her involvement in Emma's beating, in the fire, before she died. I was too afraid to say anything. I ... I couldn't believe it. She spoke of her mother like our queen was a monster. She told me what Emma was forced to do ... with you, Senator Bachman."

The entire temple gasps. Mine might've joined them.

"And you, Mr. Torrence, Mr. Andrews, Dr. Hoffman. Piper named you all." Violet bows her head, her fingers digging into my hand, but she pivots to Emma. "I'm so sorry. You endured the worst the society had to offer. You went to Piper for help, and she tried and failed. It should've landed on me next. But I was too scared. Too much of a cowardly mouse to ever be considered commanding." She looks at her friends, Willow, and Falyn. "Not anymore. I mentioned my worries to you guys, but you brushed me off. You acted like I was mistaken. And you put me up as the next princess after Ivy." Violet tilts her head. "You knew what that meant for me."

Willow looks to the side, her gaze skating across mine but never landing. I study her expression, searching for our similarities, but I find none. Not inside, or out.

Falyn glares at Violet, insolence twisting her lips.

Shifting my balance, I squeeze Violet's shoulder. She's not alone when it comes to being a recipient of Willow and Falyn's ire.

"This is all your fault."

I jerk my gaze to Falyn's.

"No. It's yours," Violet says, either not realizing Falyn's speaking to me or deciding she doesn't care. "You stand by Sabine and do her bidding like what she demands isn't despicable and belittling."

"Shut up, Vi. I'm talking to your pet possum—or should I say, everybody's pest. You refuse to be put down, Callie, instead involving our entire *school*, thinking you're doing them a favor, when all you've accomplished is ruin. For them. For *us*."

I part my lips. "That's big talk for a girl who's never been forced to fuck one of those men up there to fill Sabine's pockets."

"*Enough!*" Sabine screeches. She prowls over to me, wraps her cold, bony hand around my wrist, and holds it high. "Is this your new princess? Your future *queen*? She is as my Marquess says. A rodent. A pest. A delusional *imbecile*."

The crowd above murmurs among each other, so low in tone, it's difficult to tell which way they're leaning.

I struggle against Sabine, but she holds fast. "Allow me to put it to a vote," she says. "I'll admit to concealing Rose Briar's surviving lineage, but it was for the best interests of the Society. Rose was not well before she disappeared. Manic, untrustworthy, and mourning her multiple miscarriages and stillbirths." Sabine slants her gaze to me. "Hereditary, I'm sure. My great-great grandmother understood this and deduced that the Virtues could not endure if they were to wait for Rose's secret child to come of age. The Harringtons took over, if only to keep our women strong. To maintain their educations and discover the top girls, grooming them for successful futures—"

"Did you start back then?" I sneer. "Selling your girls to maintain your authority over the Nobles?"

"Shut up," she hisses, her nails biting into my skin. "Your credibility has long since soured, you useless, vile cunt."

My eyes widen at her open vindictiveness, my hand going slack in her hold.

But nobody saw or heard it.

"Yes, put it to a vote." Tempest saunters to center stage.

Sabine's lower lip trembles with the intense need to shut him up, but a part of her must know she can't, not if she wants to continue her charade.

"Vote with the full knowledge that I'm with Callie, as is Emma Loughrey, a legacy of the Nobles and a former Virtue Princess, adopted or not. And Eden Yurman, a recipient of the Virtue's torture." Tempest notches up his chin. "And the current Noble Prince, Chase Stone, who's authorized me as his emissary and wishes for Sabine Harrington to step down."

A rush of voices meets his statement, but one person manages to talk over him. "And the king?"

"The king stands with his queen." Tempest shrugs.

"The king should be here. As should Viscount Marron," another deep, masculine voice pipes in. "Why aren't they here representing themselves?"

"Ask your queen," Tempest answers. "She's sneaky. While we wait, let's all consider how this is looking to that NYPD guy over there, and what he might do once he's released." Tempest's forehead wrinkles. "Unless we're supposed to dispose of him? I dunno, Queen, do you want to graduate to serial killer status so soon?"

Sabine drops my hand. "You little prick."

She moves so fast, her billowing skirts are a blur until the *slap* rings out.

Tempest's head jerks to the side, the tanned skin on his cheek blooming with red.

My jaw drops open. Violet whispers, "Oh my God."

Both of us are so glued to the action in anticipation of Tempest's response, I don't see Falyn coming in time.

Until the flash of silver.

The glint of her teeth.

And the roughened edges of her scream.

35

CALLIE

Falyn's scream echoes above the rafters, ricochets off the walls, and tunnels into my ears with such murderous accuracy that my body responds before my mind figures out I'm about to be disemboweled in an effort to save Tempest.

I duck, the blade whistling above my head, and tackle Falyn at the waist until we both tumble to the ground.

Shouts and hollers follow, the heavy clomps of footsteps and the high-pitched decibels of screams, but Falyn spins me to my back, covering my face with her robe and pressing down so hard, I don't have to hear my nose crack under the pressure—I *feel* it.

The fabric quickly becomes soaked with my saliva and blood as my mouth gapes and I fight against her suffocation, the random acts and heightened ruckus becoming quieter as my sole focus turns to survival.

The knife—where's the knife?

I have the keen sense she'll be swinging it down at any moment, and I won't be joining Chase in the hospital after. It'll be the morgue.

Falyn straddles me, howling triumph over the outbreak in the temple. My arms start to tire. My vision dots with darker stars, but all I can think is: *Fight.*

I raise my knees. Blindly bring my legs forward in an attempt to cross them at the front of her chest and throw her down to the ground.

The pretzel idea works—as soon as Falyn feels my shins at her face, her arms lift and she pushes at them, but thigh muscles are *so* much stronger than arms. Bunching my abs and arching my back, I smack her onto the ground and rise to a seated position, scrambling to get the cloak off my face.

And open my eyes to a violent melee.

Cloaks stream down the back stairwells onto the main floor, some trying to stop the cluster of fights, but most starting them.

Tempest's A-list actor father stands in front of his son, screaming obscenities at whoever tries to come near them and attempting to push Tempest to the exit.

Tempest cuts his eyes to me and smirks. As Willow beelines over to me and Falyn on the ground, he kicks out his foot and she belly-flops.

Sabine? Where's Sabine?

Frantic, I search the room, but Falyn is fast recovering. I peel off her and stand, dodging her hands and running into the fray, but not before collecting the knife on the way.

It's heavy with quality. Ornate with silver. Wet with

invisible blood—Ivy's blood. Chase's blood. Tempest's and mine.

My grip tightens around the hilt. I wrestle my way into the middle of the temple, pausing. Then scream: "*Sabine!*"

As I do, my eyes travel up. I spot her on the balcony, alone, looking down. When she catches my eye, she curls a beckoning finger.

I don't hesitate. Sprinting to the nearest staircase, I take the steps two at a time, the knife sharp and heavy at my side.

I burst onto the balcony, the shouts and pummels down below somehow echoing louder up here, but I force the distraction away, centering all my senses on Sabine.

She reclines against the railing, her arms spread, her red dress lifting at every silky, invisible movement. The French twist in her hair is intact, and she's as regal as ever as she stands above the chaos she's caused.

"Your mother cried while she was dying," she purrs.

My feet turn to rocks. Immobile with the weight of the Earth.

"She did," Sabine assures, her hands trailing across the top of the railing. "And her last words were, '*Don't hurt my daughter.*' Oh, my." Sabine mock frowns as she watches me process her words. "Tough, isn't it? To realize the very nightmares you had over how she died were probably correct."

"You ... *monster.*"

"Did you think I hired a hitman, or manipulated one of my impressionable Virtues, or even James, that dear, malleable boy, to do my bidding? No, Calla Lily. I wanted your mother for myself. Our time together at Briarcliff was wrought with conflict. She had everything at her fingertips —her heritage was known by my future grandmother-in-law at that point. In fact, Prudence Harrington was grooming her for the succession, proud of Meredith's rise from nothing, and many accomplishments, despite her buried upbringing no high Noble or Virtue wanted to admit to. But then something changed." Sabine arcs her stare up to the elaborate ceiling, pondering her words as though pure chaos isn't exploding around her. "I believe she realized that if she accepted the role, she'd have to confess all her sins, including her illegal affair with a teacher. I do believe her mind started backtracking when she realized she was pregnant with you, sweet child, and she finally understood that once you enter succession, all your heirs are automatically obligated to enter the process, too. She didn't want that for you. At that point, she'd noticed the foulness, understood the dark nature that one had to possess to truly rule the Virtues. You see, she walked in on a princess and a Noble doing ... well, you're aware. Hmm. Now that I think of it, it was our newest Senator, dragging the girl's thighs toward him and positioning her to best accept his cock."

I wince, the dagger shaking by my side. "That's enough."

"Is it, my dear? Don't you want to hear how I found your mother after she ran, kept apprised of your upbringing, and waited for the perfect moment to kill both of you so there would never be a question as to my rule? Or would you rather we skipped that part and go straight to the crime scene I orchestrated when you were annoyingly late to your weekly dinner plans, and I had to MacGyver a scene of destruction *you* were responsible for."

My brain screams at me to remain standing when my knees buckle. I right myself, but my vision's blurred. My lips seize.

"How was I supposed to know you had an impressionable detective in your pocket? As an aside, you do have a knack for convincing men you're so small, fragile, and innocent. I wish you'd use that talent, but sadly, here we are. Ahmar Kazmi covered up everything I planted, forged a police report, and put his job and future on the line. All for ... you."

"Because Ahmar *loves* me." The wet whisper coats my lips. "An emotion you'll never come to understand. He believed in me so much, he couldn't let me fall for something I did not—would *never*—do. That's what you can't fathom, you witch. The idea that men love me for me, not for gain, or indecent motive, or blackmail. Ahmar loves me." I take a step. "Dad loves me." Another step. "*Chase* loves me." One more. "*My mother loved me.*"

Sabine's eyelids twitch, her lips thinning in fury. "I'm well aware of what love is, you pitiful trash. I loved my daughter! Piper was everything to me, and your meddlesome cunt took her from this world! Chase was hers. If he were hers that night, she would never have fallen."

"She was pushed by your other forgotten, neglected daughter," I retort. "Playing favorites doesn't really work when it ends in murder, does it, you felon-of-the-year?"

Sabine's face twists into haggard rage. "You wasted, undeserving slut of a girl! You're nothing! You will become nothing! I'll never give you this throne. I'd rather take your life just as I took your mother's."

"It's over, Sabine. Look around you. This chaos is yours. You're done—"

Sabine's hands wrap around my neck. She squeezes so tightly, my muscles shrink, tendons pop, and I gag on my own insides.

"Callie!" I hear Ahmar scream, and my bulbous eyes move past the railing to down below, where Ahmar is frozen between two fighting cloaks, his neck arched as he spots me and attempts to separate himself and get to me.

A red cloak swoops in just as he disentangles himself, the hood falling back and revealing Chancellor Marron, grabbing Ahmar by the arms and pulling him back. He came late to the party, but he's making his statement known.

Marron wants me to die? floats through my addled mind, but the black stars bouncing into my vision prevent me from dwelling on it.

Watching Ahmar be wrestled to the ground sends me into a fit of panic, and in a feat of pure desperation, I lift the dagger and shove it into Sabine's side.

Sabine gasps with a shocked kind of pain, her eyes widening, but she doesn't release me.

Worse, she glances down behind her at the floor below. Then she looks back at me and smiles. "Do you want to know how my daughter felt?"

"N—N—" I garble, dropping the knife as my hands flail and scratch against her forearms.

We grapple on the balcony, Sabine using her full, rage-filled force to bend me over the railing.

She doesn't resemble the groomed, sleek woman she's presented herself as all this time. Large, streaked blood vessels pop red in her eyes, the tip of her nose is a vicious scarlet, and her ruby lipstick is smeared across her too-white teeth, her canines shining with saliva.

"Piper will finally be avenged, and you'll die knowing your mother's murder will never be solved," she whispers hoarsely. "And my Virtues? They'll live *long* after you."

My side strains against the stone, my legs screaming for me to relent, but my lack of breath prevents any sort of fail-safe. I'm being forced over the rail, Sabine's stick-thin arms growing the strength of ten vengeful men...

Fight, Callie. Fight!

A chorus of voices shoot forward, silently chanting.

Chase. Ivy. Mom.

You're strong. You will be missed if you go. You don't have to come to us yet.

As if summoned, Eden and Emma appear at the top of the stairs, rushing toward me.

They're here. They're not mad, anymore.

Their faces flash in and out of a black void as they come closer. *I'm dying. When they get here, it'll be too late. I'll pass out, and Sabine will—*

NO.

A bolt of energy soars through me at the image of my friends, desperate to save me. And Ahmar down below, fighting to get to the balcony.

My hands form into a prayer at my stomach. Sabine sees the motion and smiles. "That's right, dear girl. Succumb to my inevitable triumph."

Her face wavers, in and out, and I realize it's not my blinking that's making me see black, then reality, then black.

Pressed together, my hands shoot up, between her strangling arms. Sabine doesn't expect the move and stiffens her grip, but with enough force, I pull my hands apart and break her hold.

Sabine stumbles at the unexpected show of self-defense. I give her no time to recover.

I glance at her bleeding stomach. "That was for Chase."

Then I twist her until her back smacks against the railing. "This is for Ivy."

I push her.

Her face warps with enraged panic and she swipes for my neck, but her balance is too far over the rail. Sabine's fingers hook my necklace instead, the chain ripping free and tangling into tarnished gold treasure in her palm as she falls.

Eden and Emma reach me, their palms smacking against the stone as they bend forward over the rail.

"And that?" I say dully as Sabine's scream is abruptly cut off. "That was for my mom."

36

CALLIE

TWO WEEKS LATER

"Sweetheart? You can go in and see him now."

The nurse pads quietly away after notifying me in the hospital's waiting room, and I stand, smoothing my shirt and casually wiping drool from the side of my mouth from when I tipped my head back to count the ceiling tiles, then never lowered my chin.

I'm not sure how long I slept in the chair, but my neck aches with a crick, and I massage it as I follow the nurse's footsteps into the corridor. It gives me something to do rather than focus on the nervous beats of my heart or the swarm of butterflies in my stomach.

The nurse didn't have to tell me what room he's in—I've known the number since the moment he was taken out of ICU and put in a private room. I've counted the days since he opened his eyes, the hours since he's been taken off a breathing tube, and added up every day I wasn't allowed to see him.

After a whirlwind of police, press, and parents, I've at last been granted permission from Chase's team of doctors to see him.

Creeping past the other rooms, all silent and dark save for the soft green glow of machines, I find Chase's with his door slightly ajar.

My breaths come out shaky. Phone calls with Ahmar and Dad have prepared me for this moment—a section of time where Chase may not look like himself or speak much at all, but instead of being scared, all I want to do is run to his hospital bed and grab his hand, then hold it to my cheek.

Because even through all the surgeries, a new reality to wake up to, and his recovery, he'd still be warm, and I need that assurance more than anything.

The large window is dark with night, but silhouetted with lights from neighboring city buildings. Those white lights crest over the still form in the bed, machines beeping softly beside him.

"I'm not Frankenstein's monster," comes a gristly, hoarse voice. "Unless that means you want to be my Bridezilla."

Smiling, I step through the reflection of lights across the floor and to his bedside, where I can get a closer look.

"Chase," I whisper.

His head falls to the side at my voice, his onyx eyes shimmering through the shadows. He blinks. "Hey, sweet possum."

"How are you ... I mean, do you feel okay? Can I get you anything?"

Amazing, how after weeks of mental preparation and all

the make-believe conversations I had with him in my head, *that's* what I come up with.

"Nurse just gave me my meal." He clears his throat, grimacing when his body moves with the gesture. "Wouldn't say no to a sponge bath, though."

"I'll give you all the sponge baths you want if it means you'll be okay." I'm not surprised at the break in my voice. I only wish I'd held it in longer—I don't want to fall apart in front of him so soon. "I'm sorry. You've gone through the most harrowing injury of your life, and here I am blubbering over you."

"Hey, I like a good hot chick blubber." His voice comes out soft. "C'mere."

I shuffle closer, finding that hand I was so desperate to hold, but reluctant to put it to my cheek, now wet with a mixture of terrified and relieved tears.

"More than that, sweet possum. Get up here."

"But I could hurt you."

"No more than I already am, baby."

I hesitate, but my mind's already at his side. The mattress dips when I put a knee to it, and Chase flinches again. "Maybe this isn't—"

His arm shoots out, and he pulls me the rest of the way in, nestling me into his uninjured side.

The smell of him—a mixture of hospital and forest and *him*, has me relaxing against him as easily as if we were in my dorm room.

"I missed this," he murmurs against my hair as he strokes it away from my face.

"I missed you," I counter. "I thought you were—when I got to the dock, I thought it was too late."

"Never. Well, maybe a few seconds longer and I might've been." He keeps stroking, and my eyelids fall heavy like a cat's. "Tempest told me what you did. How you fought the water and almost died of hypothermia to get to me."

"I'd do it again."

I feel his chin pull with a smile. "Sweet possum, you did. Isn't that the second time you almost drowned? I gotta start calling you Lady of the Lake."

"No way. I don't want to ever see that placid, bullshit water ever again."

His hand moves from my temple to my shoulder and squeezes. "Does that mean you're out?"

"Out of what?"

"Briarcliff. The university. Tempest also gave me the low-down on the temple, and the societies, and…"

"Sabine," I finish for him.

"Yeah."

I rise up on my elbow, wanting to see him and not just feel him. "Somebody called the police. Actually, a bunch of people did, once it was clear Sabine was losing ground and was obviously going to resort to violence to keep it. They came in right as she fell, swarming the temple. I've never seen Cloaks scatter so fast, and I thought I'd witnessed them at their sneakiest."

"I heard it was a clusterfuck."

"A lot of Cloaks had left before it got out of control—the ones called out by Violet, the powerful, older men and women. All that remained was … us. The kids. I keep trying to imagine what it was like to be one of the Briarcliff PD, walking in to a bunch of rumpled rich kids in fancy, torn velvet robes, surrounding a woman bleeding out in the middle of the floor."

"The three of you were on the upper balcony looking down." Chase shifts to get more comfortable. "You, my sister, and Eden."

"Wow, Tempest didn't leave anything out, did he? I thought we weren't supposed to upset you in your…"

"Tempest is a fucking choirboy right now who refuses to tell me shit. I've been reading the news on a tablet Rio snuck in here under a Big Mac. *Both* were very much appreciated."

The mention of his friends causes me to think about all the arrests. "I'm sorry about James."

"Stop apologizing, Calla."

My eyes tighten at the use of my nickname, previously only used by Mom and Ahmar. But as fast as they narrow, they soften. I don't correct him. I want to hear it more from him.

He says, "You're the one who endured the worst. Sabine was gonna kill you—I read the Article."

Chase refers to the Briarcliff Patch local newspaper, written by one librarian named Darla Dumphries, outlining the events of the temple showdown in scarily accurate detail. She wasn't there, but enough shellshocked new initiates spoke in detail about the allegations of trafficking against Sabine Harrington and all those in cahoots with her. Darla wasn't afraid to name names or explain how Sabine strangled an unnamed high school senior, and the two were wrestling for enough time for the girl to be forced into using self-defense before she was tossed over the railing by a very angry, very unhinged alumnus and formally respected member of Briarcliff University.

I have a lot to thank Darla for. It's because of her all those men and women who escaped were now being dragged in for police interviews. Lawyered up to their necks, of course, but the media prints their names in block letters across the nation every time another one is rounded up. Daniel Stone and Chancellor Marron are a few such individuals, brought in to explain their actions and how a club so egregious, so despicably vile, could possibly be allowed to function on private school grounds. The indictments should come any day now.

"The Nobles and Virtues are no more," Chase says, drawing me back to the present.

"This isn't what I wanted," I respond quietly. "Not like this, anyway."

"Please. This is perfect for you. The societies are dismantled, press is all over the scandal, and my father is so fucking infamous, he can't even hire drivers without them either attempting to pass on any information about him for money or refusing to go near him. It's amazing."

I lift my head. "But all you wanted was to save them, and I imploded that goal into dust."

"Yeah, you fucked it up real good, but I'm glad you did, because otherwise you'd be dead."

Chase says it so simply, but I sense his burning stare in the gloom.

"It didn't go as planned," I say.

"No shit. Nothing ever does. My psycho stepmom stabs me in the stomach—I lose my fucking gall bladder for it—and what does Father do? Stays at my bedside like a good little daddy, all the while aware of a temple ceremony where Sabine railroads you and solidifies their positions as kings and queens for fucking world domination. We can't make this shit up, and I was a fool to think a malignant society could cure itself."

"You were right about the new pledges, though. They're the ones who stood up to this mess and made it public."

"No, Calla, *you* did." He finds my hand in the tangled sheets and holds it firm. "The news about you is scarce, but I got the gist that you held your ground with Sabine in front of all the people who wanted to either destroy you, or bury you, or both. You got balls, kid."

I smile at the reference, similar to what Ahmar said to me once we both recovered enough from the all-night interviews and interrogations, and he tucked me under his emergency blanket, where we sat at the back of an ambulance and just stared out at the mess. He wasn't able to discuss the forged police report or his belief that I could actually hurt Mom. I'd searched for his hand and squeezed hard, letting him know I forgave him. All his actions after that report told me how sorry he was and how much he wanted to protect Meredith's only child. We have a lot to work out, but I'm thankful we're both alive to do it.

"Marron didn't do anything but hold Ahmar back from saving me," I say now. "He arrived near the end but didn't say anything in my defense."

"I'm not surprised."

"Do you think he knows about me? Or believes it? He hasn't said anything since he resigned. He's only speaking through his lawyers, and he hasn't bothered to get in contact with me."

"Does that upset you?"

I think about it. The first thing I saw as dawn crept up over all the flashing police lights was my parents tumbling out of their car as it screeched to a halt in front of yellow crime scene tape. Lynda's arms were flailing, and Dad was screaming at whoever was unfortunate enough to be loitering nearby. But like a boat searching for a lighthouse, they found me through the chaos. I've never seen Dad sprint so fast, or heard such an echoing, keening sob come from Lynda. They found me, they held me, and they cried until they finally believed I was safe.

"No," I answer Chase. "He's not my father. Never will be."

"I wish, in the midst of all this crazy, you could've found justice for your mom."

My gaze slides over to him. "But I did."

"Oh, yeah?"

"Sabine admitted everything and told me how she killed Mom. I've given all those details to the NYPD, but I don't know if they have enough evidence to pursue it. But you know what? I'm okay with that. I have my answers, and Sabine's getting her punishment. Perhaps she was suffering already, what with Piper's betrayal and then death. Not even Addisyn's willingness to act just like her mother was enough to convince Sabine to be satisfied with what she's gotten away with. It was always more. Just *more*. She wasn't going to stop."

Chase is silent for a moment. He changes our grip, lacing his fingers through mine. "You good?"

"About as good as you," I say.

He grumbles in agreement. "I mean about the whole self-defense thing."

"You mean my attempted murder."

"Don't call it that." A rough edge overtakes his voice. "It'll never be that. She was close to killing you."

I shrug it off, but Chase reads me better than that.

"C'mon, sweet possum, talk to me."

"It's terrible," I say eventually. "I hate thinking about it. I have nightmares, sometimes even when I'm awake. The way her face contorted and the crunch of her ... her skull. It's always here in my head. But my fear of the police not believing me because of my past—that's over now. There are enough witnesses, and Sabine made her motives clear when she screamed she wanted to kill me."

"The Article mentioned something like Eden and Emma tried to get Sabine's hands off you, and in the struggle, Sabine fell. But that's not what happened, is it?"

This is for Chase. Ivy. My Mom.

"No," I admit. "Do you think differently of me now? Now that..." *you know what I'm capable of?*

Chase speaks through my flashback. "I'm thinking what I've always thought. That you're a gorgeous, perplexing, frustrating, addictive girl who I never want to let out of my sight again."

I study him, wondering how two such screwed up people could still find happiness amid all this horror.

As if in answer, Chase shuffles to make room for me to snuggle closer. "Get back here. I'm cold."

This time, I don't hesitate.

"I love you," I whisper into his skin. "Don't ever leave me again."

He tips my chin up and kisses me, slow and light, breathy and sweet. "Remind me never to push you into a lake."

I smile, then at his goofy, lopsided grin, start laughing.

Soon, we're both shaking with painful, needed laughter, our hearts entwined with our voices as we unconsciously wish for better, lighter things to come.

EPILOGUE
CHASE

Graduation - 4 Months Later

"Are you ready yet? I feel like you should be ready by now," I say as I twirl my tie between my fingers, wearing a path in Callie and my sister's wood flooring.

"Almost!" comes Callie's faint call through her door.

There's a faint twinge in my gut as I move, my skin tight, uncomfortable, and itchy over the ache. I absentmindedly brush a thumb over the scar tissue.

Callie flings her door open. "We just have to—oh."

She gives an appreciative sweep from my feet to my head. I'm in a pantsuit, shirtless, swinging a tie around, and she looks like she wants to lick me from top to bottom.

"Like what you see?" I ask, summoning my arrogance instead of shrinking and covering the nasty mark on my abs like instinct tells me to.

"Very much." She bites her lower lip.

My pants tighten at the groin because of it.

A blush creeps across her cheekbones, and she glances behind her. "Um. Emma? You almost ready?"

Aaaaand shrinkage. Nothing like the mention of my sister to deflate the moment.

"Yeah. Hang on," Emma says, her voice faint.

I perk up, angling my head to better see into Callie's room. Callie steps aside, the deep puirple of her floor-length gown flowing across her legs as she walks. It sets off the subtle red in her hair—a copper fire I always knew was in her but never took the time to spot outside her.

My sister steps into the doorframe in a pale blue gown, her hair combed to one side and flowing over her shoulder. She chose to have her hair styled on her right to mask the scars on her cheek and neck, but I want her to wear them proudly.

As if summoned, my healing stab wound throbs a reminder that physical differences can sometimes make one shy.

Emma raises her eyes to mine. I'm about to say, "You look extravag—"

"Put a shirt on, you social media whore."

I bark out a laugh. "I'm only holding out my phone so I can constantly check the time while I wait for you angels." I peer behind her. "Is Eden ready, or am I still waiting to put on my shirt?"

"She's ready," Callie says, and I can't help but look to her and smile.

Her voice remains quiet, tentative and unsure. After the

events that transpired, and my long hospital stay, she's approached these last months as she would a viper. Cautious, suspicious, and threatened.

Especially considering Sabine is still in a coma. My hope is she'll never wake up.

The temple's showdown was told to me in spurts as I regained consciousness and how the society lost control of some members, many were hurt, and one severely injured when she was stabbed in self-defense, then folded over the second-story barrier.

That was the first story given to me by Detective Haskins. The truth was whispered in my ear, Callie curled against me and explaining how she pushed—*she* pushed—Sabine headfirst into a marble floor.

She admitted to killing my mother, Callie said. *And was unashamed about Ivy, unrepentant about all the girls she'd had molested and raped. All she cared about was Piper, a girl she could never get back. She didn't give a shit about anybody living. It's like the rage of every person wronged by her swept through me. I couldn't stop it if I tried.*

Did you try? I asked, but it wasn't with judgment.

Her hair brushed under my jaw as she shook her head in answer. *I didn't want to be a good person then. I wanted to be as bad as her.*

I kissed her head. *You'll never be like her. I love you, Callie.*

After one beat. Two. Three. *I love you, too.*

I said them. After years of refusing love, I've finally accepted it. It's with those words in mind I tilt my head back to get a better, full-on view of her as she passes me and heads to the kitchen for a trillionth cup of coffee. Callie catches on to my attention, covering her mouth with her fingers as she quiets a soft huff of embarrassment. "Stop looking at me like that. Your sister is right there." She motions to the bedroom, a place I wish *we* were frequenting right about now.

The mention of Emma sobers me. Again. "She handling everything okay?"

Callie shrugs. "Graduation day? Sure. It's nothing compared to the level of torture she endured at the hands of your father, being told she was adopted, then witnessing Sabine plunge off a balcony."

"Fair point," I muse, but I'm not convinced.

Emma and I hashed things out as much as we could with only a four-month time period between Hell and Earth. It took a lot of coaxing, but I'm pretty confident I've convinced her she'll always be my twin, no matter fucking what.

It was important to me that Emma and Callie work their shit out, too, and while it's still in progress, the fact that these three misfits are getting ready together for our final day at Briarcliff University is a big win.

"Do you regret staying at Briarcliff?" I ask her as she fiddles with the coffee machine. Emma and Eden stay in the bedroom, bickering about some sort of salmon sash—whatever the hell that means.

Callie answers with zero hesitation, "No." She stops what she's doing and looks up. "Because that would've meant leaving you."

My girl.

My girl blew the case wide open when she did what she

did that day. I wish I could tell her daily how proud of her I am, how *strong* she is, but the words always die on my lips when those haunted eyes of hers meet mine. They're burnished now, those golden greens. Torn and spent with wear.

But I love them. And I love her about as much as I can love anybody—with every fiber I possess.

"You guys ready?" Callie calls, sliding a mug over to me.

I take the shot of espresso, wishing it were tequila.

"Yes, yes, we're coming!" Eden answers and soon, the two of them shuffle out of Callie's bedroom, so uncomfortable in their fancy-ass frocks I want to bust out with belly laughter. Not wanting to lose my balls so soon after recovery, I amend by saying, "You girls look great."

"Awesome. Let's get this over with so I can find my sweatpants," Eden says.

They head to the door, attempting to corral Callie on the way.

"Hang on," I say to them. All three heads turn.

Damn. It's eerie how much these girls mirror each other's movements now. Is this what death and trauma does to a group?

"What?" my sister barks when I'm momentarily speechless.

"Callie stays with me for a minute. We'll meet you guys downstairs."

"What happened to the crankasaurus who wanted us in our finest so we could get this shit over with?" Eden asks.

"He needs a minute," I retort, and leave it at that.

"Go," Callie says to the girls. "We'll be right down."

They're not happy about it, and I'm confident I hear "topless hypocrite" muttered from one of their mouths, but they leave.

"What?" Callie asks. She moves her hands to her hips. "Dad, Lynda, and Blair are waiting. If we want to make the ceremony, we should—"

"Take the dress off."

Callie's mouth falls open. Before she can question me, I prowl toward her, reaching around for her zipper, or buttons, or whatever holds this royal purple *fuck me* gown in place.

"Chase, don't! We have to—" Her words are cut off with a kiss, one her lips instantly go supple for.

She groans, batting at my bare chest but not putting much effort into it.

Our tongues dance and grind, but instead of giving into the bliss, I pop one eye open and continue wrestling with the back of her dress. Goddamnit. I can't—it won't—

Fuck this.

I break off the kiss, lift her skirts, and place her thong-clad ass on the kitchen counter.

"Chase!" she cries. Mugs rattle on their tree.

I give her one last, searing, biting kiss, then coax her until she's lying flat. "I want your pussy, and I want it now. Oh, and I'm thirsty."

Callie struggles onto her elbows. "What? Oh, *g*—" Her head falls back, that incredible hair cascading, as soon as I push my tongue into her folds and play with the hood of her clit.

"Mm," I say into her sweetness, then lick for more.

She cries out, her legs swinging up and pretzeling around my neck, her fingers tangling into my hair to bring me deeper. I do as she requests, diving and twirling my tongue, using my fingers to spread and stroke her, until she writhes against my mouth, each moan and mewl escaping those pert lips sending my cock higher and higher.

There's not much more I can take. I push off, though I'm still parched and starving for her, to undo my belt and pants. Tossing them somewhere, I then palm my dick, aligning it to her perfectly.

She spreads her legs, as if my cock isn't a magnet to her pussy and couldn't find her anywhere.

"Are you wet for me?" I say, though her folds shine with both my saliva and her juice. I just want to hear her say it.

"Yes." When I don't move, she growls, "Goddammit, *yes*, Chase, now fuck me like you promised you would, or I'll just get myself off while you watch!"

"Don't you dare," I growl, then sink into her.

Callie's palms smack against the granite as she spreads her arms wide and tilts her chin to the ceiling, accepting my dick like a sex goddess in benediction.

It turns me on so much that I have to reel in the tingling warning at my balls, the tightening in my shaft. I want to draw this out. It's been too long, and I'm not about to play the game of delicacy when she looks so damn hot spread out on the counter.

I start hard, but I won't finish fast. Our skin smacks together. My tie hangs open at my bare neck and at each thrust, the Briarcliff colors bounce.

"More," Callie whispers through her cries, her hands

scrabbling for my pecs as she arches and pulls me closer. "More, more, *more*."

"Always," I groan near her ear, then sit her up so she's draping over me, and I clutch her thighs and pound.

The edge is near, that placid sparkling surface below begging for me to make waves.

"You with me?" I ask her between thrusts, surprisingly breathless.

I could blame it on my recovery, but...

It's her.

She's done this to me.

"Yes," she whispers back, just as starved for oxygen.

"Then come," I order, gripping the back of her neck, her hair tangling against my fingers. "Come with me."

"Yes," she says, her back arching as the first wave hits her, then the next.

I take some pleasure for my own, my lips peeling back at the first fractal impact, my vision blacking out right about the time my entire being comes alive.

When it's over, we collapse against each other, breathing heavy, the fabric of her dress curling and tickling my ass cheeks.

I take my time leaving her, since she feels so good and right, but I also don't want to take away the moment she's been waiting for—the moment we all want.

Graduation out of this motherfucking school.

I kiss her before I draw away, her lips swollen and reddened with my scruff. I love that I've left my mark on her and that when she accepts her diploma from the acting Chancellor, our sex will be all over her.

Callie pops down from the counter, smoothing her hair. "I should probably straighten up."

"You look perfect."

"Sure." She scoffs. "If you like the whole scruffy possum look."

"I *love* the scruffy possum look."

She catches my stare and smiles.

In that moment, I'm lost.

I'm hers.

"Fine, but only because we're a million minutes late," she says, then helps me dress, especially as I can't bend down so well anymore.

Callie fixes my tie around my collar in between stolen kisses, then scrapes back my hair from my face and laughs when it pops right back into the tousled position as soon as she lets go.

"I think we're as ready as we'll ever be," she says.

"Agreed. Let's go."

She takes my hand, but as we stroll to the door, something through her open door and under her bed catches my eye.

A green stem.

"Hang on a minute, would you?" I say as soon as she steps into the hallway.

"Really? Again?"

"Not for sex," I say on a huff, though when I give her the once-over, I can't promise anything. "Be right back."

I jog into her room while she waits, grab the stem, white petals escaping with my pull. I stare at the fresh bloom.

"Chase? Everything okay?"

"Yeah," I call, then break the stem in half. I stroll into the bathroom like nothing's amiss, then flush the white rose down the toilet.

"You ready?" I ask as I step into the hallway and shut the door.

"Isn't that what I should be asking you, Mr. There's Always Time For Sex?"

"I'm golden," I say with a grin, then take her warm, welcoming hand and lead us into our society-free future.

Can't get enough of the Nobles and Virtues? Read the latest spin-off, THORNE, now! Don't miss out on Ketley's darkest romance yet.

The moment I stepped into Winthorpe High, I was branded as the new girl who stole somebody else's life, and he hates me for it...

Are you desperately awaiting Tempest's book too? **BECAUSE HE HAS ONE! Here it is!**

SNEAK PEEK OF THORNE
THE THORNE OF WINTHORPE, BOOK ONE

The car slows. We turn a hard left to pass through iron gates with the twisted iron cursive of "Weatherby Manor" lining the top. Instead of a long drive leading up to the house, there's a circular driveway. While consumed in my internal rage, I'd missed our turn away from the ocean to a crowded street of mansions, each hidden behind large brush, stone, and iron, sitting five or six yards from the main road.

Malcolm slows the car in front of the black double doors, each showcasing identical, elaborate door knockers. At this vantage point, glimmering black twines around the iron circle like snakes, with bumps and ridges like the features of a face resting in the middle.

A *splat* against the window has me jumping back. Then another and another. Soon, Medusa's double heads blur into distorted ink as raindrops start falling in buckets against the car.

"Shit," he mumbles while twisting to reach into the back seat.

I flinch at the close contact, a motion he doesn't miss. For a moment, his brows sag in disappointment, but he quickly smooths his expression as he hands me an umbrella. "Marta and Dash have left for the day, so you'll have to make a break for the door without assistance."

Frowning at his notion of needing help to step out of a car, I open the door. The mansion seems close enough, so I sprint to the house, leaving the unopened umbrella to bounce against my side.

By the time I make it to the entrance, my hair sticks to my temples, and my black tank sags against my torso. Rain droplets fall into my eyes as I turn under the stone awning and watch him step out of the black sedan and head to the trunk—umbrellaless.

Did he give me his only umbrella? My fingers tighten on its handle.

He lifts the trunk, the rain drenching the top of his head and his shoulders, falling so hard it blurs the landscape into white streaks as he pulls out my luggage.

I can't very well stand here and witness him struggle with my things in a storm—though it's tempting—and I don't have a key. The umbrella *thwicks* open at the press of a button, and I jog back to the car, helping him with my two carriers.

"I got it," he says, ushering me back to the house. His previously coiffed hair falls into his eyes. The blue sky seems to have taken shelter in his irises until the storm passes.

"You're soaked," I say.

"So are you," he counters, "and without a jacket. Wait for me at the doors."

Ignoring his request, I'm about to shove the umbrella into his chest and grab one of my roller bags when movement behind him catches my eye.

The rain seems to lighten as my attention focuses across the street. A figure leans against a stone column, legs crossed at the ankle and eerily still despite the cascading rain, their umbrella tipped just enough to disguise their face. Smoke drifts from underneath the nylon canopy, the pungent smell of weed soon following, even at this distance.

Their eyes are hidden, but I *feel* this person watching my movements.

"Who's that?" I ask, a crash of thunder almost stealing my words.

Lightning flashes, placing the figure in stark relief. The person hasn't moved, as if impervious to the sharp crackle of thunder and deadly spikes of lightning.

"Ignore him."

The man grips the back of my arm and ushers me away, but I can't peel my gaze from the boy across the street— because he is a guy, I can see it now that he's raised the umbrella and his broad shoulders come into view, then his face.

Keys jangle as the front door's unlocked, but my stare remains on the figure. His features are obscured, but his pale skin and dark hair come through the rain in stark relief.

So does the moment when the joint falls from his mouth, his lips part in disbelief, and his eyes lock on mine.

He jerks back, doing a double take, but then blinks out of it, turning rigid. That face—oddly mesmerizing in the blur of the storm—hardens before his mouth turns up into a sneer, and he whirls from the stone column on one side of a curving driveway, disappearing into the thick foliage beyond.

My brows pinch together. "What's his problem?"

"When I say ignore him," the man says as he pushes open the door, "I'm not kidding around, Ember." He waits for me to step in first, but as I turn my attention to him, I notice the sky has left his eyes. "He's the son of a terrible man. You'd do best to stay away from him."

I sneak a final look across the street before stepping inside, but the boy is long gone.

Terrible man, huh? You mean, he could be an enemy of the guy who upended my life simply out of curiosity and a desire for control?

I think I'd do best knowing everything about him.

read your next enemies to lovers, dark bully obsession now.

A NOTE FROM KETLEY

Hello, my sweet possum,

Are you wondering about that final rose? Callie and Chase have their happy ending, but what about those societies?

Not to worry, Tempest's story is up next and you can **read him now**.

If you're in a completed series mood, Don't forget the Briarcliff spin-off series, *The Thorne of Winthorpe*, which you can also **read now** (and OMG this cover).

If you're looking for more books by me right now, check out my romcom, angsty romances, available on Amazon under Ketley Allison.

Thank you for reading this series all the way to the end! I love my stories, but it always feels so nice and surprising that other people love them, too. If you have the time, I'd be grateful if you left a review on your preferred platform, or tag me on social media to let me know your thoughts. Those golden little stars are what drive me to keep writing.

You can also join my new readers' group, <u>Ketley's VIPs</u>, on Facebook! I'd love to meet you!

Until next time, happy reading!

xoxo, Ket.

ALSO BY KETLEY ALLISON

all in kindle unlimited

If you want more hot villains with kinks, read:

Rival

Virtue

Fiend

Reign

Thorne

Crush

Liar

Tempest

If you like your bad boys morally gray, read:

Rebel

Crave

If you like mafia men, read

Underground Prince

Jaded Princess

If you like a grump turned into protective alpha, read:

Rock

Lover

If you like your playboys damaged with big secrets, read:

Trust

Dare

Play

If you like a psychological thriller with a side of romance, read:

To Have

To Hold

ABOUT THE AUTHOR

Ketley Allison has always been a romantic at heart and loves writing over-the-top, plot-twisty romance and characters. Ketley was born in Canada, moved to Australia, then to California, and finally to New York City to attend law school, but most of that time was spent in coffee shops thinking about her next book.

Her other passions include her two daughters, wine, coffee, Big Macs, her grumpy cat who would rather swipe at her than cuddle her, and her husband, possibly in that order.

tiktok.com/@ketleyallison

instagram.com/ketleyallison

facebook.com/ketleyallison

bookbub.com/authors/ketleyallison

amazon.com/author/ketleyallison

goodreads.com/ketleyallison

pinterest.com/ketleyallison